A WAR TRANSFORMED

WWI ON THE DOGGERLAND FRONT

———————◦———————

A WARGAME BY FREDERICK SILBURN-SLATER

OSPREY GAMES

Bloomsbury Publishing Plc

Kemp House, Chawley Lane, Cumnor Hill, Oxford, OX2 9PH, UK

29 Earlsfort Terrace, Dublin 2, Ireland

1385 Broadway, 5th Floor, New York, NY 10018, USA

E-mail: info@ospreygames.co.uk

www.ospreygames.co.uk

OSPREY GAMES is a trademark of Osprey Publishing Ltd

First published in Great Britain in 2023

A catalogue record for this book is available from the British Library.

ISBN: HB 9781472856258; eBook 9781472856265; ePDF 9781472856234; XML 9781472856241

23 24 25 26 27   10 9 8 7 6 5 4 3 2 1

Originated by PDQ Digital Media Solutions, Bungay, UK

Printed and bound in India by Replika Press Private Ltd.

Osprey Games supports the Woodland Trust, the UK's leading woodland conservation charity. Between 2014 and 2018 our donations are being spent on their Centenary Woods project in the UK.

To find out more about our authors and books visit www.ospreypublishing.com. Here you will find extracts, author interviews, details of forthcoming events and the option to sign up for our newsletter.

CONTENTS

TERRAIN 71

TERRAIN TYPES 71

DETERMINING TERRAIN TYPES 73

SKILLS – ABILITIES, RITUALS, MANIFESTATIONS, AND ORDERS 75

RITUALS 76

HERMETIC LODGES 77

MANIFESTATIONS 82

ORDERS 94

ABILITIES 98

VEHICLES 99

VEHICLES AND SHOOTING 99

VEHICLES AND MOVEMENT 100

VEHICLES AND CLOSE COMBAT .. 102

THE CURSE OF IRON 103

4

5

Chapter One
WHAT'S IN THIS BOOK?

———————◆———————

A War Transformed is a fast-paced, skirmish wargame set in an alternate reality where the First World War is changed utterly by forces far beyond human understanding. The game takes place in the Doggerland Front, a newly opened frontier in a war that already threatens to consume a weary world. Setting their small band of men against that of their opponent, players struggle to claim control over one small portion of this savage place – at least for a short time!

The game allows for two Patrols of around 30 to 50 models, controlled by opposing players, who will move, shoot, and make strategic decisions for their troops. From last stands to running skirmishes, stalwart defences of strategic resources and lighting raids on enemy installations, this book contains multiple scenarios for small-scale platoon combat. Rules are given for how your models can perform powerful magical interventions and special actions, known as Rituals and Commands, as well as how they move, shoot, and interact, with both each other and the terrain that surrounds them. Within these pages you will also find out how to deal with casualties and morale, key elements in maintaining the resolve of your own troops whilst breaking the will of your opponent's.

This book introduces the different factions vying for control of the Doggerland Front, with information on their relative strengths, their histories, and troops available to them. *A War Transformed* is a broad narrative; the mythologies and histories described herein should not be thought of as set in stone. Wargaming rewards imagination and players are encouraged to see the contents of this book not as a rigid set of constraints, but as a framework through which to explore their own dark visions of this harsh frontier.

A War Transformed takes place in a parallel universe where the natural course of the First World War is interrupted by a completely unforeseen cosmic event – an asteroid, dubbed Summerisle for its discoverer, struck the moon and tore a huge piece from it. This impact, called The Shattering, awakened the long-forgotten spirits of nature and old gods of the earth, irrevocably changing the course of history.

In ancient times, these gods had a compact with mortals. Sacrifice was exchanged for the promise of fertility; a life or two was offered and crops flourished. However, long ago, something changed. The gods retreated from this world, falling into a deep slumber. In time, man forgot his covenant and believed himself the master of nature.

Now, with the Summerisle incident, the old gods have returned to reclaim their rightful dominion. Devastated by the cataclysm caused by the Summerilse's impact, much of the world lies barren. Though nature reclaims the world with preternatural speed, nothing planted by human hands will grow. It is only the intercession of the ancient gods that feeds the world; wherever they are appeased with sacrifice and worship the earth gives up its bounty, but life must be bought with death.

Chief among these old gods is the moon goddess herself; her three aspects, Maiden, Mother, and Crone, are collectively known as the Triune Goddess. Her masculine counterpart, the Horned God, is the master of wild places. A host of other smaller gods and nature spirits abound, and all exact a tribute of human souls to sustain them. Driven to a frenzy akin to madness by both the wounding of the moon and the desecration of nature caused by the war, they command a far greater tithe in blood than seen in ages past.

But the tale grows stranger still. The Shattering provided new opportunities to prosecute the war. As the ground shook and the waters receded, the ancient ground that once connected the British Isles with mainland Europe, Doggerland, was revealed once more by the ebbing tide. Lost for 8,000 years beneath the roiling North Sea, this new and vast frontier, stretching from the Isle of Wight to Jutland, now lies open and unguarded.

An army can now march from London to Berlin dry shod. The trenches of the Western Front stretch far across what was once the bed of the sea, littered with the wrecks of ships and detritus long thought lost forever under the dark waves.

Be Warned!

Players expecting an accurate simulation of First World War combat, or even those opposed to the occasional anachronism, will find themselves disappointed!

Chapter Two
MAGIC IN A GILDED AGE

———————◆———————

Throughout this book, there are many references to occult beliefs and practices prevalent in the late 19th and early 20th centuries of our own reality. It was a time when magical and occult societies such as The Hermetic Order of the Golden Dawn sprang up across the west and spiritualists, mediums, and mystics plied their trade in fashionable drawing rooms.

Magic, folk tradition, and national identity were closely linked in this period, with the brutal reality of the war only deepening people's desire to connect with the other world in search of identity, respite, or connection with lost loved ones. As people reached out into the world of spirits, many also rejected the march of industrialisation, seeking to reclaim rural traditions and ways of life. For some, this meant looking back into the pre-Christian past or embracing the superstitious beliefs of the mediaeval world. It is around this time that anthropologists first looked at the beliefs of the ancient past and saw parallels in contemporary folklore, traditions, and beliefs.

These romantic notions fed darker undercurrents. Their focus on national myths and racial identity gave early fascists an evocative vocabulary of symbols, with disastrous consequences.

The first tentative moves towards what would now be recognised as folk-horror were made in this era, with authors like Arthur Machen and M. R. James penning weird tales of witches, unquiet spirits, and ancient, terrible gods. The horror of the unknowable and inscrutable was explored by luminaries like H. P. Lovecraft and Algernon Blackwood, who imagined worlds presided over by cosmic beings of unbelievable power and dark purpose. Artists explored folklore, symbolism, and the intersection of modern life with the spiritual and instinctive, operating at the fringes of human consciousness.

Lunar mythology and folk magic are at the core of *A War Transformed's* rich narrative setting, and this book contains information about the various belief systems of this strange new world, but none of it should be seen as a dogmatic stricture. *A War Transformed* is a fluid framework within which players can give full licence to their creativity, creating an interesting and exciting force that is fun to collect, build, and play.

THE SHATTERING

It had been the talk for weeks, even in the cut-off world of the trenches, where news was scarce and gossip rare. This giant asteroid, named for its discoverer, was hurtling towards the earth at undreamt of speed. Was this to be mankind's end?

But the earth itself was not struck. Instead, Summerisle collided with the moon and was obliterated in an instant, the impact flinging vast quantities of lunar rock into orbit and leaving a gaping scar in the moon's surface.

Reeling from the enormous blow it had been struck, The Shattering caused the moon to teeter in its orbit. As it staggered, the enormous force of its gravity wrought untold destruction upon the war-weary planet that lay prostrate below, tearing at its very shape. As the Earth writhed in the moon's embrace, the seas churned, the ground convulsed, and mountains cracked and were rent asunder.

For many months, the people of the world, kept an uneasy truce, but it could not last. The Great War, held off for a season, was soon resumed with even greater bitterness – no longer a fight for mere imperial glory, but now a terrible struggle for survival.

When the moon was wounded, an ancient force awakened. Primordial gods and ancient spirits, their names lost to history, were roused from their slumber. As these ancient deities revealed themselves, secret societies that had held safe their ways came out of their seclusion. Hidden in the shadows for countless generations, protected by rarefied splendour or rural isolation, covens of immeasurable age stepped out of the shadows to show the desperate people of the world how to appease the gods and renew the fertility of their ravaged world – how to trade blood for an endless summer.

At the front, men who once fought for King and Country, for Kaiser and Fatherland, now fight for renewal, growth, and the promise of Spring. Each drop of blood shed restores life to the dying world.

As magic returns, the world bears witness to a new kind of warfare. Above foxholes, trenches, and dugouts hangs the Sundered Moon, full and impossibly large in the sky. Her mysterious power seeps into tired limbs as masked soldiers chant and stamp, their hair woven with flower garlands.

This is a war transformed.

THE NATURE OF MAGIC

Between our reality and the spirit world is a veil, a barrier between planes of existence, a boundary between the material world that we inhabit and the aethereal one inhabited by ancient spirits and gods. The two planes exist simultaneously, one alongside the other. In some places, the veil is as thin as gossamer, the barrier between the realities considerably weakened. These places have long been known for their spiritual power – ancient groves of trees, stone circles, sacred lakes and rivers. Closer to the spirit realm, these places became sites of pilgrimage and sacrifice in ages long past.

Through magic, those with the gift can intercede with the beings that inhabit that other place, exchanging offerings or worship for power, protection, or the promise of fertility. Those with this power have gone by many names throughout history– seer, priest, even witch.

At these great loci, fertility was secured through sacrifice. A few souls were given in exchange for the harvest, their blood appeasing the spirits of the other realm. Contented with the exchange, the gods blessed the crops to grow, the animals to fatten, and the cycle of birth and death to continue. However, in time, man forgot these ancient compacts, subduing the world by force and bending it to his will. The gods, ever inscrutable in their purpose, acquiesced.

But when the moon was shattered by the impact of Summerisle, something changed. Long known to man as a source of great power, its cycles affect the ebb and flow of magic as surely as the tide. Now, across the face of the world, the veil has been torn to shreds. Powerful energies and ancient spirits are now free to pass through to wreak havoc in the material world once more. Driven to madness by the wounding of the moon, the gods have returned to demand the sacrifice that is their due, though they now ask an impossibly steep price.

There were always some who clung to the old ways. In towns and villages across Europe, the rituals and rites of the old gods were still practised by the poor, even if they were not fully understood. With the return of the old gods, patterns of belief and traditions that had faded away with the industrialisation of the previous century have come flooding back. Now, in those same towns and villages across Europe, ancient songs are sung by young and old alike and the forgotten rituals of yesterday have been reclaimed.

THE OLD GODS RETURN

In trenches and dugouts, offerings are made at makeshift shrines and fanes. When men charge headlong against machine guns and shells, charms and tokens of warding rattle to the rhythm of their pounding feet.

It is the Triune Goddess to whom many men now pledge their allegiance. The Lady of the Moon's irreparable scarring by Summerisle has woken her from her millennia long slumber.

She shows herself in three guises, though each has had a thousand names throughout history.

THE THREE ASPECTS OF THE LUNAR GODDESS

The Maiden, represented by the waxing moon, its splendour growing nightly, is the first aspect of the Triune Goddess. She is the patron of Spring, of new growth and potential. With the promise of grace and unending youth, the Maiden draws to herself those who fear to die and those who cling most tightly to life.

The second face of the Triune Goddess is the Mother, strong and warm. The mother embodies the realisation of potential, of fruitfulness and the consummation of power. Hers is the full moon and the summer, when the fruit hangs heavy on the vine and nature has fulfilled its true majesty. The Mother draws to her all who wish to hold fast to their bosom that which they have won through the strength of their arm.

Ancient and enduring, the Crone is the final aspect of the Triune Goddess, mistress of the waning moon. In her is found knowledge of all endings. An aptitude for the craft and a strong connection to the spirits is the birthright of her followers, with powerful magic and indomitable will at their command. Those who thirst for knowledge pledge themselves to her and, with dark whispers of things unknown, their loyalty is repaid.

Standing apart is her lover and kinsman, the Horned God, virile master of the hunt. He too has been known by many names, in a myriad of tongues.

THE HORNED GOD

Consort of the Triune Goddess, the Horned God is generative, vital, wild, and wrathful. His devotees throw themselves into any fight, the possibility of expressing their skill and mettle greater than their instinct for self-preservation. To the faithful he represents will, individuality, and personal prowess. Sometimes guardian, sometimes destroyer, he is capricious and untamed, instinctual and savage.

Each aspect of the Triune Goddess or the Horned God draws to them mortals with different goals and motivations. However, though the people of this transformed world may appear to worship a host of different deities, many are simply avatars of one of the three faces of the Triune Goddess or the Horned God.

A TRANSFORMED GEOGRAPHY

Revealed by the retreating waters of the North Sea, Doggerland stretches from the coast of Britain to Denmark. The shores of East Anglia and The Netherlands blend seamlessly into a wide and expansive plain stretching out far into the North Sea. In a bid to exploit the possibilities offered by the newly opened front extending from their former shores, the neutrality of the Netherlands and Denmark have been ignored and men from all sides of the conflict now fight on the ancient seabed along with the old battlefields of France and Belgium.

Doggerland is a world of silt and muck, dark pools of brackish water and undulating plains of rock-strewn sand. Occasional hills punctuate the landscape, low and squat beside the towering chalk cliffs that hem them in. The English Channel is much reduced, an accusing finger of brackish, icy water jabbing as far as Kent. It is here that both the Rhine and Thames dump the effluence of their length into the sea, mingling the waste of two warring nations, newly minted neighbours in a much-changed world.

Huge, grasping thickets of bramble and undergrowth now radiate out from the tangled wreckage left by the fighting. With every passing year, Doggerland grows greener, ploughed and harrowed by vehicle tracks, watered with men's blood.

Dotted here and there are the remains of ships, wrecked by the cold and turbulent sea that once covered this strange land. Amidst the rusting ribs of these artificial giants are the remains of the great beasts that once called this place home. Entombed beneath the waves millennia ago, great ivory tusks of long dead mammoths stick out from the sandy ground. Some say that stranger sights are there to be seen too, if you know where to look.

Both the old battlefields of Europe and the new Doggerland Front are pockmarked with shell holes, hastily dug fortifications, and the other now-familiar scars of war. Across the sandy soils of the newly revealed front, trenches are cut, earthworks raised, and the terrain modified to better suit the needs of the men defending it.

A BARGAIN STRUCK

Ravaged by war and devastated by The Shattering, the world teeters on a knife's edge. To secure crops and harvests, guarantee the fall of nourishing rain, and ensure the return of spring, a deal must be struck with the ancient gods of nature. Pernicious, cruel, or perhaps simply indifferent, the gods look upon man's plight with cold detachment, demanding supplication and sacrifice in exchange for the boon of fertility.

Through ritual passed down from the earliest time in history, the gods may be appeased. In ancient groves, songs of praise and celebration ring out in the night, while livestock is slaughtered, and gifts are offered before idols of nameless gods. In the shadow of ancient standing stones, great fires are lit and throngs of masked dancers sway and stamp until the breaking of the dawn.

Though prayer and ritual can win divine favour, life is the most precious offering. The spilt blood of animals, the finest part of a herd, or the prize of a hunt may be enough to secure a paltry blessing, but the gods most desire that which is most precious to us. Whether given by the willing or taken from foes, they hunger for human souls.

Sacrifice can take many forms, but the intention is always the same. With thick cords, sharp knives, stout clubs, or strong hands, victims are committed to the gods. As life drains from their bodies, the compact is renewed. Wherever blood is spilt becomes an oasis of green.

The favour of the gods can grant enormous power to those who know how to wield it. Those men and women with the gift are called witches, capable of wielding some scant portion of the god's power through ancient covenants. The intercession of these witches can turn the tide of battles – bending the powers of the spirit world to their whim or calling forth the eldritch creatures that exist at the margins of this transformed world.

THE HERMETIC LODGES

Worshippers of the old gods align themselves to hermetic lodges, each dedicated to the worship of a particular divinity or one of their aspects. Some are organisations of great power, their congregations numbering in the thousands, while others little more than a few individuals.

Driven underground by new and zealous faiths millennia ago, these lodges have since operated in secret, either out of a desire for rarefied exclusivity or a simple fear of persecution. As the old gods returned, they emerged from the darkness to build the world anew as it was in ages past. Many lodges have existed since the oldest days, secreted in rural idylls and practising rites little changed by the march of centuries. Others are newer, organisations born of the romantic fever of the preceding century. Seeking to wed ancient identities and new political visions, these groups have enthusiastically embraced the old ways.

There are thousands of hermetic lodges across Europe. Though they worship different gods, or at least different aspects of the same gods, they broadly follow the same path. Sacrifice is given to maintain the fertility of a world ravaged by The Shattering. In a world already brutalised by total war, the faithful are forced to take ever more drastic measures to maintain life giving crops as ecosystems crumble; more and greater offerings are often needed to win the favour of the pernicious spirit realm.

From the vast empires of Britain, France, and Germany, subject peoples bring their own ancient ways to the battlefields, their gods and guardian spirits finding comfortable niches in a new pantheon worshipped by colonisers and colonised alike. Tirailleurs, sepoys, and askaris have brought the folk religions of people drawn from across the whole surface of the earth to the shores of Northern Europe.

A NEW WORLD ORDER

Maps have been redrawn, both geographically and politically, with their comfortable assumptions upended. Though much of the line is still manned, the great trenchworks of the Somme, Passchendaele, and Verdun are completely overgrown. Choked in greenery, the grim moonscape of total war has been smoothed over by the steady march of nature as she reclaims her world. With towns and cities in disarray, the powers of the world can ill afford grand campaigns. The lines of the trenches, stretched far beyond their original limits by the receding seas, are now poorly garrisoned. What were once clear lines on a map are now fuzzy, formally impenetrable boundaries are now easily transgressed.

Forces are isolated and thinly spread, often going for long periods without orders or provisions. Skirmishes and ambushes are now commonplace, with raiding for captives, supplies, and pillage finding new currency in a world of tanks, rifles, and shells. Though those in command still love a big push, periodically gathering the men stationed on the front together to push the war towards its end, these offensives seldom accomplish much. The logistical difficulties of bringing forces to bear in any decisive way when food and material are in such short supply means that they often fizzle out after a few miles, the ill-motivated combatants disappearing back off to their foxholes and dugouts with whatever booty they can carry.

Though, in theory, the old alliances stand firm in these hard times, the forces of allied nations rub up against one another and limited fighting between them is now commonplace, though it quickly fizzles out. Many of the nations formerly involved in the war now face civil strife at home so great that they have been forced to withdraw completely from the fighting, or else scaled back their involvement to such an extent that their contribution to the war is token at best. This change in the dynamic has freed many belligerents from the threat at their back, enabling them to concentrate their efforts on a single front.

Although equipment is still being produced, the logistical challenges of the changed world have significantly impacted industry, especially those that rely on imports for raw materials. Weapons, uniforms, and other equipment are often salvaged or supplemented with civilian equivalents. Uniforms in particular may be rummaged out of stores, with many irrevocably damaged pieces replaced with old stock in an outmoded pattern. Manpower shortages are addressed with desperate appeals to the neutral powers for assistance, most notably in the United States, where recruiters from all the nations of Europe tell tales of the great adventures of service at the front to entice men to join the American Volunteer Legions.

Shortages affect the vehicles seen on the front too. With extraordinarily few tanks and armoured cars now being produced, many that were damaged have been inexpertly patched up with improvised or scrounged materials.

Though they may share a worldly master, the men that fight on the Doggerland Front can owe their allegiance to a whole host of different deities. Secret organisations devoted to magic were the preserve of Europe's social elite long before the war, but the lower echelons of society, convulsed by food shortages and political instability, are now also drawn to the old ways by poets and artists, rabble rousing political agitators, and navel-gazing mystics, all of whom co-opt the allure of these secret fraternities and interpret the events of The Shattering to their own ends.

For generations, Europe has been rent by forces even more powerful than the catastrophe of Summerisle. Lurking in the shadows, gnawing at the heart of empires, the spectres of new ideas are ever at the periphery. Across the world, the tumult caused by the return of magic has already toppled many nations and the European empires themselves hang by a fine thread. Emboldened by the power granted by the old gods, demagogues of all stripes now incite packed rallies into rapturous frenzies. Pogroms, riots, and civil strife are common in this much-changed world.

As the world sinks further into environmental collapse, the situation becomes ever more dire. More and greater devotion must be offered to secure the crops upon which all depend. The nations that still fight this transformed war teeter on the verge of collapse and society is increasingly brutalised by the need for sacrifice. With each passing month the discourse grows ever more fractious, and the calls for violence ever more frequent.

Chapter Three
HOW TO PLAY

———————————◆———————————

The following section covers how to actually play *A War Transformed*, including commanding your troops, summoning powerful magics, and firing withering barrages with machine guns, rifles, and other, more unusual, weaponry.

GENERAL PRINCIPLES

HAVE FUN

The ultimate goal of any game is to enjoy yourself, but never let your enjoyment get in the way of others'. In a competitive game like *A War Transformed*, it can be easy to let your emotions get away from you. Whether it's gloating in triumph, or wallowing in pity from a bad dice roll, neither are a good look. Always strive to be good natured in defeat, magnanimous in victory, and conciliatory in dispute.

DIE ROLLS

In *A War Transformed* **low** die rolls are generally better. A roll of one is, in most cases, the best result. Higher rolls are generally undesirable, though there are a few circumstances where bigger numbers are better.

WHEN THINGS DON'T MAKE SENSE

It is inevitable that, on occasion, situations will arise that do not seem to be adequately explained in the rules. In these cases, it is up to the players to determine the best solution. As a general rule, use common sense to agree a solution that conforms to the character of the game and the realities of war.

In instances where there are two rules which seem to contradict one another, *A War Transformed* the specific trumps the general – if two rules appear to contradict one another, the one that applies in the fewest cases takes precedence.

DEALING WITH DISAGREEMENT

It is entirely possible that both players have a sensible solution to the problem at hand but, despite their best efforts, they cannot come to an agreement. In these cases, flip a coin to decide the best solution, war is sometimes arbitrary after all.

To play *A War Transformed*, you will need a tape measure or ruler that measures inches, a selection of dice, some models representing your Patrol, and this rule book. You will also need a playing surface, approximately 6' x 4' in size, with some terrain for the models to fight over. Optionally, you can also use some additional items to act as memory aids and indicators of various game states.

ITEMS NEEDED FOR PLAY

ESSENTIAL ITEMS

Dice

A War Transformed uses a few types of dice – d3, d4, d6, and d10 – to determine the outcomes of Tests. It is best to have at least a few of each these handy and, if possible, have them in a couple of colours to make it easier to differentiate between the rolls of differently equipped models within the same unit.

Scatter Dice

Scatter Dice have arrows on four faces to indicate a direction, rather than a numerical value, as well as two faces which indicate a Direct Hit. These special dice are used to select which direction a thrown or lobbed projectile goes if it misses its mark.

Scatter Dice can be easily acquired from any retailer that sells specialist dice for wargames and RPGs. However, don't worry if you don't have any to hand, as a standard d6 can suffice instead; simply take the face with a 1 on it as indicating a direction – if it is facing straight up into the air or down onto the surface of the table that's a Direct Hit, otherwise, whichever direction that face is pointing in is the direction of Scatter.

Command Tokens

A way of recording how many Command Tokens your force has is absolutely vital. Coloured counters are the best way, but coins or similar objects can also work.

Templates

A War Transformed uses round Templates of 3" diameter (Small Template), 4" diameter (Medium Template), and 6" diameter (Large Template), as well as one Template 2" wide and 10" long (Projected Fire Template). These are used determine how many casualties will potentially be inflicted by certain weapons. These can be bought, or easily made out of tracing paper.

Models

A War Transformed uses models at 28mm scale. However, beyond that, the models that you use are up to you.

Rulebook

This rulebook will be your faithful friend and guide through the harsh and disturbing world of *A War Transformed*, so read it well and keep it close at hand when playing in case you need to check anything – there's no shame in looking up a rule if you aren't sure.

Playing Surface

Whilst a 6' x 4' is the gold standard for tabletop gaming, it isn't always the most practical thing to store. Spouses, partners, and housemates can sometimes (undeservedly) question the need for large pieces of furniture that exist solely to support a hobby. So, in the interests of keeping harmonious households, *A War Transformed* can also be played on a normal sized dining table, though it may lose some of the grand scale of a larger surface.

Terrain

No table is complete without terrain. The setting of *A War Transformed* allows for many interesting building projects, from the ruined towns and villages of Belgium and northern France to the recently drained seabed of Doggerland, strewn with hastily dug trenchworks and ancient mammoth remains; use your imagination and get creative! Tumbling churches with bomb-ravaged graveyards, shelled out towns, ancient stone circles revealed by the receding waters – the possibilities are endless!

NON-ESSENTIAL ITEMS
Tarot Cards

These cards come in a deck of 78, 22 of which are known as the major arcana – individual cards without a suit but with a number at the top. In *A War Transformed,* powerful abilities known as "Rituals" are available to some models, all of which are themed around the major arcana of a traditional tarot deck.

Some players may find it useful to have a deck on hand to remember what Rituals they have available, or which units, friend or foe, are subject to the effect of a particular Ritual. They are easily bought, or you can make your own.

Note that prior knowledge of the tarot is not required, and that these cards function purely as a memory aid. However, if you do have knowledge of tarot, you can consult the cards before a match to see if the spirit world has any tips on securing victory.

Counters

A handful of counters with a few different colours or designs can be useful for tracking certain actions or effects within the game, such as wounds, pinning, or any number of other game states. Wargames are complicated and it's easy to forget details, some of which may be crucial, in the heat of battle. A few counters, or a pen and paper, can be invaluable tools for not getting lost in the fog of war.

COLLECTING AND MODELLING

A War Transformed is chiefly a framework for players to explore a dark and mysterious version of the Great War, so your creativity and vision are paramount; much has changed since The Shattering, so don't be a slave to history when it comes to uniforms and equipment.

A multitude of different peoples fought the First World War and a suffusion of plastic and metal kits, from a range of different manufacturers, are available to you when building your Patrol. Many of the factions, powers, and troops in this volume make thematic reference to beliefs and cultures stretching all the way back to Mankind's earliest history, or at least the refraction of those beliefs through the lens of Edwardian culture. Eagle-eyed readers will note allusions to the occult and spiritualist practises of the gilded age, ancient folk traditions of Europe, folk horror literature and cinema, so kitbashes that make use of these themes are encouraged!

In many ways, the magical beliefs of the 19th and early 20th centuries were attempts to return to beliefs that were seen as national, universal, or, in some cases, racial in character, whether real or imagined. At their best, these systems of magic helped inspire great works of art and literature. However, at their worst, they played midwife to the heinous political ideologies so prominent in the history of the 20th century. Within these pages you will find much to inspire your own conversions and kitbashes, but *A War Transformed* is not prescriptive. The rules included in this volume are deliberately written to allow players the freedom to go their own way when modelling and collecting, so be creative!

KEY PRINCIPLES AND DEFINITIONS

There are some rules to engagement so fundamental that any aspiring general must learn them first, before moving on to anything else. These core rules will be referred to frequently throughout this book, so make sure to understand them fully before going any further.

WHAT IS A UNIT?

In *A War Transformed*, every model is part of a unit. Sometimes a single model will be a unit unto itself, but many units are made up of a group of models with similar training, armaments, and constitutions banded together.

A unit of models performs Actions as one, Shooting at the same targets, Moving in concert with one another, and fighting in vicious hand-to-hand combat together against the same enemies.

UNIT COHESION

A multi-model unit must maintain some semblance of a formation throughout a game of *A War Transformed*. All models within a unit must remain within 1" of at least one other model in the unit to maintain Cohesion, and no two models in a unit can have more than 6" between them.

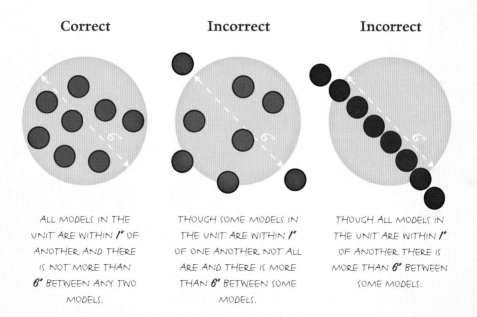

Correct

ALL MODELS IN THE UNIT ARE WITHIN 1" OF ANOTHER AND THERE IS NOT MORE THAN 6" BETWEEN ANY TWO MODELS.

Incorrect

THOUGH SOME MODELS IN THE UNIT ARE WITHIN 1" OF ONE ANOTHER NOT ALL ARE AND THERE IS MORE THAN 6" BETWEEN SOME MODELS.

Incorrect

THOUGH ALL MODELS IN THE UNIT ARE WITHIN 1" OF ANOTHER THERE IS MORE THAN 6" BETWEEN SOME MODELS.

SINGLE MODELS

Some units are composed of a single model. Generally, this will be a character model or a vehicle, but may sometimes be a group of models on a single base, such as a gun crew or procession of religious celebrants. To all intents and purposes, these models should be considered to be a unit in every respect, even though it is a single model and not a group of models.

BASES

Whatever we may wish our models are only plastic, resin, or metal. Unlike real flesh and blood soldiery, they do not move and, despite the best efforts of modellers to create dynamic posing. The models will never dive into cover, dodge, and parry in combat, or duck behind walls after taking a shot.

For that reason, all measurements in *A War Transformed* are taken from the base of a model, rather than from the model itself. This allows for a variety of poses and positions, without necessarily penalising or incentivising models that are built in a certain way.

Base Sizes

Unless otherwise stated, a model's base size is stipulated by its Keyword.

- Individual **infantry** are mounted on a base no larger than 25mm diameter.
- Individual **cavalry** are mounted on a base no larger than 50mm diameter.
- **Weapons teams** should be mounted on a base no larger than 75mm diameter, or the equivalent square base.
- **Unique** units that are mounted or on foot, are mounted on a base no larger than 50mm diameter.
- **Cars** are mounted on a 50mm x 100mm base.
- **Tanks** are mounted on a 75mm x 100mm base.
- **Behemoths** are mounted on a 75mm x 150mm base.
- **Unique** units with the Keyword **tracked vehicle** or **wheeled vehicle** are mounted on the same base as a vehicle with the same Keyword.

All units, including vehicles, should be mounted on an appropriate base. Some models in a players' patrol might require some adjustment to their base size if they do not fit with the above standards. In such cases players should use their best judgement if increasing base size and standardise as much as possible.

FACING

Units with the Keyword **cavalry** or **infantry** do not have a Facing. However, for **vehicles** and **weapons teams**, the concept of Facing is important. For these units, which may only be able to Move or Shoot in the direction which they are Facing, the "front" of the model must be clearly indicated.

In many instances, the front of the model will be obvious – gun barrels are a good indication – but with some other units it may be less clear. In those instances, it is vital that the front of the model is obviously marked and that your opponent is made aware of where the front of the model is.

For units such as these, mounting on a rectangular or square base means that the forward arc of the unit is clearly visible.

REACH

Models are in contact if they are within 1" of each other, measuring from the edge of the base of each model.

This means that models do not actually need to be touching one another, or a terrain feature, to be considered to be in contact. Wherever the phrase contact appears in this book, players should understand it to mean that the model's base is less than 1" from the object in question.

This allows some leeway for models with "sticky out bits", such as guns, bayonets and the like, to be positioned alongside another unit or a piece of terrain without physically touching it. In general, this will be important in cases where units are fighting in hand-to-hand combat, but it also has some bearing in Leadership Tests and some rules to do with Movement and Cover.

UNIT CHARACTERISTICS

A unit's profile contains vital information about how it behaves, its constituent parts, what equipment is available to it, and how effective it is at making Attacks and other Actions. In addition to any Keywords, units in *A War Transformed* have a value assigned to each of the following characteristics:

Pace (P)

Pace is measurement of how fast a unit Moves, whether on foot, hoof, wheel, or track. A unit's Pace value is equal to the number of inches that the unit moves, or half the number of inches that the unit moves when it Charges.

Martial Skill (MS)

Martial Skill is an indication of how proficient a unit is at fighting, both in Close Combat and at range. Unlike the other characteristics, which have a numerical value associated with them, a unit's Martial Skill is given as a word such as "Medium" or "High". The higher a unit's Martial Skill, the better it is at winning Close Combat or at hitting their enemies when Shooting.

Zeal (Z)

Zeal is an indication of a unit's bravery and staying power in the face of danger. The higher a unit's Zeal characteristic, the greater the chance that it has of passing a Leadership Test. A unit's Zeal score is also used to determine how many Attack Dice it generates in a Close Combat, though bear in mind that single-model and multi-model units work a little differently!

Wounds (W)/Models (Mod) Score

A single-model unit's Wounds Score represents the amount of punishment that it can take in terms of blows or injuries before it succumbs to either total mechanical failure or death. As a unit takes damage, it accumulates Wounds up to a certain value, at which point it is removed from the table. It can be useful to have some coloured markers on hand to represent the number of Wounds that a unit has accumulated over the course of the game, or you can record the number of Wounds taken by whatever other means you see fit. The higher a unit's Wounds Score is, the longer it will last.

Any unit composed of multiple models has no Wounds Score, but rather a Models Score. This is the number of models that the unit is made up of when it starts the game. All models that are part of a multi-model unit may only be subjected to one Wound before they succumb to their injuries. This means that, rather than gaining Wound Markers as they fight, a multi-model unit simply loses members until there are none left, at which point the unit is Destroyed.

Saving Throw (ST)

A Saving Throw is a measure of a unit's ability to avoid damage that would otherwise cause a Wound. A Saving Throw can be thought of as armour, agility, exceptional hardiness, or insensibility to pain, depending on the unit.

Unless otherwise stated, all models within a unit share the same characteristics even if they are armed with different equipment.

EXAMPLE UNIT PROFILE

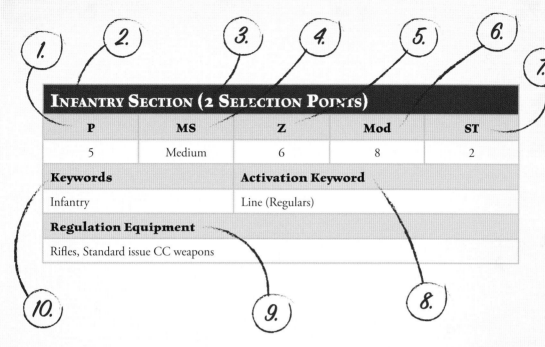

INFANTRY SECTION (2 SELECTION POINTS)				
P	MS	Z	Mod	ST
5	Medium	6	8	2

Keywords	Activation Keyword
Infantry	Line (Regulars)

Regulation Equipment
Rifles, Standard issue CC weapons

1. THE UNIT'S PACE
2. THE NAME OF THE UNIT
3. THE COST OF RECRUITING THE UNIT TO YOUR PATROL
4. THE UNIT'S MARTIAL SKILL
5. THE UNIT'S ZEAL CHARACTERISTIC
6. THE NUMBER OF MODELS IN THE UNIT, ALTERNATIVELY THE UNIT'S WOUNDS
7. THE UNIT'S SAVING THROW CHARACTERISTIC
8. THE KEYWORD DETERMINING WHEN THE UNIT ACTIVATES AND UNDER WHICH CIRCUMSTANCES IT GENERATES COMMAND DICE
9. THE WEAPONS CARRIED BY THE UNIT
10. ANY KEYWORDS HELD BY THE UNIT

Regulation Equipment

Unless otherwise stated, all models within a unit share the same equipment.

However, some units, and unit upgrades, may mean that certain models within a unit are equipped differently. In this case the specific numbers of a particular weapon will be stated.

For example, a Field Gun Team is equipped with the following weapons: Field Gun (1), Standard issue CC weapons. This means that there is one field gun, rather than each crewmember having their own field gun....

ADVANTAGE AND DISADVANTAGE

In some cases, the characteristics of a unit will be altered by the special rules of another unit. This can be the case when sustained fire reduces the Zeal of a unit by adding Combat Stress Markers, or when leaders inspire their men to greater heights of heroism or use strange magic to quicken their pace.

In these cases, the value of dice rolls that Test against that characteristic may be altered up or down. These changes are referred to as "Advantage" and "Disadvantage". Advantage modifies the result of a die roll down, thereby making the Test more likely to succeed, whereas Disadvantage modifies results up, decreasing the likelihood that the Test will be successful.

A rule that causes a roll to be counted as one lower is referred to as "rolling at Advantage 1", whilst one which causes the roll to be counted as two higher would be "Disadvantage 2" and so on. This means that if you rolled a 6 for a Zeal Test, but had Disadvantage 2 to Zeal, then your roll would be counted as an 8.

Simultaneous effects are cumulative on one another, so if a model is under the effect of a Ritual that grants Advantage 1 to its Zeal, then another Ritual comes into play with the same effect, that unit now has Advantage 2 to its Zeal. This is also the case when the effect of one interaction increases a characteristic, whilst another reduces it, resulting in the effects cancelling one another out.

> *No special rule can ever reduce any characteristic below 1 or above 10.*

BLANK VALUES

Some units will have a blank value for one or more of their characteristics. A unit with a blank value for any characteristic has no ability to perform Actions or Tests associated with that characteristic, so a unit with no value in its Pace characteristic cannot move, whilst one with no Saving Throw has no way of defending itself against incoming damage.

There are no circumstances in which a unit with a blank value for any characteristics can gain that characteristic. For example, a unit with a blank Pace characteristic cannot have their Pace modified by a Ritual or other special rule – if it starts with nothing, then it will always have nothing.

COVER
Makeshift Cover

Any solid terrain object on the table that is over 0.5" in height or any hole this 0.5" or deeper is considered to give Makeshift Cover against Shooting Attacks to any unit in contact with it.

Being in cover confers Advantage 1 to a unit's Saving Throw characteristic against Shooting Attacks. Some terrain features provide additional benefits to a unit's Saving Throw in addition to the benefit of Makeshift Cover.

> *Only units with the Keyword **infantry** receive the benefits of Cover.*

Enhanced Cover

Certain pieces or terrain afford even more protection to men huddling behind or within, granting them Enhanced Cover. Any unit occupying a piece of terrain that grants Enhanced Cover is immune to the effects of Critical Hits generated by Shooting Attacks.

Trenches

In addition to the other advantages conferred by Cover, any unit with the Keyword **infantry**, which is not also a **creature**, may reroll any Saving Throw made against Shooting Attacks if they are in a **trench**.

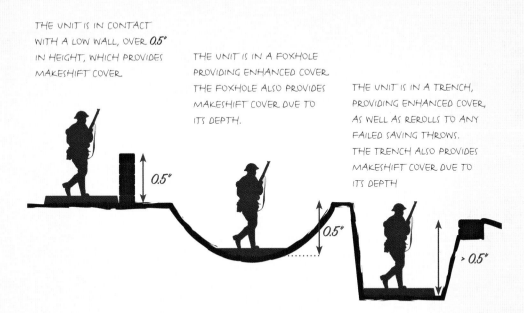

THE UNIT IS IN CONTACT WITH A LOW WALL, OVER *0.5″* IN HEIGHT, WHICH PROVIDES MAKESHIFT COVER.

THE UNIT IS IN A FOXHOLE PROVIDING ENHANCED COVER. THE FOXHOLE ALSO PROVIDES MAKESHIFT COVER DUE TO ITS DEPTH.

THE UNIT IS IN A TRENCH, PROVIDING ENHANCED COVER, AS WELL AS REROLLS TO ANY FAILED SAVING THROWS. THE TRENCH ALSO PROVIDES MAKESHIFT COVER DUE TO ITS DEPTH

0.5″

0.5″

> 0.5″

Cover And Other Attacks

Any weapon that generates an area-of-effect template when making a Shooting Attack ignores the benefit of any Cover. Enemies in Cover are far more difficult to kill with standard weapons, so entrenched units are best dislodged with **template** weapons such as grenades, mortars, and flame throwers.

Close Combat Attacks are also unaffected by Cover. Sometimes a bayonet charge is the only possible course of action, bloody though it may be.

BATTLE SHOCK TESTS

A Battle Shock Test is a special type of Zeal Test, made only under specific circumstances. When a unit must make a Battle Shock Test for any reason, it takes an immediate Test against its Zeal characteristic, including any Advantage or Disadvantage from special rules.

For every point that the test is failed by, the unit either loses a model or takes a Wound.

Where units consist of multiple models with different profiles, such as a unit with special weapons, "standard models" are removed as casualties first, then "upgraded models" in the order chosen by the controlling player.

There are many rules and circumstances by which Zeal is modified, so make sure that you keep a reference handy so that you don't miss any – a single die can be the difference between success and failure!

There is no opportunity to roll Saving Throws for Battle Shock Tests.

COMBAT STRESS

During the course of the game, some units will be exposed to conditions that damage their morale. These units gain Combat Stress, hampering their abilities until they are no longer able to function. There are a number of circumstances in which a unit may gain or lose Combat Stress, all of which will be covered in the following chapters, but which are too numerous to list here.

Combat Stress Markers

Each time a unit is subjected to Combat Stress, place a Combat Stress Marker (abbreviated to CSM) next to it. A unit can have a maximum of three Combat Stress Markers active at any time. If a unit with three Combat Stress Markers is put into a situation where it would normally receive another marker, then it must make a Battle Shock Test instead.

The unit must perform a Battle Shock Test for every Combat Stress Marker that it generates over three, applying the result of that Battle Shock Test in full every time until the unit either loses a Combat Stress Marker, or the unit is Destroyed.

This means that, if a unit that has three Combat Stress Markers receives another two, it would have to make two consecutive Battle Shock Tests. By the same token, a unit with just two Combat Stress Markers that receives a further three would also have to make two consecutive Battle Shock Tests.

Multi-Model Units

Combat Stress Markers make it more difficult for multi-model units to pass Zeal tests and Battle Shock Tests by imposing Disadvantage-1 to Zeal for each active Combat Stress Marker.

Combat Stress also helps to determine what action a unit takes at the end of a Close Combat Subphase. An exhausted unit is far more likely to break and run, or to suffer an unfavourable result at the end of the combat. Further rules for the interplay between Combat Stress and Close Combat can be found in the chapter dealing with Close Combat later in this book (see page 48).

Single-Model Units

Combat stress works differently for units composed of a single model, such as **unique** units and **vehicles**. Rather than building up Disadvantage to their Zeal when they gain Combat Stress, units such as **vehicles**, commanders, and supernatural **creatures** gain Combat Stress Effects as they accrue Combat Stress Markers. Remember that mindless units do not generate combat stress, so any single model units which are also mindless are the exception to this rule.

THE NUMBER OF COMBAT STRESS MARKERS NEEDED TO CAUSE THE ADDITIONAL SPECIAL RULE

1 CSM	2 CSMs	3 CSMs
Lamed Pace reduced to 3	**Trembling** Shooting attacks are taken at low MS	**Shaken** Aura range reduced by 5"

THE NATURE OF THE SPECIAL RULE GAINED AS A CONSEQUENCE OF THE COMBAT STRESS

The Combat Stress example diagram shows how Combat Stress Markers can hamper a unit's ability to function effectively. While the vast majority of additional rules caused by Combat Stress are negative, some may surprise you.

Single-model units may gain Advantage or Disadvantage to their Zeal by other means, but never by Combat Stress.

COMBAT STRESS AND MULTIPLE ACTIVATIONS

Unique units may be Activated once per Phase, allowing them to perform Actions up to three times per Round. This allows these leaders to perform heroic interventions, but at a cost. When Activating a unit in this way, they gain a Combat Stress Marker for each Activation after the first in any given Round. The process resets each Round, allowing **unique** units to be Activated once for free, then at the cost of one Combat Stress Marker for each Activation thereafter in that Round.

Any Combat Stress Markers generated in this way remain until such a time as the unit can lose them in some way, such as through a Ritual or a special activation, such as Resting. A Combat Stress Marker generated in this way is added to the unit after they have completed their Activation, so any special rules caused by a Combat Stress Marker do not come into play until after the unit has been Activated and has completed whatever task its commanding player gave it.

Combat Stress, Orders and Rituals

Some Orders cause a unit to generate additional Combat Stress by pushing it beyond the usual limits of endurance.

In these instances, whatever Action the Order or Ritual allows the unit to take is resolved first, then the Combat Stress Marker is added after the Activation ends.

EXTRA HITS

There are some circumstances under which additional Hits are generated. In most cases, this will be as the result of a unit's Abilities or Skills, but it may also be due to some other special rule coming into play.

For example, consider the Banish Ability:

Banish – Select an enemy **creature** within 15" to take d6 MS Low Hits – (1 Command Token)

When this Ability comes into play, a number of Hit Dice equal to the value rolled on the d6 are generated against the target **creature** and resolved as though they were made as part of a Shooting Attack. Let's imagine that the d6 roll generates a result of 4. The results of the dice are 1, 2, 4, and 4. As the stated Martial Skill of the Hits is Low, only the results of 1 and 2 would cause a potential Wound.

Unless otherwise stated, a Saving Throw is allowed against the additional Hits generated in this way.

ORDER OF PLAY

In *A War Transformed*, there are certain rules that determine what models can do and when. These rules generally have to do with Activation, which is when a player selects one of their units and performs Actions with it. The rules for Activation determine when and under what circumstances a player may have a unit Move, Shoot, or do anything else.

These Activations take place in a defined order, though certain rules allow players to break the order of Activation, but not without cost!

In order to understand the rules of A War Transformed, *it is important to know what is meant by a few terms. It may seem intimidating at first, but it is actually a reasonably simple system to grasp, though markedly different from many other popular wargames.*

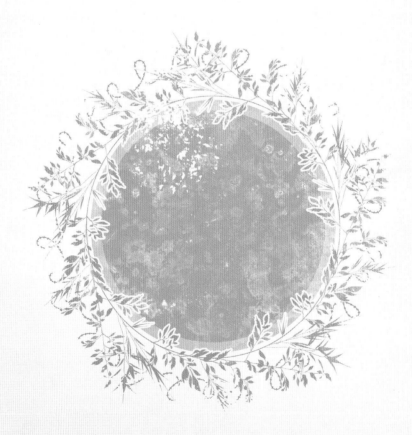

ACTIVATION GLOSSARY

ACTIVATION GLOSSARY TABLE

Term	Definition
Round	A full series of Phases, including a Close Combat and Compulsory Move subphases and four standard Phases.
Close Combat Subphase	A special Phase that takes place at the start of a Round, before any other Activations. Any units that are in contact with any enemy units fight in Close Combat – removing casualties and making any necessary Tests.
Compulsory Moves	A subphase wherein any units that Move without instruction from their commanding player, either as a consequence of Breaking or some other special rule, do so according to their own rules and Keywords.
Phase	The portion of a Round in which specific classes of model, determined by the Activation Keywords on their unit profile, undertake Actions like Moving, Shooting, or using Abilities.
Turn	One half of a Phase, in which each player Activates whatever models they have in their platoon whose Activation Keywords allow them to act in that Phase.
Activation	When a unit or units are chosen by a player and act out whatever Actions are available to them.
Activation dice	d6 dice used to contest Priority Activation, players receive these at the start of each Phase.
Command Tokens	Tokens generated each Round by a player's units after the Close Combat subphase. Some will only be generated if certain preconditions are met. Command Tokens can be spent to use Skills or converted into bonus Activation dice to boost a player's chances of taking the first Turn in a Phase.
Skills	Unusual activations available to certain units. These include both powerful Rituals and mundane Orders. Using a Skill requires spending Command Tokens.
Priority Activation	When a player wins the first Activation in any given Phase, they are said to have won Priority Activation – they take the first Turn.
Keywords	Keywords determine how a unit acts in different circumstances and conditions, either enhancing or detracting from their abilities or granting them special characteristics when undertaking actions such as Moving, Shooting or fighting in Close Combat.
Activation Keywords	A unit's activation keyword defines when it can be activated in the phase order. It also includes the unit's "type" (Support, Assault, Regulars etc.), which govern the circumstances under which it generates additional command tokens.

PHASES

Whilst many games break their Rounds into consecutive Phases, wherein all models move, shoot, then fight sequentially, *A War Transformed* runs through a sequence of Phases in which units with a corresponding Activation Keyword can be Activated by their controlling players.

Players compete to act first in each Phase, potentially gaining the upper hand or scuppering their opponents' carefully laid plans. How this bidding mechanic works is covered in more detail later, but first let's take a look at how Phases work.

Phase Order

The Phase order determines which models are allowed to perform certain Actions and when. A Round of *A War Transformed* consists of four Phases, with players using special commands in the first and units being Activated to Move, Shoot, or use Abilities in the following three.

PHASE ORDER TABLE				
1		**Command Phase**	Players can attempt to manifest creatures, perform Rituals, or issue Orders. Units that use a skill in this Phase, such as issuing an Order or performing a Ritual, do not count as having been Activated.	
1a		**Close Combat Subphase** (including Combat resolution)		
1b		**Compulsory Moves**		
2	Activation Phases	**Cannonade Phase**	Units with the Activation Keyword cannonade can be activated	Unique units may be Activated once per Phase, but gain a Combat Stress Marker for each Activation after the first.
3		**Elite Phase**	Units with the Activation Keyword elite can be activated	
4		**Line Phase**	Units with the Activation Keyword line can be activated	

MINDLESS UNITS

A small number of units can never be activated, but always move towards the closest enemy unit within Line of Sight, except those which are **camouflaged**, regardless of any intervening terrain, at their stated Pace value during the Compulsory Move Phase.

If an enemy is within range, a **mindless** unit will always Charge at them, providing it is possible. **Mindless** units do not generate Combat Stress under any circumstances and cannot be Pinned.

COMPETING FOR ROUND PRIORITY

In *A War Transformed*, players face off at the start of each of the four Phases to determine who is going first. They do this by bidding with dice. Each player is allocated one d6 Activation Die at the start of each Phase with which to contest Priority Activation.

They may also choose to spend some of their Command Tokens, exchanging them for additional Activation Dice, in order to improve their chances of winning Priority Activation, if they wish to do so. Players may convert as many of their Command Tokens to Activation Dice as they like.

At the start of each Phase, players declare how many dice they intend to bid for Priority Activation. The player who had Priority Activation in the preceding Phase declares their intentions first, with the first player to declare in the very first Round at the beginning of the game decided by a coin flip.

Once both players have decided how many Activation Dice they are bidding, it's time to roll! Total the value of all the Activation dice you rolled and (after any modifiers granted by special rules) the winner is the player with the highest result. Note that this means it is theoretically possible for just one dice to beat a whole slew of others, so always be careful not to overstretch yourself – it may not pay off!

Ties

In the event that both players get the same score when rolling their Activation Dice, the player who had Priority Activation in the previous Round goes first. The momentum of combat often rewards the player who can claim and keep the initiative.

Why Compete?

Activating first in a Phase can spell the success or failure of your carefully laid plans, so it's important to prioritise the Phases that you want Priority Activation in, whilst also considering your opponent's plans. Getting Priority Activation in a Phase that your opponent is desperate to go first in can devastate their dastardly plots and schemes, so think carefully about what you want to achieve in any given Round and how you can stop your opponent from doing the same.

Don't Overdo It!

As tempting as it is, don't get too excited and blow all your Command Tokens by converting them to Activation Dice and using them on one big Phase. Command Tokens are also necessary to use your **unique** units' Abilities, which will be vital to success on the battlefield.

Try to make sure that you have some Command Tokens handy so that you can respond to the changing reality of the battle as it progresses – being left unable to react to your opponent's unfolding plans could spell certain defeat!

GENERATING COMMAND TOKENS

At the very start of the Round, players determine how many tokens are available to them.

COMMAND TOKEN TABLE A	
Whole Force	1 Command Token if more than 50% of the force's units have neither been Broken nor Destroyed (rounded down)
Captain	1 Command Token if the Captain has neither been Broken nor Destroyed

In addition, different kinds of units generate Command Tokens depending on their Unit Type, a Keyword that determines the circumstances, if any, under which it produces Command Tokens.

COMMAND TOKEN TABLE B

Regulars	1 Command Token per Round for each unit, provided it has neither been Broken nor Destroyed
Assault	1 Command Token per Round if the unit is within 6" of an enemy, provided the unit is not Broken **OR** 2 Command Tokens per Round for if the unit is in Close Combat
Support	1 Command Token per enemy unit Pinned by this unit in the proceeding Round*, providing that the unit has been neither Broken nor Destroyed
Artillery, Tracked or Wheeled Vehicle, Leader, Creature, or Rabble	This unit does not generate additional Activation Dice under any circumstances

When Shooting with support weapons, enemy units can be Pinned, preventing them from being Activated. Each time that a support unit successfully Pins an enemy over the course of a Round, put a counter next to it – in the following Round each of these counters represents a Command Token you can now use. Note that some support units may not be able to pin enemies and where this is the case, those units cannot take advantage of this special rule.

Work out how many Command Tokens you generate in the Round and put them all together – this is called your Command Pool and will generate anew at the start of each Round.

WHAT HAPPENS IN THE COMMAND PHASE?

In the Command Phase, any Rituals or Orders a player has access to through their chosen Captain and Witch may be used. Witches may also attempt to spend any Manifestation Dice in their pool to call forth **creatures**, powerful entities from beyond the veil that excel in certain roles and can have a powerful impact on the battle. The Command Phase sets the tone for all the Phases that follow, so watch your opponent's actions carefully – they may give away what they plan to do next!

WHAT HAPPENS IN THE CLOSE COMBAT SUBPHASE?

Detailed rules for the Close Combat Subphase can be found later in this book (see page 48). For now, it is enough to know that it happens before the Compulsory Movement and Activation Phases but after the Command Phase.

In the first Round of the game, no units should be in contact with enemies, so there is no Close Combat Subphase.

WHAT HAPPENS IN THE ACTIVATION PHASES? – CANNONADE, ELITE, AND LINE

Once it's determined who is Activating first in any particular Phase, the player with Priority Activation can start using units that have the appropriate Activation Keyword on their unit profile to complete whatever objective that player has. Once a player has exhausted all of their chosen Actions in a Phase, the next player can now do the same, Activating all of their eligible models to come to the defence of beleaguered comrades or smash an advancing group of enemies.

UNIT ACTIVATION KEYWORDS

When choosing models from the selection tables later in this book, every model has an Activation Keyword that determines which Phase it can be activated in.

Unique

These individual models may be commanders or leaders and can be activated during any of the Activation Phases, provided it is your Turn. They can perform special Actions to destroy the enemy's resolve or stiffen wavering hearts by spending Command Tokens.

Cannonade

On the Doggerland Front, bombardment often presages an attack, softening the resistance of enemies and opening pathways for attacking forces to cut through. This class of models, made up of units such as artillery and machine guns, are the first to be Activated.

Elites

Fast attack units tasked with breaking through enemy lines, reconnaissance specialists who scout ahead of the main force, or elite assault troops hell-bent on entering the breaches in enemy formations made by your artillery barrage, this class of unit is next in the Activation Order.

Line

Line troops are the bread and butter of any Patrol, making up the majority of your units. A mixed class that includes infantry and powerful vehicles, Line Troops can be relied upon to accomplish many objectives and are the third class of models to be Activated.

WHAT CAN AN ACTIVATED UNIT DO IN A PHASE?

During each Phase, any unit with the appropriate Activation Keyword can be selected by a player and Activated. There are two kinds of Activation:

- ⊛ **Special Activations** – wherein a unit may perform one of the Actions from the list below.
- ⊛ **Normal Activations** – wherein the player may choose to Move the unit first, before carrying out a chosen task. Note that in a Normal Activation, the Move (if there is one) *must* be made first.

ACTIONS AVAILABLE TO UNITS WHEN ACTIVATED

Special Activations

Rest	Almost unit can take a Rest Action, but can do nothing else in this Phase. Units with the Keyword **wheeled vehicle** or **tracked vehicle** cannot take a Rest Action.
Charge	The unit charges into an enemy and engages them in Close Combat.

Normal Activation (includes a Move)

Ability (if available)	The unit uses a special innate skill to perform some feat. Any unit that has access to Abilities can use them.
Shoot (if available)	The unit makes a Shooting Attack against a selected enemy unit from afar using whatever weapons they have at their disposal. Any unit equipped with a ranged weapon may Shoot, but bear in mind Only models equipped with a weapon with the Keyword **quickfire** may both Move and Shoot.

RESTING

Any unit that is not in contact with an enemy, Broken, or a **vehicle** can choose to Rest. A unit that is resting can do nothing else in this Round, but they lose a Combat Stress Marker.

    Unique units can only be Activated to Rest if they have not been previously Activated this Round.

HOW MANY TIMES CAN A UNIT BE ACTIVATED?

- ☺ **Unique Units** – can be Activated once per Phase, but will generate a Combat Stress Marker for each additional Phase that they are Activated in after the first. This resets at the end of the Round. This means that a **unique** unit can potentially be activated three times in one Round, but in so doing they will generate a huge amount of Combat Stress, hampering their Abilities and raising the possibility of needing to take a Battle Shock Test. Note that, although Witches and Captains issue Orders and perform Rituals in the Command Phase, this does not count as an Activation and so does not count this towards the number of Combat Stress Markers they take. Commanders must carefully weigh their options, using their **unique** models to perform heroic interventions only when absolutely necessary to press home a faltering assault or shore up a wavering defence.
- ☺ **Line, Elite, or Cannonade Units** – can only be Activated once per Round in their own Activation Phase, or in another Phase as allowed by a special rule.

ACTIVATIONS OUT OF ORDER

Captains can use special Orders to break the normal sequence of Activations and allow their units to be Activated outside their native Phase.

These Orders can offer a whole new range of tactical options, allowing commanders to push forward in lightning assaults or to hammer the enemy into submission with withering volleys of fire before they have a chance to act themselves.

VEHICLES

Whilst flesh and blood fighters can be pushed beyond their limits through charisma, fear, or sheer determination, machines are limited by material constraints. In almost all circumstances, a **vehicle** can only be activated in its own Phase.

*Only Orders, Rituals, or Abilities that specifically mention **tracked/wheeled vehicles** as a valid target should be thought of as applicable to those classes of unit.*

THE ORDER OF TURNS BROKEN DOWN

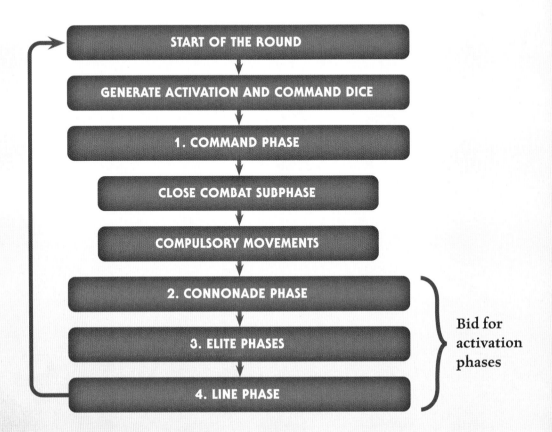

START OF THE ROUND

GENERATE ACTIVATION AND COMMAND DICE

1. COMMAND PHASE

CLOSE COMBAT SUBPHASE

COMPULSORY MOVEMENTS

2. CONNONADE PHASE

3. ELITE PHASES

4. LINE PHASE

Bid for activation phases

MOVEMENT

BASICS OF MOVEMENT

Units in *A War Transformed* can move in a few different ways.

A unit may simply Move, advancing in an orderly fashion; Charge at full pelt to engage in Close Combat with the enemy; or Pivot, turning themselves in order to bring their armaments to bear.

Moving

When a unit Moves, it may move a number of inches up to its Pace value, made as part of a Normal Activation and **preceding either a Shooting Attack or the use of an Ability**.

Charging

Charging is a Special Activation wherein units move up to **double their Pace value**, with the sole focus being to initiate a Close Combat with an enemy unit. A Charge is the only method by which opposing models can come into contact and is therefore critical for initiating Close Combat.

Pivoting

Pivoting is a type of movement made as part of a Normal Activation. Pivoting enables models with a Facing that can only Move forward to turn to face in a different direction before Moving or, alternatively, allows models that can only Shoot in a forward arc to turn to face their chosen target before opening fire.

Pivoting occurs at the start of a movement, so that a model Pivots and then Moves if it is able, ending its Activation orientated in the same direction that it moved forward in. Remember that Pivoting is part of a Move, so any model that pivots, even if it does not then travel forward, has Moved for the purposes of any other rule.

Most models do not need to Pivot, as they have no Facing, but Pivoting is an important rule and form of movement for a significant minority of powerful units, such as **vehicles**, which have firing or movement arcs.

If a player wishes to turn a model without a Facing to point at their enemy simply for a more cinematic feel and to give a sense of realism to the battle, this does not constitute Pivoting!

BOOSTING MOVEMENT AND MAXIMUM MOVEMENT RANGE

There are many ways to boost the Pace value of a unit or allow it to Move further than it generally could. Regardless of any other special rules, all units are constrained to moving a *maximum of 20" in any single Round*.

Any bonuses to Pace applicable to a unit as part of a special rule may be used to extend the maximum distance that a unit may Move, also affect Charge.

Short Movements

There are a number of occasions when a unit will Move (either compulsorily or as an active decision by their player) but will not travel as far as they are entitled to. For example, a unit with Pace 5 may move behind Cover 3" away, travelling a shorter distance than they would have done if they were simply Moving.

On these occasions, that unit still counts as having made a Move for the purposes of any other rule, so they can neither use nor be the target of any Abilities or Orders that are incompatible with them having made a Move.

MOVEMENT AND TERRAIN

No battlefield is flat, and the Doggerland Front is no exception. A host of features mark it, from the ribs of long-sunk boats to the bones of creatures from the ancient past. On either side are the innumerable towns and villages of northern Europe, some ruined, some still standing, as well as the snaking lacework of interlinked trenches cut in the early days of the war. These sites are often the focus of fighting, as Patrols strike across the front for raid or conquest.

Certain terrain features may block the path of units that are Moving, or require them to make a Test to see if they are able to continue as planned. These effects differ depending on a unit's Keywords and the corresponding terrain that they are passing through. The majority of terrain on a table will have no effect on the passage of units through it, but some features have special rules. For example, there are some special terrain features that cannot be traversed when Charging. Full rules for how units interact with terrain when moving are given below and in the chapter on setting up the table (see page 71).

MOVING AROUND OBSTACLES

In many instances, players will wish to move around something rather than through it. This may be the case when a terrain feature blocks a unit's path, or a player may wish to skirt around an enemy to attack from a flank or avoid an overwhelming adversary.

In these cases, units that do not have a Facing can divide their Movement into sections, dividing the total distance that any one model can move into parts and moving it in stages.

For the sake of their own sanity and that of their opponent, players are constrained to moving in full inches – units cannot move in halves, sixteenths, or thousandths of an inch at a time. For this purpose, a ruler that is 1" wide can be particularly useful, allowing players to "walk" their ruler along by alternately using the corners to plot points one inch apart.

Whenever players choose to Move in this way, they must ensure that no one model in the unit makes a movement that exceeds its Pace value and that the unit maintains Cohesion.

MOVEMENT INTO BUILDINGS

To units with the **infantry** Keyword, the positioning of walls and doorways is unimportant – if a ruined **building** is within their maximum Movement distance, they can Move into it without the need to plot a course through physical doorways or windows.

Buildings With Multiple Floors

Some **buildings** may have multiple floors on which a model can stand, allowing them to see further or Shoot over obstacles. There is no mechanic for climbing in *A War Transformed*, so players can choose to distribute their models over whichever floors they like without having to make any additional Moves.

Players are encouraged to be sensible in this regard, noting that the majority of **buildings** found in northern European towns in the early 20th century would be, at most, three storeys tall and that heavy shelling of the kind suffered by such towns during WWI would have put paid to the few that weren't!

MOVEMENT AND UNIT COHESION

When Moving, it is important that a unit maintains Cohesion.

If a player wishes to move a unit in such a way that it will break Cohesion, or will mean that, in order to maintain Cohesion, one or more models in that unit would have to move further than its Pace value allows, then it is an invalid Movement and cannot be carried out. When moving as part of a normal activation, no individual model within a unit may move more than its Pace value.

In these instances, the player must find another way to achieve their goal or lower their ambitions.

MOVEMENT AND OTHER UNITS

A unit may not Move through another unit under any circumstances, friend or foe.

For the purposes of Movement, a unit's borders consist of any imaginary line that you can draw between any of the models in that unit. No model from any other unit can pass through one of these lines under any circumstances. Remember to include each model's "reach" when performing these calculations, allowing for the fact that units within 1" of each another are counted as in contact.

A clever commander can use this to their advantage by screening their important or fragile units with capable fighters, or with ones that are cheap!

Incorrect   **Correct**

1" BORDER AROUND THE MODELS DUE TO THEIR REACH

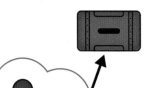

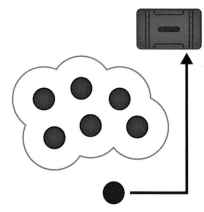

THE RED UNIT CANNOT PASS THROUGH THE BLUE UNIT TO REACH THE GREEN OBJECT.

THE RED OBJECT MUST INSTEAD SKIRT AROUND THE BLUE UNIT BY DIVIDING ITS MOVEMENT (IF THIS IS ALLOWED BY KEYWORDS)

CHARGING
The Path Of A Charge

When Charging, a unit must follow a straight path, even if that means traversing a dangerous terrain feature. As long as one model in the unit is within a distance equal to twice its Pace value from an enemy unit, then the whole unit can charge into contact, *regardless of the distance between the furthest models in the two opposing units*.

Determining A Straight Path

To determine the path that a unit must follow when Charging, first identify the two closest models in the target and the Charging unit. Once the position of these two lead models has been established, draw a straight line between the lead model in the target unit and every model in the Charging unit.

Any intervening terrain feature or friendly or enemy unit is considered to be in the path of the Charge and the rules governing these circumstances must be followed accordingly, even if that means that the Charge cannot take place.

Once this path has been established, move the lead model in the Charging unit into contact with the lead model in the enemy unit. Once the first model is moved, bring every model in both units into contact with another model in their unit, as close to their respective 'lead model' as possible and in contact with a model in the enemy unit wherever feasible.

If some feature of the table prevents you from positioning a model in contact with the lead model in their own unit, place it as close as possible to them and in contact with at least one other model in their unit. All models in the Charging unit can join in the resulting huddle, *regardless of the distance they must travel to do so.* Don't worry about any models that are not in contact, they'll still get to take part in the combat – the whole unit fights together.

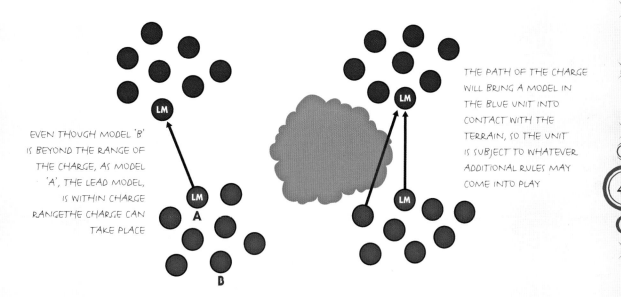

EVEN THOUGH MODEL 'B' IS BEYOND THE RANGE OF THE CHARGE, AS MODEL 'A', THE LEAD MODEL, IS WITHIN CHARGE RANGETHE CHARGE CAN TAKE PLACE

THE PATH OF THE CHARGE WILL BRING A MODEL IN THE BLUE UNIT INTO CONTACT WITH THE TERRAIN, SO THE UNIT IS SUBJECT TO WHATEVER ADDITIONAL RULES MAY COME INTO PLAY

Across Special Terrain

In the instance that a unit travels through a special terrain feature as it Charges, it must follow the rules for moving through that type of terrain (see pages 71 and 72 for more detail).

If even one model in the unit would have to traverse that terrain, then the whole unit must act accordingly.

In some instances, this will necessitate making a Test, but in others it will prevent a unit from Charging at all. In such instances, the unit must first manoeuvre itself in order to Charge from a more favourable position whenever the opportunity presents itself.

Into Buildings

If a unit wishes to make a Charge against a unit inside a **building**, then as long as the two closest models in each unit are within range of one another and no intervening terrain will stop the Charge, then those models can move into contact.

*Measurements between models on different planes, such as a unit in a street assaulting an enemy on the first floor of a **building**, are made without any reference to differences in height.*

From Buildings

Exactly as if they were moving into a **building**, a unit can leave a **building** through any part of the **building's** structure. As with Charging into **buildings**, measurements between the lead models in the Charging and defending units are made "as the crow flies" without any consideration for height discrepancies between the two.

From Special Terrain

Units occupying some terrain features, such as a **mire** or **broken ground**, cannot make Charges, or incur some form of penalty for doing so (see pages 71 and 72).

In situations where a unit wishes to Charge but is partially within a terrain feature that prevents them from doing so, they may not make the Charge. Units which include models whose bases are partially within such terrain, no matter how slim a fraction of their base it is, must first be moved out of that terrain as part of a Normal Activation before the Charge can take place (see page 37) for a table of Normal Activations).

Into Units Engaged In Close Combat

Although a unit cannot Charge through another unit, they may Charge an enemy unit that is currently engaged in Close Combat and where the straight line path would take them through one of the friendly units they are engaged with.

Provided that any one model in both the target unit and the charging unit are within range of one another, the whole unit can complete a charge into their target and can join the Close Combat alongside their compatriots.

If the Charging unit will not come into contact with the friendly unit when completing its Charge in a straight line, then it may complete its Charge without any further ado, but in cases where the two friendly units would occupy the same area then further rules for these circumstances, which can be found on page 45, will apply.

Into Multiple Units

Any player wishing to make a Charge must establish a single lead model in both the target unit and the charging unit. For this reason, a unit cannot target two units to Charge at simultaneously.

However, any friendly units that are in contact with the target of a Charge must join the Close Combat themselves, following the rules for a Charge into a unit that is already engaged in Close Combat. They do this by making an immediate, Out-of-Turn Charge (with no penalty incurred if the movement takes place outside of their native Phase) into the unit that just Charged their allies. Do this before any other units are Activated.

Unique units in this situation may also choose to join the Close Combat as a supporter instead, should their commanding player wish.

MAKING WAY

When a unit Charges to join a Close Combat that is already in progress, the models already in it may need to "Make Way". In instances where friendlies block the straight line path of a unit charging into Close Combat, it is still possible for the Charging unit to complete its Charge

TO MAKE ROOM FOR THE GREEN UNIT, THE RED UNIT MUST MOVE ACCOMMODATE IT.

LEAD MODELS ARE IN CONTACT, ALL MODELS ARE IN CONTACT WITH ANOTHER FROM THEIR UNIT AND ALL ARE AS CLOSE TO THEIR UNIT'S LEAD MODEL AS POSSIBLE.

So long as a model in the Charging unit is within range of one model in the target unit, friendly units can be moved to accommodate the Charging unit so that their lead model is in contact with the targets of their attacks.

Identify the lead model in the target unit and move the lead model in the Charging unit into contact with it. Once this is done, move all the models that are taking part in the Close Combat (remembering that individual models do not need to be in contact with enemies in order to fight) to accommodate all units. Except for the lead model, models in the attacking unit may move beyond their Pace value, but all models must be set up in contact with another model from their unit and as close to the lead model as is physically possible whilst maintaining Cohesion.

When moving any units that are already in Close Combat to accommodate a Charging unit, the same principle applies. To determine the lead model, simply select any which is contact with the model in the enemy unit that has been determined to be the lead. It does not matter which model is selected, but if multiple models are in contact with the enemy lead model and there is a disagreement, the choice can be randomised.

The chosen lead model is moved in such a way as to accommodate the unit joining the combat. Once moved, the lead model is used as a focal point for the other models in its unit to be moved themselves, following the principle that all models must be in contact with another from their own unit and as close as possible to their respective lead model.

Note that this procedure is only necessary if the friendly unit will physically need to be moved in order to accommodate the straight line path of the advancing unit. In all other instances, the normal procedure for Charging can be followed.

Making Way And Terrain

Units that are Making Way may do so into a special terrain feature, provided that it is not a terrain type that a unit with their Keyword cannot traverse. An example being cavalry entering into buildings or vehicles moving into woods. In instances where a unit that is Making Way enters terrain in which it would normally incur a penalty for traversing, such as vehicles in a mire, then that unit must make any necessary Tests associated with entering that terrain.

COMPULSORY MOVES

Sometimes a unit is forced to Move without any input from their commanding player. These special movements are called Compulsory Moves. Broken units, **mindless** units, units under the effect of a certain ability, and rampaging **creatures** all must make Compulsory Moves.

Compulsory moves happen at the end of the Close Combat Subphase. In all other respects, Compulsory Moves follow the same rules for movement as given in this chapter, so a unit that is making a Compulsory Move must make a Test if necessitated by their Keyword when traversing special terrain.

Order of Compulsory Moves

If both players have units that need to make Compulsory Moves, the player who had Priority Activation in the Command Phase takes the first Turn, choosing for themselves the order in which those Moves will occur. The next player then takes their Turn, choosing the order in which their units will complete their Compulsory Moves in the same way.

Broken Units

In the case of a Broken units, fleeing is a Compulsory Move that takes that unit directly towards its starting table edge by the shortest possible route. The path of the unit is measured from the model closest to the table edge in question. If two models are equidistant, the model furthest from the closest enemy is the model from which any measurement is taken.

In all other respects, such as unit Cohesion, the unit Moves in exactly the way it would if it were Moving normally.

Into Friendly Units

If a unit makes a Compulsory Move into a friendly unit, then they come to an immediate stop, no matter how many inches they would normally move. What happens next is determined by the special rule that caused that unit to make the Compulsory Move.

Broken units are governed by the rules on leaving combat due to Breaking given in the chapter on Close Combat conclusion (see page 52). Rampaging **creatures** are governed by those given in the chapter on Skills (page 93). In all other cases, a **mindless** unit, or one that is making a Compulsory Move, whose path is blocked by a friendly unit simply Moves as far as it is able and then stops, ending its Movement.

CLOSE COMBAT

Once battle is joined, fighting at close quarters is almost inevitable.

Whether it is scouting parties creeping up on their unprepared quarry in the night with keen blades or raiders storming a trench, insensible to the bullets flying all around them as they swing vicious clubs at the heads of their foes – at some point in any engagement, there is bound to be some fighting that gets up close and personal.

In *A War Transformed,* Close Combat, alongside Shooting, is one of the principle means of destroying your enemies, so getting to grips with these rules is a vital step in becoming a successful commander.

WHAT IS CLOSE COMBAT?

Close Combat pits one side against another in a Test to see who will prevail, with Wounds generated as the Close Combat is fought.

Players simulate the Close Combat by determining how many attacks their unit generates, then simultaneously rolling dice to determine how many of their blows land and how many fall wide of the mark. After that, both players have the opportunity to try and shrug off, deflect, or otherwise avoid the damage that their unit will receive by rolling their Saving Throws.

Depending on the success or failure of either player in this exchange, casualties are removed and the Close Combat is resolved once any other necessary Tests are performed.

No matter how many units are involved in a single clump of models, whether it is 2, 5, or 100, a contiguous area of models containing units from both sides in contact with each other is considered to be a single Close Combat.

Unique units can join a Close Combat as a **supporter**, bolstering the will of their compatriots by their presence. Any **unique** unit that is in contact with a unit in a Close Combat is considered to be part of that Close Combat as a Supporter, even if it is not actively taking part in the Close Combat itself.

WHEN DOES CLOSE COMBAT HAPPEN?

As outlined in the chapter on Activation (page 32), Close Combat occurs in the Close Combat Subphase. Any units that enter into contact with an enemy unit during one of the standard Activation Phases do not fight in Close Combat immediately, but must wait for the next Close Combat Subphase. Likewise, any unit that joins an existing combat will have to wait for the next Close Combat Subphase to make its presence felt.

WHO CAN FIGHT?

Any unit in *A War Transformed* can fight in Close Combat, provided that it has not been Destroyed – clearly units that are no longer on the table cannot engage in hand-to-hand fighting!

LEAVING COMBAT

A unit that has engaged in Close Combat, even as a supporter, can never move out of Close Combat until it is Broken or emerges as the victor.

In some exceptional circumstances, such as **template** weapon fire Scattering in an unexpected direction and removing one set of belligerents as casualties, a Close Combat may end in a way that does not necessarily include hand-to-hand fighting. In these instances, the Close Combat ends, with any units that were taking part able to be Activated in the remaining Phases of the Round.

Victorious units that are no longer in contact with an enemy unit at the end of the Close Combat Subphase, due to the enemy being either Destroyed or Broken, may be Activated in any way that the player sees it in the Round's following Activation Phases.

SUPPORTING UNITS

Unique units that are in contact with a friendly unit taking part in a Close Combat, but which are not themselves in the contact with the enemy, are considered to be **Supporters**. For all other purposes, Supporters are considered to be in Close Combat, but they do not generate attacks and cannot be attacked.

Only units with the Activation Keyword **unique** may act as Supporters, though there is nothing stopping you having them join the fray if you so wish.

Using **unique** units as Supporters to stiffen the resolve of troops fighting in a Close Combat can be an effective strategy for ensuring a favourable result. Some **unique** units can boost the effectiveness of Close Combat fighters whilst keeping themselves out of harm's way.

UNITS IN CONTACT

If a friendly unit is in contact with a unit that is the target of a Charge, that unit is compelled to Charge into the Close Combat as well, unless it has the Activation Keyword **unique** and may act as a Supporter.

In instances where Charging into the combat will require the unit to pass through the friendly unit, it does so according to the standard rules on Charging (see page 42).

CLOSE COMBAT ATTACKS

The number of Attack Dice that a multi-model unit generates is determined by its Zeal, including any modifiers, according the following table.

UNIT STRENGTH AND ATTACK DICE GENERATION TABLE	
Unit Strength	**Number of Attack Dice**
Full Strength (No Casualties)	Attack Dice equal to Zeal
More Than Half Strength	1 fewer Attack Dice than Zeal
Half Strength	2 fewer Attack Dice than Zeal
Less Than Half Strength	Attack dice equal to half the unit's Zeal (rounded down) or 3 fewer Attack Dice (whichever is the least)
Sole Survivor (1 Remaining Model)	1 Attack Die

Units engage in Close Combat as a whole, rather than as individual models. For that reason, the actual positioning of physical models is unimportant for determining how many Attacks can be made.

Each Attack Die generated is rolled in the Close Combat Subphase. Note that only units that are in contact with the enemy generate Attack Dice, so Supporters do not – they are merely there to provide a boost in the case of Morale Tests, or some other benefit determined by their special rules.

Single-Model Units

Single-model units that do not have the Keyword **tracked vehicle** or **wheeled vehicle** use a different table for generating Attack Dice, based on their Keyword. Generally, the larger the model, the more Attack Dice it will generate. However, **creatures** are far more deadly than mortals, with roughly man-sized **creatures** generating 4 Attack Dice apiece.

49

SINGLE-MODEL UNIT ATTACK DICE GENERATION TABLE

Unit	Attack Dice
Lieutenants, Witches, and Captains	2 Attack Dice
Weapon Team	2 Attack Dice
Tiny Creature	2 Attack Dice
Man-Sized Creature	4 Attack Dice
Large Creature	6 Attack Dice

Always be sure to check the entry for the unit for any additional rules caused by Combat Stress when generating Attack Dice for single-model units.

ROLLING TO HIT

Once you have determined how many Attack Dice your units in Close Combat generate, it's time to see if they can cause some injuries. For each Attack Die that your unit generates, roll a d6.

All units taking part in a fight roll their Attack Dice simultaneously. There is no order in which Attacks take place, so it is very handy to have some differently coloured dice on hand in order to help keep track of which Attack Dice belong to which unit.

There is no onus on players to actually roll simultaneously if they prefer to do so in sequence, but the results of all Attack Dice must be resolved before any casualties are removed and any further actions are taken in the Close Combat Subphase.

The result required to achieve a Hit is determined by a unit's Martial Skill, as shown on the following tables.

LOW MARTIAL SKILL, ROLL TO HIT (CLOSE COMBAT)

d6 result	Effect
1–2	Hit
3–6	Miss

MEDIUM MARTIAL SKILL, ROLL TO HIT (CLOSE COMBAT)

d6 result	Effect
1–3	Hit
4–6	Miss

HIGH MARTIAL SKILL, ROLL TO HIT (CLOSE COMBAT)

d6 result	Effect
1–4	Hit
5–6	Miss

Critical Hits

Some units have Keywords that allow them to make Critical Hits in Close Combat, sometimes including preconditions that must be met to do so. If a unit has a Keyword that enables it to make Critical Hits in Close Combat, then any roll of 1 is considered to be a Critical Hit.

Critical Hits immediately deal a Wound to a unit. A Saving Throw is only possible if the target unit has the appropriate Keyword or Keywords.

Players should think of Critical Hits as blows that are powerful enough to dismember, or lucky thrusts that find their way through a teeny gap in a foe's armour – anything that would instantly incapacitate or kill an enemy in a fight.

SAVING THROWS

Once both players have rolled all of their Attack Dice and generated any successful Hits, their opponent now has the opportunity to roll for Saving Throws. A Saving Throw stands in for both agility and armour, with some largely unarmoured units having a better Saving Throw on account of their dexterity. Others are simply well covered by plates of steel or a tough hide!

Regardless of the actual source of the protection, the Saving Throw roll works in the same way. For every Hit made against the unit (with the exception of Critical Hits) roll a d6 and compare it to the unit's Saving Throw characteristic. If the result is either equal to or lower than that unit's Saving Throw characteristic, it avoids the consequences of the Hit.

For example, if a unit requires a Saving Throw of 2 then it will need to roll a 1 or 2 on a d6 in order to successfully protect itself. Any rolls that are equal to or under the unit's Saving Throw characteristic succeed and no further action is taken, any that exceed fail and the unit takes a Wound or loses a model.

There are some instances in which a unit's Saving Throw may be made with Advantage or Disadvantage due to a special rule or ability. *However, a roll of 1 on a die is always a success, whilst a roll of 6 on a die is always a failure, no matter the Advantage or Disadvantage at play.*

TAKING WOUNDS

For every failed Saving Throw roll made by a multi-model unit, one of its models is removed as a casualty. When the unit has no models left, it is Destroyed. In instances where removing models disrupts unit Cohesion, other models within the unit can be rearranged to maintain both the Cohesion of the unit and also of the Close Combat in which they are fighting.

Single-model units with a Wounds Score gain a Wound Marker for every failed Saving Throw roll. When a single-model unit has an equal number of Wound Markers to its Wounds Score, it is Destroyed.

Distributing Wounds In Multi-Model Units

Some units can be upgraded to carry special weapons, granting individual models or groups of models in that unit special rules. When a unit loses models due to Wounds in Close Combat, the unit's commanding player decides which individual models are removed as casualties. This means that you can choose when your unit loses its special weapon models when it loses models.

CLOSE COMBATS WITH MULTIPLE UNITS

Numbers confer a huge advantage in Close Combat, and piling reinforcements into an ongoing Close Combat can be an excellent way to tip the balance in your favour. A unit only generates Attack Dice once per Close Combat Subphase, so an individual unit can only inflict so much damage each Round.

Nominating Targets

When in a Close Combat involving multiple units, you can opt to target a proportion of the Attack Dice your units generate at a specific enemy unit that your unit is in contact with. This can be useful in instances where your unit has a significantly better chance of inflicting casualties on one of the units it is in contact with over the other. A unit's Attack Dice cannot be targeted against an enemy unit it is not in contact with.

Divide your Attack Dice in any way that you see fit with just one caveat – in a Close Combat involving both **vehicles** and other troop types, **infantry** and **cavalry** must prioritise assigning Attack Dice to enemy **infantry** and **cavalry** units, leaving the **vehicles** until last. In this way vehicles can be "screened" with **infantry** and **cavalry**.

AFTER CLOSE COMBAT

After the Close Combat Subphase has been resolved, it's time to ascertain what happens next. In some instances, a unit's will to fight will be so shattered that it will simply turn and run, in others, a unit might stand its ground and the Close Combat will continue into the next Round.

At the end of any Close Combat Subphase, each unit that was involved in a Close Combat calculates its Morale. A unit's Morale determines which Combat Result Table the unit uses. These tables have different sets of results, which model the unit's reaction to the course of the Close Combat so far, whether that be running away, fighting to the bitter end, or revelling in their success.

Close Combat Conclusion Order

The order in which units act out their Close Combat Conclusion is determined by their Zeal. The unit with the lowest Zeal calculates its Morale and carries out its Close Combat Conclusion results first, then the process repeats with the next unit in ascending Zeal order until all units have acted out their Close Combat Conclusions, ending with the unit with the highest Zeal characteristic.

In cases where each player has a unit with the same Zeal score, the units belonging to the player who has the fewest models involved in the Close Combat acts first. If both players have the same number of models in the Close Combat, decide with a coin flip.

If a player has several units with the same Zeal, they decide the order in which those units act for themselves.

Calculating Morale

To calculate a unit's Morale, take its Zeal as a starting point, remembering to include any modifiers from Combat Stress Markers and any other factors. Next, use the following table to calculate the unit's Morale by either subtracting from or adding to the unit's Zeal.

Morale Calculation Table		
Close Combat Performance	**Modifier**	**Condition**
The unit has suffered more Wounds than it inflicted	-1 Morale	For each Wound suffered over the number inflicted on the opponent.
	-2 Morale	For each friendly unit Broken or Destroyed in the Close Combat this Round.
	+1 Morale	For each friendly unit fighting in the Close Combat or acting as a Supporter.
	-1 Morale	If the unit has the Keyword **infantry** and the Close Combat involves an enemy unit with the Keyword **cavalry** (except as a Supporter).
The unit inflicted more Wounds than it suffered	+1 Morale	If the unit has inflicted more Wounds than it suffered.
	Plus 1 to morale for each	For each enemy unit Broken or Destroyed in the Close Combat this Round

If a unit's Morale is 0 or less, it immediately becomes Broken, fleeing from the Close Combat in the Compulsory Moves Subphase.

Units with Morale equal to their Zeal simply continue the Close Combat into the next Round without any further calculation, but where there is a difference between Morale and Zeal, whether higher or lower, the Close Combat Conclusion rules below are used to determine what happens next.

If a unit's Morale is *lower* than its Zeal, it rolls on the Lower Morale Table and if its Morale is *higher* than its Zeal, it follows the rules for Higher morale.

Close Combat Conclusion – Lower Morale

For each point of Morale below the unit's Zeal characteristic (without modifiers), roll a d6, totalling the results.

LOWER MORALE TABLE	
Result	**Effect**
1–3	Fight On
4–7	Getting Tired
8–11	Exhausted
12 or more	Shattered

Fight On
Though they are losing, the unit's resolve holds and they continue to fight. The unit remains in place as though nothing has happened.

Getting Tired
Despite the grave situation, the unit fights on, though they are starting to flag. The unit takes a Combat Stress Marker (immediately resolving a Battle Shock Test if necessary).

Exhausted
The unit has fought hard, but the strain of fighting has ground them down. The unit takes two Combat Stress Markers (immediately resolving any Battle Shock Tests as necessary).

Shattered
Hard fighting has brought the unit to the brink of collapse and their will to fight teeters on a knife's edge. The unit takes three Combat Stress Markers (immediately resolving any Battle Shock Tests as necessary).

Close Combat Conclusion – Higher Morale

Units with high Morale generate additional Manifestation Dice, as their triumph over their enemies gains the attention of the denizens of the spirit world.

For each point of Morale above its Zeal characteristic (without modifiers), the unit rolls a d3, gaining a Manifestation Dice for each result of 1.

Some units have special rules relating to Combat Conclusion, which can be found in their specific unit profile, allowing them to forego their opportunity to generate Manifestation Dice and to enact a special result instead. Some units may also purchase Upgrades with similar effects.

What Units Are Affected By Close Combat Results?

All units that took part in a Close Combat, whether they actively fought or were only Supporters, must calculate their Morale and Close Combat Conclusion at the end of the Close Combat Subphase.

> Supporters only calculate their Morale for the purposes of determining whether or not they Break from having 0 Morale, so do not have Close Combat Conclusion effects for the difference between their Morale and Zeal.

Vehicles And Weapons Teams

If a Close Combat seems to be going against them, the crew of a **vehicle** or a **weapons team** will simply abandon it, resulting in it being Destroyed. **Vehicles** and **weapons teams** never roll for Close Combat Conclusion effects, but if their Morale goes below 0 they are still immediately Destroyed.

Mindless Units

Mindless units are not subject to Morale and so never roll for Close Combat Conclusion effects; they simply continue to fight until the unit has been completely Destroyed and, therefore, do not have to calculate morale.

Supporters Left In Combat

Sometimes, friendly units will Break and leave a Supporter out of contact with any units still in the Close Combat. In these instances, the Supporters Move back into contact with another friendly unit still in the Close Combat as part of the Compulsory Movement Subphase. If no units remain, they simply stay in place.

Though any Supporters that consolidate the Close Combat in this way will Move into contact, they do not count as having been Activated by this Movement.

BREAKING AND RALLYING

Whilst bullets, bombs, and bayonets do the killing, it is morale that wins battles. Building momentum, fostering belief in the certainty of victory, or else inspiring spirited resistance in the face of incontrovertible defeat – these are the hallmarks of a truly great leader. On the Doggerland Front, there are sights that could lead even the strongest of men to madness, but a good commander can get the best out of their men in even the most desperate of circumstances!

Break Tests

Under certain circumstances, a unit must take a Break Test. A Break Test is made against the unit's Zeal, with the Testing unit attempting to get a score of equal to or less than their Zeal characteristic on a d10, with a roll of 1 is always being a success and that a roll of 10 is always being a failure.

Any unit that fails a Break Test immediately becomes Broken.

Broken Units

A Broken unit's only goal is to leave combat completely, fleeing at full speed towards its starting table edge.

Broken units move at their Pace value in inches in a straight line towards the closest point on their starting edge as a Compulsory Move, doing so at the end of the Close Combat Subphase in exactly the same way as any other Compulsory Movement. This continues until the unit is either brought under control, Destroyed, or reaches the table edge, at which point it is immediately removed from play as though it had been Destroyed.

A Broken unit cannot be Activated, nor does it contribute to Command Token generation.

Attacking Broken Units

A Broken unit will be Destroyed immediately if it is engaged in Close Combat during the next Close Combat Subphase. For this to occur, the unit must be targeted as part of a Charge or come into contact with an enemy unit as a consequence of a Compulsory Move. This means that, for the purposes of giving and receiving Orders, making Activations, or performing Rituals, the attacking unit is counted as in Close Combat until the next Close Combat Subphase.

Broken units can be shot at normally, provided they are within line of sight and any other preconditions are met. Further rules on shooting can be found on page 56.

When a unit destroys a Broken unit in close combat, it generates d4 Manifestation Dice.

Terrain

A Broken unit cannot make any decisions about the path it takes to reach a table edge – it must always travel in a straight line towards the nearest point. Sometimes this means that a Broken unit will encounter terrain that will either slow it down or require it to make a Test, such as **infantry** moving through wire. In such cases, a Broken unit must make the Test in the prescribed manner, taking whatever penalties it incurs in so doing.

Impassable Terrain

If a Broken unit comes up against any terrain it cannot traverse, such as **impassable** terrain for any troop type or **buildings** for **cavalry**, then it takes a Battle Shock Test. The unit cannot move from this position until it is able to be rallied. A unit stuck in this way must make a Battle Shock test in the Compulsory Movement Subphase every Round until it is either able to rally or is Destroyed by shooting, an enemy engaging it in Close Combat, or failed Battle Shock Tests.

Friendly Units

A Broken unit that moves into contact with a friendly unit as part of its Compulsory Movement cannot pass through it and treats the unit as though it were **impassable** terrain, coming to a stop and taking a Battle Shock Test in the usual way.

When a Broken unit comes into contact with a friendly unit, it forces that unit to make an immediate Break Test as well.

Friendly vehicles

A broken unit which comes into base combat with a friendly vehicle follows all the rules above, but the vehicle does not have to perform a zeal test.

Other Broken Units

If, for whatever reason, a Broken unit collides with another Broken unit, then both must make a Battle Shock Test. In all other respects, the Broken unit that Moved into the other unit acts as though it came into contact with another friendly unit and will not move again until its path becomes clear, making a Battle Shock Test at the start of every Compulsory Movement Subphase that it is unable to continue along its path.

Vehicles And Weapons Teams

If a unit with the Keyword **tracked vehicle**, **wheeled vehicle**, or **weapons team** makes a Break Test for any reason and fails, it is immediately Destroyed.

Rallying

A Broken unit can be brought back under control by Rallying it. Rallying takes place during the Command Phase as an Order that is available to Captains and Lieutenants.

SHOOTING ATTACKS

The fierce hiss of a passing bullet, the steady beat of a machine gun firing, the high whine of an incoming shell – the very air of the Doggerland Front is alive with swarms of deadly projectiles.

Alongside Close Combat, Shooting is one of the surest methods of dispatching your enemies in *A War Transformed*. Different kinds of Shooting Attack are governed by different rules, impacting how shots are targeted, how accurate they are, and what kind of damage they do. Shooting governs all attacks made at range, whether the projectile in question is fired, loosed, or thrown and whether it issues from the barrel of a small firearm or a massive piece of ordnance.

WHAT IS SHOOTING?

Shooting is a special kind of combat which takes place over a distance. Unlike Close Combat, Shooting does not occupy its own Subphase, but happens as part of a Normal Activation, after an optional Movement.

Shooting Attacks are distinct from Close Combat in that they are one-sided – when a unit makes a Shooting Attack against an enemy, that enemy may only return fire in their own Turn, rather than both units fighting simultaneously as in Close Combat. Shooting Attacks can be devastating and, as they happen sequentially as part of the normal Turn order rather than in a Subphase, it is a good idea to try and get Priority Activation to avoid your units being Destroyed or Pinned before they can fire themselves!

The majority of Shooting Attacks are made using a unit's Martial Skill. Unlike a unit's other characteristics, its Martial Skill is given as a Keyword rather than a numerical value, with the different Martial Skill characteristics determining which of a series of tables a unit rolls on when Shooting.

Some special weapons function slightly differently, with any model armed with one of these special weapons rolling on a table specific to that weapon when Shooting. Some Shooting Attacks are made with d10s, whilst others are made with d6s.

When making a Shooting Attack, particularly for large units or ones armed with rapid-fire weapons, it can be extremely useful to have multiple dice of each of these types. A variety of colours can be handy to have in instances where two models within a unit have different unit profiles with different Keywords.

WHAT UNITS CAN SHOOT?

Any unit that is armed with a **ranged** weapon may make Shooting Attacks as part of their Activation. A unit may **not** Shoot if:

- ☺ It is in Close Combat
- ☺ It does not have the Keyword **quickfire** and has Moved this Phase
- ☺ It is Broken
- ☺ It is Pinned
- ☺ It is subject to specific special rule that prevents them from Shooting.

MAKING A SHOOTING ATTACK

Shooting in *A War Transformed* is simulated by using dice rolls for each model in a unit that is making a Shooting Attack. Any models in a multi-model unit that have been removed due to Wounds do not make a Shooting Attack.

Every model that is armed with a **ranged** weapon may Shoot, so there are no tables with which to generate Attack Dice, though some weapons may generate more than one Attack Die in a single Activation.

Once all Hits have been resolved, then your opponent can make any Saving Throws to which they are entitled, taking a Wound for each failed Saving Throw.

Lastly, the target unit makes any Tests that are necessary due to the Shooting Attack, such as Pinning or Devastating Tests.

WEAPON CHARACTERISTICS

Weapon characteristics are part of a unit's profile, displayed alongside information on their Pace, Zeal, and any equipment. They typically look like this:

Name	Keywords	Weapon Type | Number of Shots/Template Type | Effective Range/Maximum Range
Rifle	Small Arms	Standard Issue | (1) | 25"/30"
Hand Grenade	Small Arms, Arcing shot	High Explosive | Small Template | 8"

Different weapons have different characteristics, simulating their strength, accuracy, and rate of fire. Some weapons may require the rolling of just one die when Shooting, whereas others will necessitate rolling several. Other weapons have special rules that govern the circumstances in which they can be used to Shoot.

A small number of weapons use templates when making a Shooting Attack. **Template** weapons do not roll to see if they Hit. Instead, they generate a template that mimics the blast radius or path of their attacks. Any model caught under this template is automatically Hit, even if they are an unfortunately positioned ally!

The exact position where these templates land is often randomised, so shots can sometimes fall in unintended places. It pays to be wary when shooting **template** weapons in the vicinity of friendlies!

Though the majority of weapons in *A War Transformed* use d6s for Shooting Attacks, others, particularly **template** weapons like mortars and grenades, use d10s. Some unique classes of armament may also function slightly differently, so be sure to consult the weapon's profile for more information on how specific weapons work, including any Keywords that a particular weapon may have.

SELECTING A TARGET

The first thing to do when Activating a unit to Shoot is to decide which enemy unit you want to traget. With the exception of **vehicles**, no unit can split its Shooting Attack at more than one unit. All models within a unit must attack the same target when Shooting. **Vehicles** that have different weapons on different Faces are able to target different units on each Facing with their weapons.

What targets a unit can Shoot are governed by a few rules, so a unit equipped with a ranged weapon cannot simply pick any target on the battlefield and start firing away. In some cases, a target won't be visible, while in others another target must take priority when Shooting.

UNITS IN CLOSE COMBAT

No unit can Shoot at an enemy unit that is in Close Combat. This is due to the fear of hitting their compatriots with a stray round! Any unit that is in contact with an enemy unit, or is acting as a Supporter, cannot be targeted by Shooting Attacks until they leave Close Combat.

Occasionally a Scattered round may hit a unit that is in Close Combat. In these cases, resolve the Hits normally and inflict any Wounds as appropriate, but ignore any Near Misses. A unit that is in Close Combat can never be pinned; they are too busy fighting to take much notice of what else is going on around them!

LINE OF SIGHT

Most Shooting Attacks require Line of Sight. The exception to this is weapons with the Keyword **arcing shot**, which are generally missiles or munitions that are thrown, lobbed, fired, or loosed in a parabolic arc. Line of Sight means just that – if one unit can see another, then there is Line of Sight between them. In cases where Line of Sight is unclear, players will need to assume a model's eye view, getting their eyes as close to the models in question as possible and taking a look. If you can see a model, then it is in Line of Sight, no matter how slim a portion of it is actually visible. If one model can see another and vice versa, then the two units are in Line of Sight.

In cases where the profile of a model conveys a particular advantage in this regard, such as where infantrymen have been modelled in a crouching or prone position, it can be useful to have a generic 28 mm figure standing to attention that can be quickly substituted in for the purposes of checking for Line of Sight.

FACING

A unit that has a Face has Line of Sight in a 90-degree arc from that Face. A large **vehicle**, such as a heavy tank, might have side-mounted sponsons allowing it fire from either its left or right flank, or a cannon may only point in a particular direction such that it would have to spend a Turn Pivoting in order to Shoot at its intended target.

Determining Line of Sight in instances where a model has a Facing is as easy as measuring an oblique line at a 45-degree angle off the corner of the base on each side of the face that you wish to Shoot from, with any unit within that arc being in Line of Sight for that weapon.

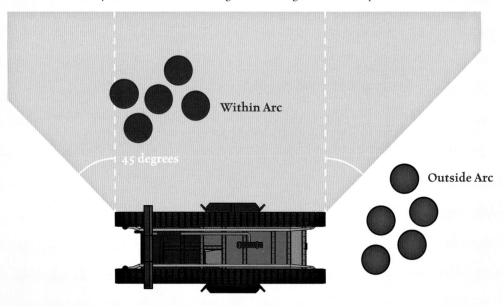

Some units may have different armaments available to them depending on their Facing and some may only be able to fire certain weapons from a particular Facing. At the same time, many vehicles have significantly more protection on the front than the sides, and virtually none on the rear. Thinking ahead and presenting the best possible Face to the enemy at all times is a valuable skill for a commander to have, so cultivate it well!

OTHER UNITS

A unit cannot shoot through another unit, regardless of whether the intervening unit is friend or foe. However, a unit that is elevated can fire over the heads of other units on the battlefield, provided that that unit is at least 1.5" or more above the surface of the table and is higher relative to the position of both its target and the unit that is wishes to shoot over. Line of Sight must still exist between the Shooting unit and its target.

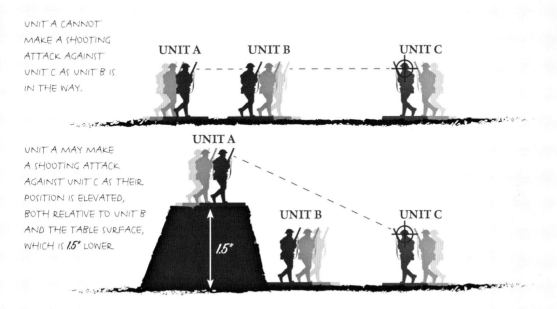

UNIT A CANNOT MAKE A SHOOTING ATTACK AGAINST UNIT C AS UNIT B IS IN THE WAY.

UNIT A   UNIT B   UNIT C

UNIT A MAY MAKE A SHOOTING ATTACK AGAINST UNIT C AS THEIR POSITION IS ELEVATED, BOTH RELATIVE TO UNIT B AND THE TABLE SURFACE, WHICH IS *1.5"* LOWER

UNIT A

UNIT B   UNIT C

1.5"

Arcing shot weapons do not require Line of Sight to Shoot, so may fire over intervening units should they wish. The other exception is units with the Keyword **sniper**, which can ignore intervening enemy units when choosing a target, but not other friendly units.

RANGE

All **ranged** weapons have a Maximum Range. Any unit that is wholly outside the Maximum Range of a weapon cannot be targeted. Standard issue weapons also have an Effective Range, within which the weapon is considerably more accurate. The Maximum and Effective Ranges of any weapon is expressed in inches, measured from base to base.

PRIORITY TARGETS

A unit must always Shoot at an enemy unit that is within 10" of them as a priority, except in a small number of cases. Soldiers in *A War Transformed* prioritise any target that presents an immediate danger to them when selecting who to Shoot at. Consequently, if any enemy units are within 10" inches of a unit armed with **ranged** weaponry then they can only target another unit if:

- ⊕ The enemy unit within 10" is engaged in Close Combat.
- ⊕ The enemy unit within 10" is Broken.
- ⊕ The Shooting unit has the Activation Keyword **cannonade.**
- ⊕ The enemy unit within 10" is completely outside the Shooting unit's Line of Sight.
- ⊕ The Shooting Unit must pivot in order to Shoot at that target and it does not have the Keyword **quickfire**.
- ⊕ The enemy unit which is within 10" has the Keyword **armoured** and the Shooting unit is equipped with **small arms**.

If any two models in opposing units are within 10" and none of the above exceptions apply, then that nearby unit must be the target of the other's Shooting Attack, if it chooses to make one. If more than two units are within 10" of a unit wishing to make a Shooting Attack and the above exceptions do not apply to either unit, then the controlling player may choose which one of them to target.

DIFFICULT SHOTS

There are a number of situations in which hitting another unit with **ranged** weaponry becomes more or less difficult. With weapons that fire at an extraordinary rate, or that are only effective at very close ranges, these circumstances matter little, but with the sort of weapons carried by the average soldier these factors can greatly impact whether a shot will find its mark. These circumstances are:

- The unit has moved in this Phase
- The target is beyond the weapon's Effective Range
- Less than 50% of the target is visible (see text box, Visibility)

Units armed with **standard issue** weapons will only ever Hit on a roll of 1 when making a Difficult Shot.

Visibility

With single-model units, this means that less than 50% of the surface area of the model is visible. In cases where the target is a multi-model unit, it means that if more than half of the models in the unit are only partially visible, with more than 50% of the surface area those models obscured, it is a Difficult Shot.

HARROWED A

THIS UNIT IS COMPLETELY IN THE OPEN – NO PENALTY IS INCURRED WHEN SHOOTING

HARROWED B

THOUGH THIS UNIT IS PARTLY OBSCURED, MORE THAN HALF OF THE UNIT IS MORE THAN **50%** VISIBLE – NO PENALTY IS INCURRED WHEN SHOOTING

HARROWED C

MUCH OF THIS UNIT IS OBSCURED, WITH MORE THAN HALF THE UNIT HAVING LESS THAN **50%** VISIBLE DUE TO THE TERRAIN – ANY SHOT TAKEN IS A DIFFICULT SHOT

HAUNTER A

N THIS CASE, THE HAUNTER IS IN THE OPEN, UNOBSCURED BY ANY OBSTACLE – THE SHOT IS TAKEN NORMALLY

HAUNTER B

THOUGH THE HAUNTER IS PARTIALLY OBSCURED, MORE THAN **50%** OF THE MODEL IS VISIBLE – THE SHOT IS TAKEN NORMALLY

HAUNTER C

THE HAUNTER IS ALMOST COMPLETELY HIDDEN BY THE BUSH, WITH LESS THAN **50%** OF THE MODEL VISIBLE – THE SHOT IS ROLLED ON THE DIFFICULT SHOT TABLE

SHOOTING TABLES

All units that have Line of Sight to shoot use a d6 on the appropriate table below to determine whether they hit their target. Some weapons have considerably higher rates of fire or are designed for use in close quarters and therefore do not use the **standard issue** weapon tables, having their own tables that do not take account of the unit's Martial Skill.

Critical Hits are only ever generated by natural rolls of 1, so a roll of 2 made with Advantage-1 does not count as a Critical Hit, even though that roll would be read as a 1.

STANDARD ISSUE (LOW MARTIAL SKILL)

Roll To Hit	Effect
1–2	Hit
3–6	Miss

STANDARD ISSUE (MEDIUM MARTIAL SKILL)

Roll To Hit	Effect
1–3	Hit
4–6	Miss

STANDARD ISSUE (HIGH MARTIAL SKILL)

Roll To Hit	Effect
1 (Natural)	Critical Hit
1–4	Hit
5–6	Miss

RAPID FIRE

Roll To Hit	Effect
1–2	Hit
3–6	Miss

CLOSE QUARTERS

Roll To Hit	Effect (Within 6")	d6 result	Effect (Outside 6")
1 (Natural)		Critical Hit	
1–4	Hit	1–2	Hit
5–6	Miss	3–6	Miss

MACHINE GUN

Roll To Hit	Effect
1–2	Hit
3–4	Near Miss
5–6	Miss

PRECISION

Roll To Hit	Effect
1 (Natural)	Critical Hit
1–3	Hit
4–5	Near Miss
6	Miss

ANTI-TANK RIFLE

Roll To Hit	Effect
1 (Natural)	Critical Hit
1–3	Hit
4	Generates Combat Stress Marker on Target
5-6	Miss

For any unit that includes soldiers equipped with different kinds of weapons, it is extremely useful to have a few differently coloured dice to help distinguish between the rolls of different models within the unit.

Every dice that meets its Roll To Hit will inflict a Wound. Once you've determined how many Wounds have been inflicted by the Shooting Attack, your opponent can roll to see how many successful Saving Throws they can make. Any successful Saving Throws negates a Wound and the Shooting Attack can be resolved to see if the unit that was under fire must make any Tests as a consequence.

SMALL ARMS AND ARMOURED TARGETS

Most weapons have the Keyword **small arms**, meaning that they are effective against unarmoured or lightly armoured targets like **infantry** or **cavalry**, but can do little to worry a steel-clad behemoth like a **tank**. A weapon with the Keyword **small arms** *cannot* cause Wounds to a unit with the Keyword **armoured**, only those armed with a weapon with the Keyword **ordnance** can. For that reason, no unit armed with **small arms** is ever compelled to fire on an **armoured** target.

INFLICTING WOUNDS

Once all of the Shooting unit's dice have been rolled, it's time for their opponent to see how many of their soldiers they can save. Check the profiles of the weapons used to see if any of them apply Advantage or Disadvantage to Saving Throws, noting which of the successful Attack Dice represent

Shooting Attacks made with these weapons. The targeted unit may roll a Saving Throw for each successful Hit (unless they have certain keywords) made against it, with each successful Saving Throw negating one Hit.

After all Saving Throws have been made, any Hits that remain become Wounds inflicted on the unit.

Distributing Wounds In Multi-Model Units

Within some units, there may be some models with slightly different unit profiles, such as an infantryman with a special weapon. When removing casualties from a multi-model unit, any model that is not **upgraded** is removed first, then models with special weapons are removed in the order chosen by the controlling player.

CRITICAL HITS

A Critical Hit is one made with pinpoint accuracy, hitting an exposed area or a gap in armour, and killing an enemy instantly. Saving Throws cannot be made against Critical Hits, unless granted by a specific Keyword held by the unit.

NEAR MISSES

Some weapons generate a special result called a Near Miss. Near Misses represent the powerful psychological effect that being under fire can have on a unit, even if none of the shots find their mark. For each Near Miss generated during a Shooting Attack means that the target unit is more likely to be Pinned.

Pinned units cannot be activated for the remainder of the Round, as the psychological stress of so much fire being poured down on them takes a heavy toll on the unit's willingness to fight. For the purposes of inflicting Wounds Near Miss results can be ignored, but do count for the purposes of Pinning Tests.

PINNING TESTS

When Near Misses are generated against a unit, it can cause that unit to become Pinned. A Pinned unit cannot be Activated, even to Rest.

Each Near Miss generated in the course of a Shooting Attack is used to calculate a Pinning Test, with every Near Miss functioning as a Disadvantage-1 modifier to Zeal. This means that a unit with Zeal 6 that has suffered 2 Near Misses in this Round of shooting must roll 4 or less on a d10 in order to succeed. If the unit passes the Pinning Test then they may be Activated as normal. If the unit fails then they are Pinned and can do nothing of any kind. Many unique models have special rules that can help them resist being Pinned.

The Pinned status only lasts until the start of the next Round, so in order to keep a unit Pinned they must be fired upon again and they must fail their Zeal Test for a second time.

With each new Shooting Attack any Disadvantage from previous Near Misses is discarded, so only calculate a unit's Disadvantage using Near Misses generated in the current Shooting Attack.

A unit that is already Pinned suffers no ill effects from any Near Misses inflicted upon it, but can still have Wounds inflicted upon it by shooting.

UNITS IN CLOSE COMBAT

There are some rare circumstances in which a unit that is in Close Combat will take Near Misses. In these instances, resolve any Near Misses as though it were an actual Miss – in the heat of combat no one will notice a bit of whizzing shrapnel!

DEVASTATING TESTS

For every Wound caused by a Shooting Attack made with a weapon with the Keyword **devastating**, the Shooting unit rolls a d10. For every result of 1, the target unit takes a Combat Stress Marker.

Devastating Tests are made after any Pinning Tests, so any Combat Stress Markers generated as part of a Devastating Test do not modify the unit's Zeal when making a Pinning Test for the same Shooting Attack.

If the unit is down to half or less of its Wounds or Model Score, then the Test is made with a d6 instead. Some units have special rules that force their opponent to make all of the Devastating Tests made against them on a d10 instead of a d6, with the target number still being 1.

BECOMING SHAKEN

When a unit is reduced to half, rounded down, of its starting Wounds or Models Score by a Shooting Attack, the unit becomes Shaken. Shaken units automatically gain a Combat Stress Marker, generated *after any Devastating Tests have been resolved.*

If a unit has some of its Wounds regenerated by some means and is then reduced below the threshold by a Shooting Attack once again, it does not become Shaken and is not required to take a Combat Stress Marker.

ARCING SHOT WEAPONRY

Some weapons have the Keyword **arcing shot** and work differently to **small arms** weapons. They do not require Line of Sight to fire, as they are either shot or lobbed in a parabolic arc. This class of weapons includes trench mortars, hand grenades, and other similar munitions.

Arcing shot weapons roll d10s rather than d6s to determine the effect of any shot that finds its mark. Instead of each model generating a certain number of shots determined by its weapon. **Arcing shot** weapons generate templates of varying size depending on the explosive payload of the ordnance that they fire.

Each template is placed over where the ordnance lands (see page 66 for how this is determined) and a d10 rolled for every model caught underneath it, including any friendly units that are unlucky to be caught in the blast of an inaccurate volley! Only the scantest portion of a model's base must be under the Template in order to register as a Hit.

Some units may generate more than one template in a single Shooting Attack. In these cases, it's best to make each roll individually, or with different coloured dice, to avoid any confusion further down the line.

Arcing Shot Weapons and Cover

All **arcing shot** weapons ignore any bonuses to their target's Saving Throws that are conferred by terrain such as Makeshift Cover from obstacles, Enhanced Cover from foxholes or the reroll conferred by trenches. As the missile is launched parabolically, it bypasses any object put between the Shooting unit and its target.

This makes **arcing shot** weapons such as grenades particularly adept at clearing fortified positions. Many an assault on the Doggerland Front begins with a hail of grenades falling among the hapless defenders of a trench!

Targeting With Arcing Shot Weapons

A unit that is equipped with an **arcing shot** weapon must follow all of the same procedures for target selection as any other unit – if an enemy unit is within 10" of it, they must target that enemy unit. Otherwise, the unit may Shoot at any point of ground that is within its range.

A unit can choose to target its Shooting Attack with an **arcing shot** weapon anywhere, even at an open spot of ground if the commanding player so wishes.

Sometimes, a player will choose to target their shot right in the midst of the enemy. In others, the spirit world may intercede with advice about the likely outcomes of rolling a Scatter Die (always keep those tarot cards handy), causing a player to target their shot slightly off to the side, or perhaps seemingly in the middle of nowhere!

Scattering

Once you have selected where you are targeting your shots, place a die or other suitable Template Marker on each of those points, where the dead centre of the Template will be. Templates with a small hole in the centre can be useful for this reason.

Roll a Scatter Die and an accompanying Distance Die for each of your Templates. The size of the Distance Die depends on the size of Template that the **template** weapon generates.

SCATTER DISTANCE TABLE	
Template	**Distance Die**
Small Template (3")	d3
Medium Template (4")	d4
Large Template (6")	d6

If the result is a Direct Hit then there is no need for the next step, simply resolve the Shooting Attack as normal, taking the marker that you put down as the centre of your Template and rolling a d10 for any model caught underneath it.

If the Scatter Die indicates a direction, then reposition the Template Marker in the nominated direction by a number of inches equal to the value rolled on the Distance Die.

Do this for each individual Template generated – some may score a Direct Hit whilst others fall far wide of their mark!

Hitting Weapons Teams

Weapons teams, such as Mortar and Machine Gun Teams have multiple models on a single base. When a Template falls over a **weapons team** unit, the number of Hits generated is dictated by the proportion of the base covered by the Template.

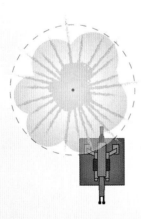 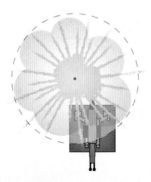 

A GLANCING HIT – LESS THAN *50%* OF THE BASE IS COVERED BY THE TEMPLATE – 1 HIT IS GENERATED

A MODERATE HIT – GREATER THAN *50%* OF THE BASE IS COVERED BY THE TEMPLATE – A NUMBER OF HITS EQUAL TO HALF THE TEMPLATE SIZE IN INCHES, ROUNDED UP, IS GENERATED

A GOOD HIT – THE ENTIRE BASE IS COVERED BY THE TEMPLATE – A NUMBER OF HITS EQUAL TO THE TEMPLATE SIZE IN INCHES IS GENERATED

Hitting Single-Model Units

When a single-model unit that does not have the **weapons team** Keyword is under a Template, hit generation works in the same way that it would for an individual model in a multi-model unit, so only one hit is generated.

To Hit Tables For Non Standard Weapons

When rolling for Hits with **non standard** weaponry, refer to the following sections as per the weapon's Keywords.

High Explosives

High explosives can be devastating against **infantry** and **cavalry**, easily shredding enemies. However, even though great care is taken in the production of these munitions, sometimes a shell or grenade will simply fail to explode due to either mechanical failure, the timely intervention of magic, or just sheer bad luck.

When rolling for Hits with **arcing shot** weaponry, a pair of "duds" will result in the projectile failing to explode or cause any real damage. Take all the rolls together – two or more 10s will invalidate any other results, even Critical Hits.

HIGH EXPLOSIVE TABLE	
d10 result	Effect
1	Critical hit
2–5	Hit
6–9	Near miss
10	Dud (two are needed, if only one is generated consider the result a Near Miss)

ANTI-TANK WEAPONRY

Anti-tank weapons are designed to penetrate armour before exploding, filling the cabin of the targeted **vehicle** with shrapnel or flame, but will sometimes fail to do so. This can result in shells exploding on impact or simply bouncing off. However, in some cases, a projectile will find its mark perfectly, causing a huge amount of damage. Some **vehicles** have more protection, meaning that **anti-tank** weaponry is less likely to cause such damage, but all **vehicles** are particularly susceptible to this kind of fire.

Against Cars and Tanks

CAR AND TANK ANTI-TANK TABLE					
d10 result	Effect (front)	d10 result	Effect (either side)	d10 result	Effect (rear)
1–4	Hit	1	Vital Component	1–3	Vital Component
		2–5	Hit	4–5	Hit
5–6	Spall	6–7	Spall	6–7	Spall
7–8	Fails To Penetrate	8–9	Fails To Penetrate	8–9	Fails To Penetrate
9–10	Deflection	10	Deflection	10	Deflection

d10 result	Effect (front)	d10 result	Effect (either side)	d10 result	Effect (rear)
BEHEMOTH ANTI-TANK TABLE					
1–3	Hit	1–4	Hit	1–2	Vital Component
				3–4	Hit
4–5	Spall	5–6	Spall	5–6	Spall
6–7	Fails To Penetrate	7–8	Fails To Penetrate	7–8	Fails To Penetrate
8–10	Deflection	9–10	Deflection	9–10	Deflection

- **Vital Component** – The round strikes the hull just above a vital component! The hit causes d3 Wounds.
- **Hit** – The shot is effective, damaging the **vehicle** and causing a single Wound.
- **Spall** – Smashing into the armour and deforming it, the round sends red hot shards of metal zipping mercilessly through the cabin, damaging equipment and shredding flesh. The **vehicle** recieves a Combat Stress Marker.
- **Fails To Penetrate** – The round explodes against the side of the armour, generating a Template on the hull at the point of impact that acts like a Hand Grenade (see page 65), inflicting a Hit to any unarmoured models within the Template.
- **Deflection** – The round hits part of the hull designed to turn them aside, pinging uselessly off into the aether instead.

No Saving Throws are allowed against **anti-tank** hits, the armour has already done its work in turning the round aside, or else it has been penetrated completely.

DIRECT FIRE WEAPONS AND SCATTERING

Direct fire weapons, such as anti-tank cannons, shoot a large projectile directly at their target rather than in a parabolic arc. Consequently, they Scatter differently than **arcing shot** weaponsand also require line of sight..

When firing with **direct fire** weapons, select a position on the perimeter of the target model's base and then, depending on the distance between the Shooting unit and its target (measured base-to-base), use the tables below to ascertain the effect of Scattering on the shell. Roll a d10 and compare the result against the appropriate table. The projectile will either score a Direct Hit, impacting the enemy unit exactly where directed, or will Scatter to the left or right by a small number of inches. The closer the target unit is, the more likely the round is to score a Direct Hit.

Left and right are defined relative to the starting table edge of the Shooting unit.

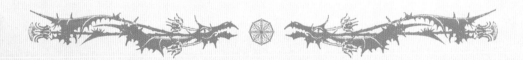

UNDER 20" SCATTER TABLE

1" Left	Direct hit	1" Right
1–2	3–8	9–10

BETWEEN 20" AND 40" SCATTER TABLE

2" Left	1" Left	Direct hit	1" Right	2" Right
1	2–3	4–7	8–9	10

OVER 60" SCATTER TABLE

3" Left	2" Left	1" Left	Direct hit	1" Right	2" Right	3" Right
1	2–3	4	5–6	7	8–9	10

Any shots that are Scattered beyond the perimeter of their target's base have missed. These shots are lost completely, so there is no need for any further action to be taken.

Armoured vehicles have considerably more armour on their fronts, so hits to the side and the rear are generally preferred. Think carefully about your shot placement – one aimed at the side of a vehicle may do less damage than one to the rear, but it may also be more likely to hit!

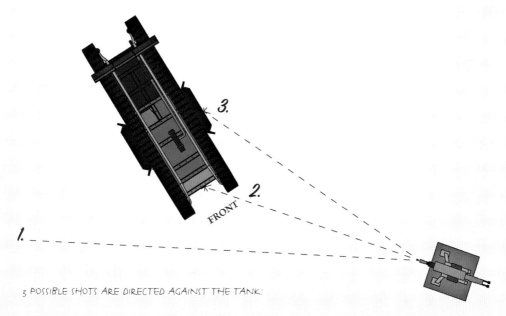

3 POSSIBLE SHOTS ARE DIRECTED AGAINST THE TANK:

1. SHOT NUMBER 1 SCATTERS 2" TO THE LEFT, MISSING THE TANK
2. SHOT NUMBER 2 IS A DIRECT HIT, TESTING AGAINST THE TANKS FRONT ARMOUR
3. SHOT NUMBER 3 SCATTERS 2" TO THE RIGHT, HITTING THE TANKS SIDE ARMOUR

FLAME WEAPONS AND PROJECTED FIRE TEMPLATES

Fire has always been used on the battlefield in some capacity, causing terror and mayhem wherever it is employed.

Some flame weapons use a standard round Template, whilst others generate a Template directly in front of the Shooting model's base called a Projected Fire Template. Both varieties of flame weapon use the same table for ascertaining how many wounds are caused by a Shooting Attack.

Like any **template** weapon, a Hit is generated for any model caught underneath the Template, regardless of how little of the model and their base is covered, with the result of each Hit generated using the following table:

d10 result	Effect
FLAME TEMPLATE SCATTER TABLE	
1–9	Hit
10	Miss

A projected fire weapon produces a Template 2" wide and 10" long from any point on the base of the model armed with it.

Chapter Four

TERRAIN

The battlefields on which *A War Transformed* is fought are varied, with features that are both alien and familiar to us in the real world. Many of these terrain types have special rules which may help or hinder units passing through or occupying them.

TERRAIN TYPES

OBSTACLES

A battlefield will contain several terrain elements too small or numerous to give much consideration to in the course of a game. These small, individual pieces of terrain are referred to as **obstacles**.

Though all unit types may move through **obstacles** without penalty, they provide Makeshift Cover to **infantry** in contact with them.

OPEN GROUND

Flat and featureless, **open ground** can be easily traversed without hindrance. Whether it is the salt-soaked plains of the recently drained sea, cultivated farmland, flower strewn meadows, or paved streets, **open ground** will form the bulk of the area of any battlefield.

All troop types may pass over **open ground** with no penalty or bonus. Small streams, shallow pools, and puddles should also be considered as **open ground**.

BROKEN GROUND

Pockmarked by mortars, scattered with debris, or even just heavily ploughed, **broken ground** presents little challenge to **infantry** or **tracked vehicles**, but can be a hazard to other unit types.

Cavalry can traverse **broken ground** without any penalty when Moving, but they must roll a d6 when Charging, gaining a Combat Stress Marker on a roll of 6. **Wheeled vehicles** cannot cross broken ground at all and treat it as **impassable** terrain.

FOXHOLES

Explosions can carve out huge scoops of ground, leaving deep indentations in which men may huddle for shelter from bullets, shells, and other projectiles.

Infantry within a **foxhole** have Enhanced Cover. **Foxholes** can be traversed by all models as though they were **open ground**.

TRENCHES

Trenchworks and revetments may be hastily dug before an expected engagement, or else be maintained, expanded, and inhabited over a number of years with saps, culverts, and machine gun nests.

Infantry that occupy a **trench** have both Enhanced Cover and Makeshift Cover. In addition, **infantry** in **trenches** may reroll any failed Saving Throws generated against a Shooting Attack (once per failed Saving Throw). **Trenches** can be traversed by all models as though they were **open ground**.

For the very largest trenchworks, consider whether it makes sense to designate them as some other terrain type – a light tank or horse would be able to drive over or jump a narrow trench, but not a huge gap!

WIRE AND THICKETS

Festooned with scraps of hanging uniform, windblown detritus, and other grisly baubles, barbed wire criss-crosses the old lines of engagement. Elsewhere on the Doggerland Front, huge thickets of bramble and thorns have grown quickly where the fighting has been fierce, and vegetation is returning with preternatural speed.

Wire and **thickets** present a huge obstacle to most units but none whatsoever to **tracked vehicles**, which can even destroy it simply by moving through it (page 71).

Cavalry and **wheeled vehicles** cannot traverse this terrain at all, nor can **infantry** Charge through it. **Infantry** trying to Move through **wire** or **thicket** as part of a Normal Activation must make a Test on a d6 for each model in the unit, gaining a Combat Stress Marker on each roll of a 6.

WOODS

In this transformed world, the **woods** of Europe have become dark and foreboding places; they are now home to things that once dwelt only in the darkest corners of men's imaginations.

Woods cannot be entered by units with the Keyword **tracked vehicle** or **wheeled vehicle**. **Cavalry** can traverse **woods** without any penalty if Moving, but must make a Test on a d6 to Charge as though they were crossing **broken ground**.

LOCUS

Across the front, traces remain of the ancient peoples that held the old gods sacred. As civilization crashes around them, the people of the 20th century looked to the forgotten customs and rituals of their forebears, rediscovering the ancient sites in their midst.

Infantry and **cavalry** at least partly within 3" of a **locus** count their Zeal as 1 higher.

MIRE

Wherever water sits on the battlefield, it becomes churned into a sticky mess by vehicles, men, and animals passing through it. In time, great pools of muck and sludge can form, becoming an obstacle to the steady passage of units of all types.

No unit may Charge through **mire**. Both **wheeled vehicles** and **tracked vehicles** Moving through **mire** must make a Test to ensure that they pass through it without getting Stuck (page 102).

BUILDINGS

Whether they are completely ruined or still partially standing, **buildings** dot the surface of the Doggerland Front. Even the most tumble-down structure can afford some protection against enemy fire, though doorways and ceilings render **buildings** inaccessible to some troop types.

Infantry have Enhanced Cover when occupying ruined **buildings** and may traverse them without penalty, but units with the Keyword **cavalry**, **tracked vehicle**, or **wheeled vehicle** cannot move through or into **buildings** under any circumstances.

IMPASSABLE TERRAIN

Some features of the landscape present such a formidable obstacle to movement that they are effectively out of bounds to any units.

Impassable terrain cannot be traversed by any unit under any circumstances and units must Move around it instead. **Impassable** terrain includes rock formations, deep rivers and ponds, and buildings that units cannot enter.

DETERMINING TERRAIN TYPES

Once your terrain is set out, it is a good idea to go around the battlefield with your opponent, surveying the topography and agreeing on exactly what type of special terrain each feature represents. In many cases this will be obvious, but the guide below provides some indication of what should be counted as what to help decide in any borderline cases.

It is good practice to do this in advance of rolling any dice to head off the possibility of any misunderstandings occurring.

IS THIS A BUILDING?

Players should carefully consider whether a feature of terrain constitutes a **building**, a collection of **obstacles**, or separate elements of **impassable** terrain, agreeing before the game begins and abiding by that ruling throughout.

A **building** may take many forms, but there must be space for one model on a 20 mm base to stand within it with at least 1" of space all the way around it.

A **building** is essentially an open or partially open topped box, the sides of which are impassable to all but **infantry**. A good rule of thumb to follow is that if the walls of a ruin do not form a box that is both enclosed (at least partially) and in which models can easily stand, then it is not a **building**.

Players are also encouraged to make sure that no **building** is too large – if a **tank** can easily fit inside it, then it shouldn't be classed as a **building**.

For large and impenetrable structures where it doesn't make sense for models to be clambering about with ease, or where the inaccessibility of the building is the point, such as with fortifications, consider another terrain type, such as **impassable**, even if only for particular parts of the structure.

IS THIS BROKEN GROUND?

A good rule of thumb is that if you wouldn't want to sprint over it for fear of losing your footing, then it is probably **broken ground**. **Broken ground** can be any area of the battlefield that seems to present a challenge, so don't constrain yourself just to rocky footing – rubble, tall grass, scree, and crop fields can all be **broken ground**. Players are encouraged to use their initiative to create battlefields that feel real and are fun to play on – the more variety, the better!

IS THIS A LOCUS?

A **locus** is a special category of terrain features, including things like menhirs, shrines, barrows, and sacred sites redolent with ancient power. A tumulus or cromlech might be **impassable**, whereas a looser collection of standing stones, such as a henge, could be a **building**.

Many types of terrain could be nominated as a **locus**, so that a sacred pool may perform double duty as both a **mire** and a **locus**, or a venerated grove of trees both a **locus** and a **wood**. If a **locus** has a second type assigned as well, it follows all rules for both.

IS THIS AN OBSTACLE?

Objects like trees, broken walls, and fences, commonly referred to as scatter, are counted as **obstacles**.

Any narrow linear object, such as a low wall or fence, or small single object, such as a tree, tractor, or telephone box, counts as an **obstacle** – if a reasonably fit man on foot could easily vault over or skirt around it without breaking their stride, it is an **obstacle**. For walls of more solid construction, or larger objects like omnibuses, or ruined tanks, players should consider whether it is more fitting to consider them as **impassable**.

IS THIS A WOOD?

A **wood** is any group of trees too densely packed to be considered a collection of **obstacles**, but diffuse enough that a group of models can actually occupy it. Once again, a good rule of thumb is to imagine yourself shrunk down to the size of one of your models and being tasked with sprinting through it – if that seems like a difficult proposition, then the terrain feature is **woods**, but if it sounds relatively easy then it should be considered to be a series of **obstacles** instead. For stands of trees that have been shelled to little more than stumps, **broken ground** can also be an appropriate terrain type.

Should your collection of terrain include any stands of trees too forebodingly impenetrable for a group of models to be placed inside, it should be considered **impassable**.

Chapter Five
SKILLS – ABILITIES, RITUALS, MANIFESTATIONS, AND ORDERS

In *A War Transformed,* many units have access to powerful Special Activations, called Skills, that can dramatically alter the course of battle. These skills themselves, both magical and mundane, are split into four types: Rituals, Orders, Manifestations, and Abilities.

SKILLS PHASE TABLE	
Command Phase	
Rituals	Magical rites that can be performed to give special bonuses to your units or hinder the units of your opponent.
Orders	Prosaic actions or instructions that officers can give to units, such as letting them to Activate out of sequence, but are essentially non-magical in character.
Manifestations	An effort to call through the veil one of the many creatures awakened by The Shattering.
Activation Phases	
Abilities	These Activations may be used whenever the unit that holds them is Activated. They range from feats of physical strength, mental fortitude, or dexterity to the use of minor magic. As with any normal Activation, they include a movement at the unit's standard Pace.

All these Skills have an Activation Level of some kind. Some are a simple exchange, costing a defined number of Command Tokens. Others are more complex, requiring a player to convert their Command Tokens into dice and roll to meet a particular threshold.

The criteria that must be met to use a Skill is listed alongside its effects, as well as any specific preconditions that must be in place before it can be used. These are given either in the following pages, or on that unit's entry in the army selection lists. Some Skills are shared between different units and selected from a pool, whilst others are unique to a specific unit type.

Some Skills have a stated range at which they work. This measurement is calculated from the base of the unit utilising that skill, in a straight line.

Any skill that has a stated range requires Line of Sight to the target of the Skill.

RITUALS

PERFORMING RITUALS

Once believed to be nothing but hocus pocus cherished by rubes and rustics, the reality of magic is now undeniable to all who have seen the changed face of war.

Rituals are magical ceremonies that can help your forces or harm those of the enemy. They are performed in the Command Phase and always take immediate effect. To perform a Ritual, a Witch must roll dice to simulate their attempt to call upon the favour of the gods.

To be successfully cast a Ritual requires a certain number of 1s to be rolled, with this requirement being stated on the entry for the Ritual. *Command Tokens used to cast a Ritual are rolled as d3s*, with the controlling player able to dedicate as many as they chose to ensure that the Ritual will be successful.

Each Ritual may be cast once per Round. Most rituals will only last for the duration of the Round in which they were performed, but some have different durations that will be stated alongside their effects.

A Witch in Close Combat, even if they are only a supporter, cannot perform Rituals – great concentration and the performance of certain symbolic actions are luxuries for which the cut and thrust of melee simply does not allow!

A Witch that wishes to perform a ritual must first leave Close Combat by some means. Only then will they be able to perform a Ritual, provided that it is still possible for them to do so. Additionally, a Witch that is Broken cannot perform rituals – they are too focused on running for their life!

TARGETING RITUALS

Provided they meet any specific criteria listed, are within range and which have Line of Sight (if necessary), and they are a valid target for the chosen Ritual, any unit may be chosen by a player to be the target of a Ritual. This means which units that are fighting in Close Combat or which are Broken *may* the target of a ritual.

GENERATING MANIFESTATION DICE

The drone of incantations, the scent of blood, the rhythmic beat of a drum or stamping feet – all these are powerful beacons to the creatures of the other world.

When Rituals are performed, there is a chance to generate Manifestation Dice. For every paired result generated when attempting to cast a Ritual, add one of the dice to your Manifestation Pool. For example, a roll of three dice that produced 1, 2, and 2 would generate a Manifestation Dice on account of the pair of 2s. See page 82 for full details in regard to Manifestations.

Magic and Vehicles

Magics that corrode the flesh or corrupt the mind would have little effect on a **vehicle**. Only commands, rituals, or abilities which specifically mention tracked/wheeled vehicles as a valid target should be thought of as applicable to these classes of unit.

HERMETIC LODGES

In addition to its nationality, a Patrol will owe its allegiance to a particular aspect of the Triune Goddess or her consort. Membership of these different Hermetic Lodges, clandestine organisations with a history stretching back far beyond the transformational events of The Shattering, confers access to different Rituals and bonuses.

When creating your Patrol, you must pick the Hermetic Lodge to which your Witch belongs. Membership of the different Hermetic Lodges dictates which Rituals your Witch has access to, with each having its own strengths and weaknesses, which will suit different playstyles.

RITUALS OF THE MAIDEN

The Maiden grants her followers unrivalled speed and attacking potential through her movement-focused Rituals. The powers associated with The Maiden are balanced in terms of cost and will be most appealing to players with an aggressive play style.

The Chariot (Level 1)

As the skies darken, the thunder of hooves will soon be heard again.

Select a friendly **vehicle** to receive d3 extra Pace for the remainder of this Round.

The Hanged Man (Level 1)

One man falls and one is driven onwards. If they are willing, is it punishment or sacrifice?

Select a unit that is not engaged in Close Combat and perform a Zeal Test as if for Battle Shock. For every point that the Test is failed by, remove one model from the unit. For every model removed, a friendly unit within 20" may immediately be moved 6" in any direction and gains the Keyword **insensible** for the remainder of the Round. Any unit moved in this way does not count as having been Activated.

The Fool (Level 1)

A fool may rush in, but cunning is no ward from a bullet.

Select a unit within 12" of your Witch. For the remainder of the Round, that unit gains the Keyword **foolhardy**.

The Moon (Level 1)

The light of the moon can be treacherous, and those who walk the path must watch their step.

Select an enemy unit within 25". In the coming Round, that unit loses d4 from its Pace.

The High Priestess (Level 2)

What is a machine but a body of steel? What is a piston but a brazen limb dancing?

A unit with the Keyword **tracked vehicle** may be activated in the Cannonade Phase, as opposed to its stated Activation Phase.

The Lovers (Level 2)

A lover's touch can cool an aching limb or kindle a burning heart.

Select a unit with one or more Combat Stress Markers that is not engaged in Close Combat and remove d3 Combat Stress Markers.

RITUALS OF THE MOTHER

The Rituals associated with The Mother focus on protecting your troops. Rituals of The Mother are inexpensive and will appeal to players with a more cautious style, but they have little to offer in terms of offensive flexibility.

The Empress (Level 1)

Love is a tonic and a mother's care can soothe any ache.

Select a unit that is not engaged in Close Combat and remove one Combat Stress Marker from it.

The High Priest (Level 1)

The bones are cast, the entrails incised and the ashes scried.

Select a friendly unit with the Activation Keyword **unique**. For the remainder of the Round that unit may reroll all failed Saving Throws.

The Moon (Level 1)

The moon's pale light embraces all and steers us to our destiny.

Select a friendly Broken unit anywhere on the table to immediately return to the fight.

Temperance (Level 1)

A mother's children are like the limbs of one body.

Select two units with the Keyword **infantry** or **cavalry** that are within 12" of one another. For the remainder of the Round, any Wounds inflicted on the first unit can be transferred to the second on a roll of 3 or less on a d6. A roll must be made individually for each Wound, and any Saving Throws must be made using the profile of the second model.

The Tower (Level 1)

The world's refuge. A stout fortress and a strong arm prevail against all woes.

Select a piece of special terrain, such as **woods** or **mire**, anywhere on the table. For the remainder of the game, any unit of **infantry** that occupies that terrain feature may reroll their Saving Throws as though they occupied a **trench**.

Justice (Level 2)

Measure for measure, drop for drop.

Select a single-model unit within 25" of your Witch. For the remainder of the Round, any unit that makes a Shooting Attack against it is inflicted with a Devastating Test for every casualty that it inflicts. This Test is made according to any existing modifiers to Devastating Tests in play on that unit.

RITUALS OF THE CRONE

The Hermetic Lodge of The Crone focuses on Rituals that can sway the balance of power through cunning and guile – her Rituals tend to be powerful, but expensive, in comparison to the rituals of her sister goddesses.

The Hermit (Level 1)

The craft is an ocean, deep and wide. The powerful are each an island, isolated by their knowledge.

Select a unit with the Activation Keyword **unique** within 25", for the remainder of this Round *all* successful Hits generated by Shooting Attacks made against it must be rerolled.

The Moon (Level 1)

In the radiance of the moon's light are all things seen and known.

Select an enemy unit within 25". In the coming Round, that unit loses the benefit of any Cover it may have.

Death (Level 2)

The scythe is swung, the pendulum stops.

Select an enemy unit within 20" of your Witch that does not have the Keywords **vehicle** or **mindless**. That unit must immediately take a Battle Shock Test.

The Magician (Level 2)

What is power but the means to remake the world as you see fit?

Select two friendly models within 25" of your Witch that have the Activation Keyword **unique** and that are not engaged in Close Combat. Swap their positions on the table.

The Star (Level 2)

Brilliance beyond measure, glory without end. Those who shine brightest often fade soonest.

Select an enemy unit. For the remainder of the Round, any failed rolls generated by Shooting Attacks against that unit may be rerolled.

Judgement (Level 2)

The trumpet sounds and the dead arise, to see on what page their names are writ.

Select a multi-model unit within 25" that has suffered losses in the previous Round, then roll a d6 and consult the Judgement Result Table.

JUDGEMENT RESULT TABLE	
D6 Roll	**Result**
1	The target unit is returned to its starting strength and gains the special rule terrifying for the remainder of the game.
2–3	The target unit is returned to its starting strength.
4–5	The target unit regains d6 models.
6	All units within 10", including the target unit, must make a Battle Shock Test.

RITUALS OF THE HORNED GOD

Members of the Hermetic Lodge of The Horned God prize strength over all else, prioritising personal renown over sound strategy. Their Rituals reflect this and tend to focus on bolstering the combat prowess of their adherents.

The Devil (Level 1)

His is the fire that cannot be quenched, the unslakable thirst. Though a million souls are thrown in after him, the pit will never fill.

Select a friendly multi-model unit and roll as though for a Battle Shock Test. For every point that the roll is failed by, the unit loses one model and you gain one Activation Die.

The Emperor (Level 1)

My will be done – power speaks, and the world obeys.

Select a unit within 25" inches to gain the Keyword **freakish strength**.

Strength (Level 1)

Might begets might.

Select a unit with the Activation Keyword **unique**. For the remainder of the Round, the unit gains the Keyword **mighty blow**.

The Sun (Level 1)

As the sun's light burns through you, all that is weak is burned away.

Select a single unit within 25" of your Witch. That unit may reroll any misses in the next Close Combat Subphase.

Wheel Of Fortune (Level 1)

The wheel spins and the mighty are bought low, it tumbles on and the lowly are made high. Such is the fickle whim of fate.

Select two friendly units with the Keyword **infantry**. Select one to gain d3 to their Zeal and Pace and the other to lose d3. You must make a separate roll for each unit, declaring which of the two units you intend to roll for prior to doing so.

The World (Level 2)

On the isle there is a tree and of that tree there is a fruit and of that fruit there is a seed and of that seed there is a tree...

Select a single piece of terrain, such as a **building** or **wood** within 25". For the remainder of the game, any friendly unit fighting a Close Combat within 6" of that terrain gains the Keyword **freakish strength**.

MANIFESTATIONS

Any Witch can attempt to summon **creatures** to the battlefield – powerful but fickle allies with potent abilities. Creatures may be lesser spirits connected with a specific place that your Witch coaxes or flatters across the veil between worlds with offerings of blood, or some of the many bestial creatures that have slipped through gaps in the veil throughout history, passing into the folklore of men.

Some creatures are terrifying beasts, defying explanation or description, while others are twisted imitations of humanity, their needle teeth and distended bodies betraying their otherworldly nature.

Manifestation attempts, wherein creatures are called forth, are made during the Command Phase by rolling up to six Manifestation Dice in an attempt to reach a certain threshold of the totalled result. Less powerful creatures manifest easily, whereas more powerful ones require a considerably greater sacrifice.

For example, if a creature's Manifestation Level requires a roll of 14, then the player must roll a total of 14 with the Manifestation Dice that they throw to manifest that creature. Naturally, this means that throwing more dice will lead to a greater chance of manifesting a higher Manifestation Level **creature**, but beware – the more that dice you roll, the more likely you will be to fall afoul of the many perils that can strike the would-be manifester.

USING MANIFESTATION DICE

Each time that you roll two of the same result when using a Ritual, you gain a Manifestation Die, which are put aside to spend whenever you want to attempt to Manifest a creature. Manifestation Dice are also generated by successfully combats, or by cutting down fleeing enemies.

You may roll up to a maximum of six Manifestation Dice in a single Manifestation attempt. So long as you have at least two Manifestation Dice in your Manifestation Pool and a Witch on the table, you can make a Manifestation attempt. All Manifestation Dice must be rolled simultaneously and the creature that the player intends to roll for must be clearly stated. A witch may only make one Manifestation attempt per Round.

CREATURES

The wild places of the post-Shattering world are where the veil between our world and that of the spirits is thinnest, Sometimes, the realities have overlapped so completely that the boundary no longer exists at all. In these untamed spots, many strange creatures can be drawn near with offerings of fresh blood, then bound to the will of a powerful Witch. Creatures drawn to the battlefield in this way are coerced into fighting for one side or another, but though their free will is suppressed by the command of the Witch, the moment that that link is severed, they may become more of a liability than an asset.

Creatures are elite units that can be summoned to the table as temporary allies in the fight against the enemy. Manifesting a creature counts as a special form of casting a Ritual, so the unit that is attempting the Manifestation must follow all of the rules applicable to conducting a Ritual.

Though they are extraordinarily powerful, creatures make fickle allies. Whilst the player who initially Manifests a creature can exert some control over it, these avatars of the old gods manifest for the sole purpose of exacting a bloody harvest. If the Witch that manifested them loses control for even a split second, then the creature will act instinctively. For some creatures, this means slinking back off to the nearest forest, but others will rampage across the battlefield, attacking friend and foe unlike until either their thirst for blood is slaked or they are brought down by overwhelming fire.

Manifesting creatures in this way is about managing risk and reward, with the huge power and special Abilities possessed by creatures being an obvious draw, albeit somewhat mitigated by the possibility of losing control and finding one of these horrors at your own throat! Despite the danger, creatures prove irresistible to some commanders, their timely intervention able to bolster an ailing force or deliver the coup-de-grace that brings a bloody end to spirited resistance.

There are six classes of creatures, from weak and diminutive Snatchers to towering colossi known as Crushers.

SNATCHER – MANIFESTATION LEVEL 8

Kobolds, Brownies, and other imp-like creatures

Diminutive and cowardly, most Snatchers are similar to a human in appearance, but some may take stranger forms. They are the most intelligent variety of creature, but also the most pusillanimous, preferring to fight from the sidelines by hurling rocks and insults in their unintelligible tongues. Snatchers generally avoid the presence of mankind, but will endure brief contact under certain circumstances, such as to steal an unattended newborn, or to make good some perceived slight through an act of petty theft or vandalism. They carry this predilection to the battlefields of the transformed war, where they can take the special items of nearby units or sabotage large weapons, at least on the rare occasions that they can be cajoled into it.

SNATCHER

P	MS	Z	W	ST
5	Low	6	1	3

Keywords	Activation Keyword
Tiny Creature, Cowardly, Bramblekin, Fast Target	Elite (Creature)

Regulation Equipment

Standard issue CC weapon

Abilities

Snatch – 1 Command Token – Select an enemy unit with the Activation Keyword unique within 6" and roll a d3 – on a roll of 1, that unit loses whatever piece of special equipment it is carrying. If the Test is failed, the Snatcher gains a Combat Stress Marker.

Sabotage – 1 Command Token – Select an enemy unit within 6" with the Activation Keyword cannonade. For the remainder of the game that unit must pass a zeal test before shooting.

1 CSM	2 CSMs	3 CSMs
Stumbling: Loses Keyword bramblekin	**Hiding:** Can no longer move, but gains the Keyword camouflage	**Hiding:** Can no longer move, but gains the Keyword camouflage

BEGUILER – MANIFESTATION LEVEL 10
Rusalka, Melusine, and other drowning spirits

Beguilers are strange, fragile **creatures** that inhabit bogs, swamps, streams, and pools. They often take the form of a beautiful youth, beckoning their victims into the water with the promise of carnal delight before revealing their true, hideous nature. Other tactics, such as imitating a person calling out for help, the voice of a loved one, or a strange light in the fog, are commonplace, but the end result is always the same – a grisly demise in a pool of stagnant water.

BEGUILER				
P	**MS**	**Z**	**W**	**ST**
6	High	7	2	3

Keywords	Activation Keyword
Medium Creature, Aquatic, Undine	Elite (Creature)

Regulation Equipment
Brutal CC Weapon

Abilities

Enchant – 1 Command Token – Select an enemy unit that does not have the Keyword vehicle within 25" and Test against the unit's Zeal. If the Test is failed, the unit must make an immediate Move towards the Beguiler as though advancing into contact. When the unit ends its Move, it is Pinned for the remainder of the Round. The enchanted unit must Test for any intervening terrain as dictated by its Keywords. The selected unit can be one which has already been Activated to move this Round.

1 CSM	2 CSMs	3 CSMs
Fading Glamour: Zeal Tests made by enchanted enemies are rolled with Advantage-1	**Blinded:** MS reduced to Low	**Broken Facade:** Can no longer use Abilities

HAUNTER – MANIFESTATION LEVEL 12

Feldgeists, Leshy, and other feral spirits

Wherever man lives alongside the wild, the spirits of these untamed places must be placated, lest evil fortune befall him. Inscrutable and immensely powerful, Haunters have the most alien motivation of all the creatures that patrol this bleak frontier. Often appearing amongst the stands of shell-blasted trees or in overgrown and long-abandoned fields, Haunters will taunt their prey for days or even weeks, relishing in the fear that they generate in their intended victims as they are slowly driven out of their wits.

HAUNTER

P	MS	Z	W	ST
6	Low	6	1	3

Keywords	Activation Keyword
Medium Creature, Wisp, Disturbing	Elite (Creature)

Regulation Equipment

Standard issue CC weapon

Abilities

Torment – 1 Command Token – Select an enemy unit with the Keyword infantry or cavalry within 20". The selected unit must take a Zeal Test with Disadvantage-1 if the Haunter is within 20", Disadvantage-2 if the Haunter is within 10", or Disadvantage-3 if the Haunter is within 6", gaining a Combat Stress Marker if it fails.

1 CSM	2 CSMs	3 CSMs
Shackled: Can no longer Move	**Enfeebled:** The target of a use of Torment may reroll any failed Zeal Test	**Unbound:** Gains an additional two Attack Dice and MS increases to High

PROWLER – MANIFESTATION LEVEL 14

Black Shuck, the Beast of Gévaudan, and other great animals

Prowlers are huge beasts, alike in shape to the material creatures they resemble, but of considerably larger size. Though they are creatures of instinct, they are not without guile, and may even display a crude, but entirely cold, cunning, taking those who think of them as little more than animals by surprise. Prowlers attack with all the viciousness and speed of a wild beast, tearing and goring their foes with terrible fangs, claws, and horns until nothing but a bloodied wreck remains.

PROWLER

P	MS	Z	W	ST
7	High	7	3	3

Keywords	Activation Keyword
Large Creature, Terrifying, Camouflage	Elite (Creature)

Regulation Equipment

Fearsome CC weapon

Abilities

Lair – 2 Command Token – The Prowler may be picked up and placed in a piece of wood terrain anywhere else on the board. After having done this, the Prowler may not be Activated again in this Round under any circumstances as though Pinned.

Leap – 1 Command Token – The Prowler can "jump" up to 8", ignoring any intervening units, friend or foe, as well as any special terrain (except impassable terrain). The Prowler cannot end this movement within 1" of any other unit.

1 CSM	2 CSMs	3 CSMs
Injured Paw: Pace is reduced to 3	**Madness:** Gains the Keyword impetuous	**Blinded:** MS reduced to Low

DEVOURER – MANIFESTATION LEVEL 16

Hags, Trolls, and other anthropophagous monsters

Most Devourers are a hideous parody of the human form, covered in filth-matted hair and smeared with muck and gore, but some take stranger forms. Their hatred of mankind runs deeper than in any other creature. Their principal desire seems to be to eat human flesh in a desperate attempt to sate a hunger that will never end. However, some, particularly those that are more selective when choosing their victims, may have more complex motivations than simple hunger, choosing their meals on the basis of some inscrutable criteria.

DEVOURER

P	MS	Z	W	ST
5	Medium	7	4	4

Keywords	Activation Keyword
Large Creature, Enhanced Protection, Elemental Resistance, Unnaturally Tough, Terrifying	Elite (Creature)

Regulation Equipment

Fearsome CC weapon

Special Rule

Feast – A Devourer which rolls on the High Morale Combat Conclusion Table can ignore any results it generates and can choose instead to "feast". In so doing, it becomes a Pinned for the remainder of the Round, but regains d3 lost Wounds.

1 CSM	2 CSMs	3 CSMs
Enraged: Gains the Keyword Dumb Brute	**Blinded:** MS reduced to Low	**Injured:** Loses Fearsome CC weapon regulation equipment

CRUSHER – MANIFESTATION LEVEL 18

Giants, Titans, and other gods made flesh

Huge creatures that are festooned in ancient totems and daubed in mystic symbols, Crushers stride across the battlefield destroying everything in their path. Immensely strong, a Crusher can easily obliterate all but the strongest of armoured vehicles with overwhelmingly powerful blows. To face a Crusher is to stand before the might of the old gods manifested.

CRUSHER				
P	**MS**	**Z**	**W**	**ST**
5	Medium	7	5	3

Keywords	Activation Keyword
Large Creature, Enhanced Protection, Elemental Resistance, Mighty Blow, Terrifying	Elite (Creature)

Regulation Equipment		
Fearsome CC weapon		

1 CSM	2 CSMs	3 CSMs
Enraged: Gains the Keyword Dumb Brute	**Lamed:** Pace reduced to 3	**Berserk:** The Crusher is no longer affected by the Curse of Iron (see page 103), but permanently trades the Activation Keyword Elite for Mindless. This is not the same as if the Crusher were Rampaging, so it will not attack or move towards friendly troops. However, should the controlling Witch be killed the Crusher will still enter the Rampage state.

WHERE DO CREATURES MANIFEST?

When declaring your intention to attempt a Manifestation, indicate where on the board you want the creature to appear. The chosen location must be along one of the edges of the table, at least 6" away from any enemy units and 12" away from the enemy Witch.

There are two exceptions to this rule:

- ☻ **Prowlers** – You may choose a **wood** for the creature to Manifest in, at least 6" away from any enemy units and 12" from an enemy Witch.
- ☻ **Beguilers** – the player may choose a **mire** for the creature to Manifest in, at least 6" away from any enemy units and 12" from an enemy Witch.

In both instances the player should place a marker on a spot wholly within the terrain feature and in the exact position where they intend for the creature to manifest.

Unintended Positions

In some instances, a creature will be forced to Manifest in a position other than where you intended. Sometimes this can be a result of the Manifestation itself going slightly askew, or it may be the result of another factor. In these instances, the normal rules governing where a creature may Manifest are ignored.

In Enemy Units

If a Manifestation results in the creature coming into contact with any enemy unit, or even Manifesting within an enemy unit, then it counts as having made a Charge in this Round and must fight in the Close Combat Subphase.

To identify exactly where the creature will Manifest, identify the closest model in the targeted enemy unit to the Witch that is attempting the Manifestation. The creature should be placed as though it were the Witch themselves charging and the enemy unit must make a Battle Shock Test.

Into Special Terrain

Unusual situations can also lead to a creature Manifesting in a piece of special terrain. In such cases, the creature must make any Tests associated with moving through that terrain type.

If the creature's Keywords mean that it cannot occupy a particular terrain type, or it attempts to Manifest in **impassable** terrain, then the creature must be placed elsewhere. In the event of this, place the creature on the outside of the terrain feature, following the straight line in which the creature's Manifestation was Scattered.

Into Friendly Units

If a creature is forced to Manifest in contact with or within a friendly unit, then that unit must make a Battle Shock Test. To place the Manifested **creature**, draw a straight line between the Witch performing the Manifestation and the closest model in the targeted friendly unit. The **creature** should be in contact with the closest model in the targeted unit to the Witch performing the Manifestation.

THE DANGERS OF MANIFESTATIONS

To perform a Manifestation, a Witch must use offerings of blood to break through the material world and reach into the realm of the spirits.

Once they have passed through the veil, they must call out to the creatures that reside beyond and bind them to their will. This battle of raw spiritual power would shatter the minds of lesser men; such is the danger of reaching out into the spirit world that only those of iron-hard purpose would even attempt it.

Rolls that produce pairs, three-of-a-kinds, and so forth, can lead to unforeseen consequences. The Creature Manifestation Table lists the effects of rolling these sets of dice, with different tables for when the Manifestation attempt is successful and when it fails.

Some of these effects are best avoided, but others can be a fitting reward for pushing your luck right to its limits! Players must think carefully about the potential ramifications of their rolls as, once they have thrown their dice, there is no going back.

The effect of each of these combinations is cumulative, so if you get two pairs of dice in a single roll, that creature is Scattered by 2d6". If you get a pair and a three-of-a-kind then the manifester takes a Combat Stress Marker *and* the creature is Scattered d6".

CREATURE MANIFESTATION TABLE

Dice Rolls Include	Result	
	If Creature Manifests	**If Creature Does Not Manifest**
Pair	The creature is Manifested, but not where they were called! Scatter the unit d6" in a random direction along the table edge. If the creature is a Prowler or Beguiler and the player has chosen for the creature to Manifest from a piece of terrain, use a Scatter Die to determine the point d6" away from the intended position where the creature Manifests.	The manifester loses concentration, breaking their trance. They must take a moment to regain their composure and can do nothing else for the remainder of this Round.
3-of-a-Kind	The creature is Manifested, but the spiritual strain of binding it to the Witch's will has taken a terrible toll. The manifester gains a Combat Stress Marker and the creature immediately enters a Rampage.	The manifester attempts to subjugate the creature in a battle of wills, but fails utterly. Scarred by the encounter, the would-be manifester gains a Combat Stress Marker and can do nothing else for the remainder of this Round.

4-of-a-Kind	The Witch has tamed the creature utterly and gorged themselves on its spiritual power. In addition to Manifesting the creature, the player gains thee additional Activation Dice to be spent in this Phase.	The Witch is unsuccessful in Manifesting the creature and has left a part of their spirit in the other world. The Witch gains the Keyword **wisp** but can do nothing else for the remainder of this Round.
5-of-a-Kind	Drawn to the scent of so much blood, additional creatures are pulled through the veil. In addition to the creature Manifested by the roll, the commanding player may place another creature of their choosing, up to the same Manifestation Level as the summoned creature, anywhere on the board.	The extreme stress of attempting to pull this creature through the veil between realities destroys a part of the Witch's mind and corrupts their body. The Witch can no longer make attempts to Manifest creatures, but they gain the Keywords **bloodthirsty**, **terrifying**, and **man-sized creature**.
6-of-a-Kind	The energy of the spirit world courses through the would-be manifester, but the power is too great to be channelled and the manifester's body and mind are transformed! With an earth-shattering roar, they become an avatar of the gods themselves. Remove the manifester, replacing them with a Crusher. This Crusher will never Rampage, but any special rules or equipment held by the Witch prior to the transformation are lost for the remainder of the game.	

RAMPAGE

It takes considerable force of will to exert control over a creature, more so than many can muster. When the link of control is severed and the will that was dominating a creature is broken, that creature is free to act according to its nature, which is generally a bad thing for anyone standing nearby!

If the Witch that Manifested the creature is Destroyed or flees the battlefield, the creature that they were controlling goes into a Rampage. A Rampaging creature gains the Activation Keyword **mindless** and will Move in the Compulsory Moves subphase. The creature will move towards the closest unit of either side, foe or erstwhile friend, except for those that are **camouflaged**. Note that this might mean that the creature may switch targets from one Round to the next, so a smart commander can try and keep their units just far enough away from a Rampaging creature to keep them safe.

In every respect, a Rampaging creature follows the rules that govern units with the Activation Keyword **mindless**, so the creature will Charge any unit that is within range. If the creature comes into contact with another unit, then they fight in Close Combat, regardless of which side that unit belongs to. As mindless creatures are unaffected by combat stress, any markers held by the unit are discarded when it enters the rampage state.

Though they are no longer in control of the creature, the player who initially Manifested it makes any rolls on its behalf, including for Close Combat against their own troops! Opponents will likely want to watch these rolls carefully, so that they can gloat ever harder as the powerful entity tears its way through the ranks of its erstwhile allies!

Rampaging creatures never use Abilities, however, any other special rules that apply to the creature remain in play

Ending Rampage

A creature that is Rampaging will only stop if it is Destroyed or is brought back under control.

Targeting Rampaging Creatures

Some creatures, particularly higher Manifestation Level ones, are simply too dangerous to be left alive if they enter a Rampage. You can choose to target any Rampaging creature that was previously under your command with a Shooting Attack or, if you so wish, you can direct a unit to a Charge at it in its own Activation Phase.

In this way, players are able to remove dangerous Rampaging creatures from the field, though engaging such creatures in Close Combat can be costly.

Control

A Witch can use a special ability called "Control" to bring a Rampaging creature under its influence. A Witch can attempt to bring any Rampaging creature under their control, meaning that a canny commander can set themselves up to steal an enemy's creature if the opportunity presents itself.

Further rules for the Control Ability are found under the entry for Witches in the force selection lists (see page 122).

ORDERS

It is no mean feat to ak soldiers to go to their death. Men must be forged like swords, their resolve beaten to a cruel point. Discipline is the hammer, drill the anvil; it is by these that an officer makes a weapon of a man.

Orders give **leader** units access to many powerful abilities that are essentially non-magical in character. The vast majority of Orders simply have a cost in Command Tokens. Provided a player has sufficient tokens to pay for it, an Order can be issued by simply discarding the required tokens, after which the Order is automatically carried out. In your Command Phase your **leaders** may issue as many Orders as you desire and the same Order may be issued to more than one unit.

Some particularly strong Orders, called Ruses, can only be used in the first Command Phase of the game. Though they are powerful, many Ruses come with the possibility of causing unforeseen damage to your own forces, so think carefully before committing to using one! Ruses represent initial bombardments, chemical attacks, or subterfuge made against enemy positions in order to soften them up before an assault.

Ruses work slightly differently to regular Orders in that they require the user to convert a number of their Command Tokens into d3 dice and roll them in order to meet a threshold. Players are looking for a target number and a corresponding number of results to the Ruse's level, just as seen with Rituals. For example, a Level 3 Ruse requires three results of 1 on however many d3s the player chooses to commit to the roll. A Ruse may only be attempted once.

Any roll that does not meet the threshold is simply failed; the planned bombardment is mistimed or off-target, interceptors are caught and killed before they can get in position, or one of any number of other logistical mishaps that could occur to spoil a commander's carefully laid plans.

With the exception of Ruses, all Orders have a range of 10", so **leaders** must stay close to their men. Once an Order is in play on a unit, that unit does not have to remain within 10" of the **leader** to enjoy its benefits and may be moved freely should you choose to do so. As they are little more than a shouted instruction, even units that are fighting in Close Combat can issue and receive Orders, however, Broken units cannot.

CHOOSING ORDERS

When selecting your force, choose from the Orders listed in this chapter to customise your **captain** and determine which tactical possibilities are available to them. All **captains** may choose a defined number of Orders from the list, some more and some less.

Some **leaders** may have unique orders, specific to that particular troop choice. These Orders may not be exchanged for any other, though in some cases additional Orders may be taken if the unit profile allows for it.

RUSES (FIRST COMMAND PHASE ONLY)

Gas Barrage (Level 3)
Divide the board into six 12" square segments then roll a d10 and consult the Gas Barrage Table. Gas is generated in whichever segment is produced by your roll, according to the table. Every unit, friend or foe, that is at least partly within that segment must make a Zeal check. Any unit that fails takes 6 MS Low Hits, resolved immediately.

Once all of the Hits for gas have been resolved, it is possible that the gas will either dissipate completely or be blown around the table by the wind. In the next Command Phase, after Command Tokens are generated but before any other actions are taken, roll a d6. On a result of 6, the gas remains on the table and the process of randomising the segment in which it appears begins again. Repeat this step until the gas dissipates naturally or the game ends.

Gas Barrage Table

d10 Roll	Result
1	The segment of your choice
2–3	The left-hand segment on your opponent's side
4–5	The right-hand segment on your opponent's side
6–7	The central segment on your opponent's side
8	Your left-hand segment
9	Your right-hand segment
10	Your central segment

Smoke Screen (Level 1)

Select a position anywhere on the board within 24" of the **leader** in their Command Phase to place a Projected Fire Template, Scattering it d6". This area is now covered by a smoke screen, with any models behind it being partially obscured. Note that the smoke screen works both ways, affecting both your troops and the enemy. A smoke screen will remain on the board for d3+3 Rounds.

Barrage (Level 3)

Select three positions on the board and place a Large Template on each of them, Scattering as normal and resolving as for **high explosives**.

Infiltrators (Level 1)

Pick up a friendly **infantry** unit and set it up again anywhere on the table, within 12" of any enemy unit.

Vanguard (Level 1)

Pick up a friendly **cavalry** unit and set it up again anywhere on the board, within 16" of an enemy unit.

Mine (Level 2)

Select a section of terrain with the Keyword **trench** anywhere on the board and place a large template on it, resolving as for **high explosives**. Any unit within 10" of the centre of the Template is inflicted with four MS Low Hits.

STANDARD ORDERS

All of these Orders may be used during any Command Phase but remember that only Orders that specifically mention units with the Keyword **tracked vehicle** or **wheeled vehicle** may be used on those units.

Clear Them Out!

1 Command Token

In the coming Round, all Infantry Sections within 10" of the **leader** may reroll any grenade Scatter Dice produced by their bomber teams.

Silence Those Guns!

1 Command Token

Select a **sniper** unit within 10" of the **leader** to be activated in the Cannonade Phase.

Spirited Assault

1 Command Token

A single unit with the Activation Keyword **elites** within 10" of the **leader** may reroll any failed Pinning Tests in the coming Round.

Unrelenting Barrage

1 Command Token

Select a **cannonade** unit within 10" of the **leader** to generate a Near Miss dice for each Critical Hit roll they generate when Shooting in the coming Round.

Advance!

2 Command Tokens

All friendly **infantry** units within 10" of the **leader** may immediately move up to 3" in a chosen direction. The units may not enter into Close Combat by this means under any circumstances but can Charge if activated to do so in the Phases that follow and do not count as having been Activated.

Break Their Lines!

2 Command Tokens

A unit with the Activation Keyword **elite** within 10" of the **leader** may be Activated in the Cannonade Phase instead.

Forced March

2 Command Tokens

A single unit within 10" of the **leader** that is not **unique** may move at up to twice its Pace in the next Phase, but generates a Combat Stress Marker. This is not a Charge, simply a Move at double speed. The unit may still Shoot at the end of its Move if it is able, following any rules for Shooting Attacks and Moving applicable to units with its Keywords.

Keep Firing!

2 Command Tokens

A single unit within 10" of the **leader** with the Activation Keyword **cannonade**. That unit may make two Shooting Attacks when it is Activated, but generates a Combat Stress Marker if it does so. If you wish to Move the unit as part of its Activation, Move it once, up to its stated Pace value and following any other associated rules, then make a Shooting Attack twice in succession. No second Move is allowed.

Move Up!

2 Command Tokens

A unit with the Activation Keyword **line** within 10" of the **leader** may be Activated in the Elite Phase instead.

Stormtroopers

2 Command Tokens

In the coming Round, any Infantry Sections within 10" of the **leader** may reroll all natural To Hit rolls of 6 in the Close Combat Subphase.

Enfilade

3 Command Tokens

All Machine Gun Teams within 10" of the **leader** generate Critical Hits on rolls of 1 during this Round.

FACTION-SPECIFIC ORDERS

The following orders are specific to their faction, and may only be used by those shown.

British Empire
Jai Maa Kali!
1 Command Token

A unit of Colonial Infantry within 10" of the **leader** may be Activated in the Cannonade Phase, but only to Charge.

French Republic only
Elan
1 Command Token

A unit of Cuirassiers within 10" of the **leader** may be Activated in the Cannonade Phase, but only to Charge.

German Empire only
Load K Bullets
1 Command Token

Select an Infantry Section within 10" of the **leader**. Any Saving Throws made by a **vehicle** in Close Combat with this unit in the coming Close Combat Phase subphase is made at Disadvantage-1.

Freikorps only
Godspeaker
1 Command Token

Roll a d6 for each unit within 10" of the **leader** that is in Close Combat. For each result of 1, you gain an additional Activation Die.

American Volunteer Legions only
Fanning
1 Command Token

Any unit of Gunslingers within 10" of the **leader** generates an additional d4 shots in any Shooting Attacks made in the coming Round. Roll separately for each unit.

Russian Empire only
For the honour of the Tzar!
1 Command Token

Any Conscripts within 10" of the **leader** may reroll failed Pinning Tests in the coming Round.

ABILITIES

Abilities are used in the same way as orders, requiring players to discard a number of Command Tokens in order to use them, but are performed during a unit's Activation in one of the three standard Activation Phases.

Just like other Normal Activations, an Ability Activation includes the option for the unit to Move before triggering the Ability if you so choose. Unlike Shooting, the choice to Move imparts no detriment to using the Ability, but any measurement of range for Abilities that have one must be taken after the Move has been made, exactly as a Shooting Attack must follow on from a Move.

As they are used as part of a Normal Activation, a unit cannot use Abilities in any circumstance in which it may not be Activated normally, such as if they are in Close Combat or Broken.

Any Abilities that must target an enemy unit can be used against any unit that is within Line of Sight, even if that unit is in Close Combat.

Chapter Six

VEHICLES

"Engines rumble, ejecting great gusts of smoke from their exhausts. Some vehicles thunder across the battlefield, quick as a lightning bolt, whilst others are iron-clad leviathans crawling inexorably forward, the earth shaking as they go."

Though the **vehicles** used in the First World War were relatively crude by the standards of later fighting vehicles, they had an undeniable effect on the conflict. On the Doggerland Front, the enormous potential of fighting **vehicles** makes them an attractive prospect to commanders who want to smash aside any token of resistance. But beware – though powerful, **vehicles** have their limitations.

Sluggish movement, high recruitment cost, and a particular vulnerability to certain weapons and Close Combat means that **vehicles** are best used in concert with **infantry** or **cavalry** that can offer them protection from attack in exchange for cover and much needed firepower!

VEHICLES AND SHOOTING

As a stable weapon platform, any unit with the Keyword **tracked vehicle** or **wheeled vehicle** can always Shoot any of its weapons after having moved, regardless of whether those weapons have the Keyword **quickfire** or not.

Many **vehicles** have weapons on a number of different Faces, such as a **tank** that has a front mounted Heavy Machine Gun and other armaments on its side sponsons. A **vehicle** may fire any and all of its weapons at whichever targets are viable.

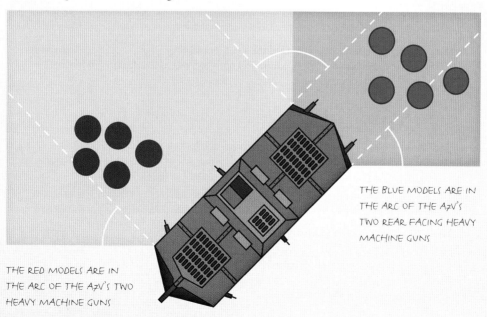

THE BLUE MODELS ARE IN THE ARC OF THE A7V'S TWO REAR FACING HEAVY MACHINE GUNS

THE RED MODELS ARE IN THE ARC OF THE A7V'S TWO HEAVY MACHINE GUNS

VEHICLES AND MOVEMENT

Units with the Keyword **vehicle** move differently to **infantry** and **cavalry** units. Some **vehicles** are light and manoeuvrable, like armoured cars, whilst others are ponderous behemoths, slow and difficult to manoeuvre but extremely resistant to damage and boasting impressive weaponry.

Vehicles cannot make Charges, and so can never enter Close Combat of their own volition, though they can themselves be the target of a Charge.

All **vehicles** have Facing, and so can only travel forwards. Pivoting allows **vehicles** to turn before moving, so you will want to be sure to orient your **vehicles** in such a way as to both move them in the direction of your choice, but also to bring as many of their weapons as possible to bear against their targets.

Tracked vehicles and **wheeled vehicles** move in markedly different ways, with **wheeled vehicles** being considerably more manoeuvrable than their more ponderous **tracked vehicle** cousins.

ORDER OF MOVEMENT FOR TRACKED VEHICLES

1. Pivot freely in any direction
2. Move directly forward up to the unit's Pace value in inches

STEP 1: PIVOT ON THE SPOT

STEP 2: MOVE DIRECTLY FORWARD, PARALLEL WITH FIGURES INITIAL POSITION.

ORDER OF MOVEMENT FOR WHEELED VEHICLES

1. Pivot freely in any direction.
2. Move directly forward, parallel with the unit's position, at least 1" and up to 1" short of the unit's Pace value in inches.
3. Pivot freely in any direction.
4. Move directly forward, parallel with the unit's position, for as many inches as desired, so long as the total Movement does not exceed the unit's Pace value in inches.

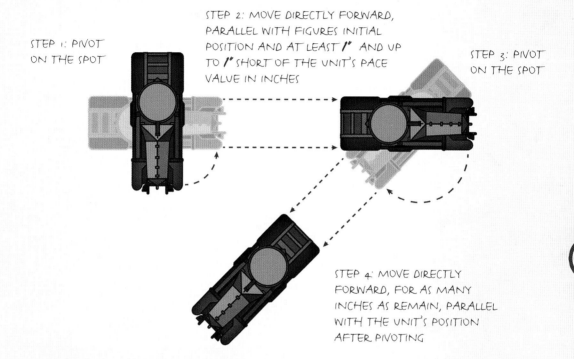

STEP 1: PIVOT ON THE SPOT

STEP 2: MOVE DIRECTLY FORWARD, PARALLEL WITH FIGURES INITIAL POSITION AND AT LEAST 1" AND UP TO 1" SHORT OF THE UNIT'S PACE VALUE IN INCHES

STEP 3: PIVOT ON THE SPOT

STEP 4: MOVE DIRECTLY FORWARD, FOR AS MANY INCHES AS REMAIN, PARALLEL WITH THE UNIT'S POSITION AFTER PIVOTING

A vehicle must move at least 1" after Pivoting both times and can only move a number of inches up to its Pace value. However, the second Pivot can be to face in the exact same direction as before if you want to drive straight ahead for the full Movement.

Some more unusual types of units, such as horse-drawn carts, share some Keywords with **vehicles** but are treated as **cavalry** for the purposes of rules to do with Movement, though like a **vehicle** they cannot Charge.

VEHICLE MOVEMENT AND TERRAIN
Moving Through Wire and Thicket
Being large and heavy, some **vehicles** can punch through all but the most stubborn of obstacles. Units with the Keyword **tracked vehicle** can traverse **wire** and **thicket** terrain without penalty, and additionally have the chance to destroy it, making breaches for **infantry** and **cavalry** to pass through freely.

When a **tracked vehicle** moves into contact with **wire**, even if it does not cross through it completely in a single Move, roll a d10. On a roll of 1, the wire is Destroyed – remove the whole piece of terrain or, if possible, just the section that the **vehicle** has passed through.

Units with the Keyword **behemoth**, which by their nature are larger and heavier, may remove the terrain feature on a roll of 1 on a d6 instead.

Moving Through Mire
Bulky objects can struggle with thick mud, becoming trapped easily. All **vehicles** that Move through **mire** must Test to see if they become Stuck. **Wheeled vehicles** are particularly susceptible to the dangers of traversing **mire**, becoming Stuck on a d6 roll of 6. Tracked vehicles are less likely to become Stuck, rolling on a d10 and getting stuck on a roll of 10.

A **vehicle** that fails this Test and becomes Stuck may not Move, including to Pivot, for the remainder of the game, though it may still make Shooting Attacks as normal.

VEHICLES AND CLOSE COMBAT

Vehicles are extremely exposed when in Close Combat with **infantry**. Their main advantage lies in their manoeuvrability, their resistance to enemy fire, and their powerful weaponry. Wherever possible, try to keep your **vehicles** out of Close Combat, where they will be quickly disabled.

VEHICLE CLOSE COMBAT ATTACK DICE GENERATION
Vehicle crews have few means of defending themselves against targets in extremely close proximity. Enemy **infantry** can fire through vision slits, set fires, or even attempt to throw grenades into opened hatches. By contrast, the crew of a **vehicle** are sitting ducks who must attempt to fight back with very limited options. Some other unusual unit types, which broadly fall into the category of a **vehicle** but may be powered by other means, pose similar issues to their defenders.

Rather than generating Attack Dice with reference to Zeal, these units generate a set number of Attack Dice in Close Combat determined by their size, as described by the table below. The number of Attack Dice generated by these units in Close Combat therefore cannot be increased or decreased by any means.

VEHICLE CLOSE COMBAT ATTACK DICE	
Vehicle Type	**Number of Dice**
Behemoth	3 Attack Dice
Tank	2 Attack Dice
Car	1 Attack Die

Always remember that this class of unit is best used in support of **infantry** as mobile gun platforms and to provide hard cover on the move. Keeping them out of Close Combat should be a priority for any commander.

THE CURSE OF IRON

The inimical nature of iron to witches has long been recognised – a simple charm to keep away the fey folk, iron bands to seal a ward, a few crude nails banged in above the lintel, the list goes on. Iron dampens and absorbs the power of Witches, soaking up their energy like a sponge.

Large quantities of iron have such an effect on practitioners of magic, be they man or something else, that it is impossible for them to perform Rituals when it is nearby; the presence of great masses of iron renders Rituals nothing more than words, stripped of power.

No unit may perform a Ritual if it is within 6" of a **vehicle**, the heavy presence of that much iron in the spiritual world is too great to ignore.

EFFECT ON CREATURES

As beings of the spiritual world, creatures abhor the presence of iron and react to it even more strongly than Witches. A unit with the Keyword **creature** cannot Move when it is within 6" of a **vehicle**, including as part of a Charge, unless they pass a Zeal Test. If the Test is passed, then the unit may move. If the Test is failed, the unit becomes Pinned.

Creatures that are rampaging are no longer subject to the Curse of Iron, their unshackled minds experience no sensation except fury.

103

DESTROYED VEHICLES

Unlike other classes of unit, when a vehicle is Destroyed its model is left in place, rather than being removed from the table. From now on, treat the model as **impassable** terrain that blocks Line of Sight and provides Makeshift Cover to any unit which is in contact with it.

Destroyed Vehicle Markers

Many wargamers like to make smoke plumes from cotton wool, or fashion other markers that can be placed alongside or on top of Destroyed **vehicles**, both to remind players what has been destroyed and to give some cinematic colour to their battlefields.

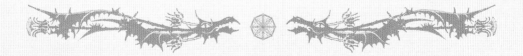

Chapter Seven
KEYWORDS

This section contains a list of all Keywords that confer special rules on a unit.

───────────────── ◆ ─────────────────

KEYWORD LIST

Aquatic
An **aquatic** unit treats **mire** as though it were **open ground** and can reroll all failed To Hit rolls made in Close Combat when wholly in a **mire**.

Armoured
This **vehicle** is so well protected that standard weaponry cannot touch it, only Shooting Attacks made by a weapon with the Keyword **ordnance** can cause damage to **armoured** targets

Armour-Piercing
This ranged weapon is utterly deadly to even heavily protected foes, bypassing even the stoutest defences. Saving Throws made against Shooting Attacks from this weapon are made at Disadvantage-1.

Big Hitter
When a **big hitter** inflicts a Wound with a Shooting Attack, it causes d3 Wounds rather than one. A d3 roll must be made for each successive successful Wound, including Critical Hits.

Bipod
A weapon with **a bipod** has two profiles when making Shooting Attacks, one for when the unit is in Cover, and another for when the unit is not.

Bloodthirsty
A unit with this Keyword may not act as a Supporter in Close Combat.

Body Armour
This piece of equipment means that a unit may reroll failed Saving Throws made in Close Combat

Bramblekin
A **bramblekin** unit can traverse wire and thicket as though they were open terrain.

Camouflage
If this unit is in contact with an obstacle that provides it with Makeshift Cover, then it cannot be targeted by Line-of-Sight-based Shooting Attacks made from more than 10" away.

Charger

Rather than generating Manifestation Dice, a **charger** unit can choose the special Close Combat Conclusion result "Reform" when it ends Close Combat with High Morale. This allows the unit to make a free Move in the direction of its choice at the end of a successful Close Combat. This does not count as the unit having Activated, so it may Charge again in the following Round.

Cowardly

A **cowardly** unit is immediately Destroyed if it is subjected to a Break Test.

Devastating

Any unit hit by a **devastating** weapon must take a Devastating Test for each Wound suffered.

Disabling

For any **tracked vehicle** or **wheeled vehicle** caught under the Template of a **disabling** weapon, roll a d3. Whatever result the d3 produces, the **vehicle** receives an equal number of Combat Stress Markers, up to a total of three. No Battle Shock Test is ever taken as a consequence of a Disabling Test, so if the unit is already subject to Combat Stress any additional Combat Stress Markers over three are discarded.

Disturbing

There is something about this unit that is not quite right! Any unit that wishes to Charge against a **disturbing** unit must first make a Zeal Test. If the test is failed, that unit becomes Pinned instead of Charging.

Divinely Favoured

This unit can make Saving Throws against Critical Hits made during Close Combat, treating them as though they were a normal Hit.

Dumb Brute

If this unit is more than 10" from a friendly Witch, then it gains the Keyword **impetuous**.

Elemental Resistance

Simultaneously existing in this world and on the other side of the veil, **creatures** have an innate resistance to many weapons used in modern warfare. Bullets are of more limited use against these monsters than Close Combat weapons, but the largest munitions are barely affected!

Units with **elemental resistance** have Advantage-1 for any Saving Throws made against Shooting Attacks from a unit using **small arms** weaponry.

Enhanced Protection

A unit with **enhanced protection** can make Saving Throws against Critical Hits generated by both Shooting Attacks and Close Combat, treating them as though they were a normal Hit.

Far-Sighted

Far-sighted units do not have to make a Difficult Shot when Shooting at units that are beyond their weapon's Effective Range with **standard issue** weapons.

Fast Target

This unit's small size and great speed makes it difficult to hit. Regardless of any other modifiers and special rules, Shooting Attacks made against this unit with **standard issue** weapons are always Difficult Shots.

Foolhardy

Devastating Tests made against a **foolhardy** unit are always made on a d10 (the target number remains 1). **Foolhardy** units also ignore the effects of the Keyword **terrifying** when making Charges.

Fortress

This unit is well-armoured enough to present a barrier to any oncoming fire and to afford a modicum of protection to any advancing units. Any unit with the Keyword **infantry** that is in contact with a **fortress** gains Advantage-1 to any Saving Throws made against Shooting Attacks.

A unit with the Keyword **fortress** effectively provides Makeshift Cover on the move.

Freakish Strength

This unit is preternaturally strong! Saving Throws made against this unit Close Combat have Disadvantage-1.

Healer

If this unit is acting as a Supporter to a friendly unit that ends a Close Combat Conclusion with High Morale, that unit can choose to "Tend to the Wounded" – a special Close Combat Conclusion action.

To Tend to the Wounded, roll a d10 for each model lost in the Close Combat Subphase. On a roll of 1, return that model to the board. This replaces the usual Close Combat Conclusion Manifestation Dice generation.

Hit and Run

When an enemy unit carries out a Charge against a **hit and run** unit, the **hit and run** unit can choose to withdraw from the enemy, keeping itself out of harm's way. If this option is chosen, the commanding player should roll a d6, retreating a number of inches equal to the die roll directly to their starting table edge.

In all respects, the **hit and run** unit follows the rules for Broken units whilst withdrawing.

The enemy unit continues its Charge in the direction of the **hit and run** unit. Add the result of the d6 roll to the distance between the lead model in each unit and compare it to the Pace value of the Charging unit. If the combined value of the d6 result and the distance between the lead models in each unit is less than twice the Charging unit's Pace value, the **hit and run** unit is caught by the Charging and immediately Destroyed. In this instance, after removing the Destroyed unit from the board, move the lead model of the Charging unit to the position previously occupied by the lead model in the **hit and run** unit, then a number of inches equal to the value rolled on the d6 towards the target's starting table edge.

Likewise, if the Movement away from the Charging unit takes the **hit and run** unit into contact with its starting table edge, then it is immediately removed from the board.

Horrifying

Being fired upon by a **horrifying** weapon is a terrifying ordeal, likely to cause a general rout. A multi-model unit that has Wounds inflicted on it by a **horrifying** weapon must make a Break Test *for each model removed as a result*.

Intimidating

Any Shooting Attack made with **standard issue** weapons against this unit from under 10" is counted as a Difficult Shot.

Impenetrable

This unit can make Saving Throws against Critical Hits made by Shooting Attacks, treating them as though they were a normal Hit.

Impetuous

If an enemy unit is not **camouflaged**, within range, and within Line of Sight, an **impetuous** unit must Charge at it. If intervening terrain prevents the Charge, the unit may be activated as normal.

Impetuous units ignore the effects of the Keyword **terrifying** when making Charges.

Insensible

This unit can never become Shaken and is immune to Pinning, ignoring any Near Misses generated by Shooting Attacks made against it.

Mighty Blow

When a unit with **mighty blow** inflicts a Wound during a Close Combat, it causes d3 Wounds rather than one. A d3 roll must be made for each successive successful Wound, including Critical Hits.

Open Top

A **vehicle** with an **open top** can be used as a mobile firing platform for its crew. Any weapon on the unit's profile that does not have a stated Facing can be fired in any direction.

Shooting Attacks made with **standard issue** weapons by **open top** units do not make Difficult Shots as a consequence of having Moved.

Ophite

This unit coats its weapons in poison, or else secretes its own venom. The unit can make Critical Hits in Close Combat, but their opponent gains Advantage-1 to all Saving Throws made against any regular Hits.

Quickfire

A unit using a weapon with this Keyword may Move and Shoot in one Activation.

Small Calibre

This ranged weapon fires a comparatively small round. No less deadly against exposed flesh, it is nonetheless more likely to be deflected by body armour or a helmet. Saving Throws made against Shooting Attacks from this weapon are made at Advantage-1.

Sniper

This unit is terrifyingly accurate with firearms and can pick a target out in a crowd, striking down their quarry before they even see them. A sniper can make Shooting Attacks at enemies through another enemy unit, but not through a friendly unit.

Swift

Swift units do not have to make a Difficult Shot when Shooting with **standard issue** weapons after having Moved.

Sylvan

A **sylvan** unit may reroll any failed Saving Throws if it wholly occupies a **wood**. However, if it receives a Wound as a result of a Shooting Attack made by a unit armed with a Flamethrower or Fire Bottles, it will immediately Break without a Test.

Sylvan units treat any unit that is armed with a Flamethrower or Fire Bottles as **disturbing**.

Trick shot

Trick Shot units do not have to make a Difficult Shot when Shooting at single-model units that are partially obscured with **standard issue** weapons.

Terrifying

This unit is so hideous, or carries such a vicious weapon, that their very presence on the battlefield quails the hearts of their opponents! All units in Close Combat with this unit, even if they are only Supporters, take -1 to Morale. Units that are themselves **terrifying** always ignore this effect.

Turret

A **turret** weapon may fire in any direction, regardless of the unit's Facing.

Undine

This unit automatically passes any Zeal Test (except for Battle Shock Tests) if it occupies a **mire**, but gains a Combat Stress Marker every time that it is Activated when it is not within a **mire**.

Undisciplined

This unit suffers an additional -1 when calculating Morale, in addition to any other Keywords or conditions that affect Morale.

Unnaturally Tough

For every Wound successfully inflicted on this unit, roll a d6. On a roll of 1, the Wound is ignored.

Unstable Projectile

Regardless of the Template size generated when firing this weapon, it uses a d6 for its Distance Die when determining Scattering.

Unyielding

This unit does not roll on the Close Combat Conclusion table, regardless of Morale – it will never break from Close Combat, but will continue to fight until completely Destroyed

Vanguard

This unit is not placed with the others when both players set up their Patrol at the start of the game. Instead, it is placed after all other units have been positioned and can be set up anywhere in the controlling player's half of the table, providing that it is not within 12" of an enemy unit.

If both players have **vanguard** units, take it in turns to place them on the battlefield, with the player who places their first **vanguard** unit first being the player who also placed the first unit of the game when setting up.

Wisp

A **wisp** is a thing of mist and shadows rather than a physical object. As such, it can never be targeted or even damaged by Shooting Attacks and is unaffected by terrain, crossing through any features like **wire**, **wood**, or **buildings** as though they were **open ground**. This means that a unit with the Keyword **wisp** can move through any terrain in a straight line without penalty. The only exception is **impassable** terrain, which must still be navigated around in the usual way.

As a **wisp** unit exists simultaneously in the spiritual and material world, it is even more affected by the presence of iron than usual. If an enemy **vehicle** moves within 6" of a **wisp**, then it must make a Zeal Test. If the Test is passed, then the unit remains in place and may be Activated as normal. *If the test is failed, then the unit is immediately Destroyed.*

Chapter Eight
CREATING A PATROL

Now that you understand the rules of *A War Transformed*, it's time to start building your Patrol! The following chapter covers the rules for how to create a legal and effective Patrol.

UNIT TYPES

There are a number of different unit types available to recruit when building your Patrol.

UNIQUE UNITS

Unique units serve as the commanders of your Patrol, capable of issuing Orders and enacting Rituals.

Captain

Your Captain is the individual in supreme command of your whole Patrol. Captains can issue any Orders that they have access to in the Command Phase. Captains also have powerful Auras around them that act on all units within a specified radius, except when Broken. Some also have Abilities, which can be used in the standard Activation Phases as per the usual rules.

Each Patrol must contain exactly one Captain, taken from either the Common Unique Units List (see page 118), or from the Faction Specific Unit Lists.

Witch

Witches can perform Rituals and attempt Manifestations during the Command Phase, making them a powerful force on the battlefield. What Rituals a Witch can perform are dictated by the Hermetic Order that the platoon belongs to.

Each Patrol may contain up to one Witch.

Lieutenant

Lieutenants come in one of two varieties, Infantry Lieutenants and Cavalry Lieutenants, each with access to a different set of Abilities and Auras.

A Patrol may contain multiple Lieutenants, all of whom act independently of one another as individual units. Just like Captains, Lieutenants also generate an Aura, except when Broken.

Lieutenants must be recruited at a cost of one Selection Point each when building a Patrol.

STANDARD UNIT TYPES

A Patrol is made up of more than just **leaders**, it must also include troops for them to command! The vast majority of units in *A War Transformed* are either **line**, **elite** or **cannonade** units, with only a slim minority being **unique** or **mindless**. Many of these other units may be upgraded by spending Upgrade Points (UP). These Upgrades provide standard units with access to special weapons and equipment that can alter their battlefield role, make them slightly tougher, or give them unique capabilities.

Infantry

Infantry will form the core of any Patrol. They are able to stand toe-to-toe with most other unit types, provide localised specialist fire power, and capture Objectives.

Some **infantry** units will be classed as **line** and others as **elite**. Many **cannonade** units and **weapons teams** also have the **infantry** Keyword, including large ordnance like Field Guns and man-portable Anti-Tank Rifles.

Cavalry

Fast-moving but vulnerable to Shooting Attacks, **cavalry** can provide a lightning-fast hammer to smash lightly defended positions, but are best used in a flanking role due to their fragility.

All **cavalry** are classed as **elite**, with the exception of **unique** units that players choose to put on a Mount.

Vehicles

Huge, thunderous machines bristling with guns or hastily converted civilian vehicles, **vehicles** can offer an extraordinary amount of firepower, but must work in concert with **infantry** or be quickly overwhelmed in Close Combat.

The majority of **vehicles** are classed as **line**, but are comparatively expensive to recruit. However, a small few are classed as **elite** or **cannonade**, typically lighter **wheeled vehicles** such as armoured **cars** as opposed to heavier, slower **tanks** and **behemoths**.

Creatures

Creatures are powerful units with unique Abilities, living denizens of the spirit world powerful enough to pass through the veil between realities.

The vast majority of creatures cannot be recruited by players, rather they must be Manifested during battle by a Witch with offerings of blood.

BUILDING A PATROL

In order to build a Patrol, first you must agree with your opponent how many Selection Points (SP) you will each have to spend – more Selection Points means larger and more powerful Patrols.

To do this, it can be useful to agree to a Scenario beforehand (see page 205 for a full list of scenarios). Different scenarios work best with differing numbers of troops, so the **Trench Raid** and **Recovery** Scenarios favour a smaller number of units, whilst **Gas! Gas! Gas!** and **The Big Push** Scenarios support much larger forces. Some Scenarios also have rules that affect which units may be recruited to your Patrol.

Once you and your opponent have decided on a Scenario and number of Selection Points, it is time to build your Patrols. All units in *A War Transformed* have a value in Selection Points next to their name in their profile, showing how much they will cost a would-be commander to recruit to their Patrol. The vast majority of units cost either 1 or 2 Selection Points, but some particularly impressive units have much higher costs reflecting the enormous impact that they can have on the battlefield.

As an example, let's say that you agreed to take a Patrol worth 10 Selection Points. This would mean that you would be able to recruit five units that cost 2 Selection Points each, or one that costs 4 Selection Points and three at 2 each. Additionally, you get both a Captain and a Witch for free.

Different kinds of units can be recruited in varying quantities, but the core of your Patrol must always be **line** units. Use the Building a Patrol Table to determine what proportion of your points may be spent on the different classes of unit:

BUILDING A PATROL TABLE	
Unit Type	**Number Allowed**
Line and Mindless	As many as desired
Elites	Up to an equal number of Selection Points as spent on line units
Cannonade	1 Selection Point per 2 Selection Points spent on line units
Unique	1 Selection Point per 3 Selection Points spent on line units

For example, if you spend 11 Selection Points on **line** units, you may have up to 11 Selection Points' worth of **elite** units, 5 of **cannonade** units, and 3 of **unique** units.

In addition to Selection Points, Patrols also get Upgrade Points. These points can be spent on non-standard equipment for your troops, giving them additional capabilities or changing their battlefield role entirely. Whilst it is entirely up to you and your opponent to agree how many Upgrade Points to allow in a given game, or even whether to have them at all. The standard recommendation is to use between 25% and 50% (rounded up to the next whole number) of for the number Selection Points you are using. For example, in a game with 20 Selection Points, the recommended number of Upgrade Points ranges from 5 to 10.

CHOOSING A FACTION

The different Factions of *A War Transformed* have strengths and weaknesses that will fit different playstyles. Choosing the right Faction can be as simple as collecting models that particularly speak to you, or as complex as playing multiple games to see which best suits you!

Your Faction choice determines your access to certain units, Orders, special items, and even Upgrades, so pick wisely!

CHOOSING A HERMETIC LODGE

In addition to choosing a Faction, players must choose a Hermetic Lodge. This has no bearing on the kind of units that you can recruit, but radically impacts which Rituals your Witch has access to. The different Hermetic Lodges can suit different playstyles better, so be aware of how your choice of Hermetic Lodge plays with your Faction choice and the composition of your Patrol.

UNIT AVAILABILITY

Common Units

The vast majority of units in *A War Transformed* are Common Units, meaning they are available to multiple Factions.

You may include as many Common Units in your Patrol as you wish.

Some Common Units and infantry section unit upgrades are locked to specific Factions – these units state which Factions they are available to, but the majority are freely available for Patrols of any Faction to recruit, which are marked as "No Restrictions".

Faction-Specific Units

By choosing a Faction, players gain access to powerful additional Faction-Specific Units as well as Faction-Specific Captains.

Just as with Common Units, there is no restriction on the proportion of your forces that can be recruited from the Faction-Specific Unit Lists. As long as players have the points and their choices conform to the other rules governing recruitment, then they may take as many units from their Faction's list as they like.

No player may recruit Faction-Specific Units that do not correspond to their Faction.

CUSTOMISING UNIQUE UNITS

There are many rules for customising Captains, Witches, and Lieutenants, notably by choosing Upgrades and Zodiac Signs. These choices, which have powerful and wide-ranging effects, are used alongside Faction choice and the overall composition of the Patrol. In this way it is possible to tailor the way your Patrol fights to suit your playstyle. Experiment with different combinations to make a Patrol that feels uniquely yours!

ZODIAC SIGNS

The signs under which men are born exert a powerful influence throughout their lives. Many a leader's destiny was forged at the moment of their birth, with a propitious alignment signalling a golden future.

You may choose a Zodiac Sign for your Captain, but not for any other units.

Each of the Zodiac Signs conveys a powerful bonus to your Captain, but some are not without cost! Choose wisely, for a Captain can only be born under one sign.

Leo
This Captain has the Keyword **impetuous**, but once per game, a friendly unit within 10" may use the Captain's Zeal for a Battle Shock Test instead of their own.

Virgo
Once per game, this Captain may perform the Ritual "The Lovers" (see page 77) without spending any Command Tokens or having to roll.

Aries
Once per game, this Captain may be Activated to Charge without gaining a Combat Stress Marker when it usually would.

Cancer
This Captain can ignore the first Wound that it receives in any game.

Pisces
This Captain gains the Keyword **aquatic**.

Sagittarius
This Captain can reroll any failed To Hit rolls made by their Shooting Attacks against creatures. Dice rerolled using this effect may not be rerolled a second time.

Gemini
Once per game, this Captain may perform the Ritual "The Magician" without spending any Command Tokens or having to roll.

Capricorn
If this Captain is acting as a Supporter in a Close Combat, both it and any allies within the Close Combat count as having Cavalry CC Weapons..

Libra
Once per game, this Captain may perform the Ritual "Justice" (see page 78) without spending any Command Tokens or having to roll.

Taurus
When this Captain Charges into an enemy unit, it gains an additional d3 Attack Dice at low MS in the first subsequent round of close combat.

Scorpio
If this Captain is acting as a Supporter in a Close Combat, any allies within the Close Combat gainthe Keyword **ophite**.

Aquarius
This Captain has the Keyword **healer**.

Zodiac Signs and Rituals

Rituals that are granted follow all the criteria that normally govern performing Rituals, but treat the Captain as the caster rather than a Witch. Just like normal Rituals, they take place in the Command Phase, cannot be used by a unit in Close Combat, and are subject to the Curse of Iron rule (see page 103).

MOUNTS

A Captain may choose to ride a Mount. This can give them a chance to keep up with other mounted units or enable them to move up and down the battlefield at speed to make them more responsive to the leadership needs of their troops. Being mounted does have drawbacks however, as Captains that choose to ride a Mount lose the Keyword **infantry** and gain the Keyword **cavalry**, along with all the detriments and bonuses associated with it (see page 111 for more on Cavalry).

Horse
The common horse makes a fine Mount for a commander.

CAPTAIN HORSE UPGRADE			
Keywords	Pace	Additional rules	Cost
Cavalry (replaces Infantry)	7	N/A	Free

Kelpie
A kelpie is a spirit of the waters. Full of malice, they commonly drown those foolish enough to be enticed onto their backs, but the strong may bend their will for a time.

CAPTAIN KELPIE UPGRADE			
Keywords	Pace	Additional rules	Cost
Cavalry (replaces Infantry), Aquatic	7	If Charging through mire, make a Zeal Test, suffering a Wound on a failure	1 UP

Gytrash

These huge black beasts may change shape at will, though they often inhabit the form of a great, dark stallion. It is said that to look upon one is to know of an impending death.

CAPTAIN GYTRASH UPGRADE			
Keywords	**Pace**	**Additional rules**	**Cost**
Cavalry (replaces Infantry), Terrifying	7	N/A	1 UP

Unicorn

A proud and haughty beast, only the pure can tame them.

CAPTAIN UNICORN UPGRADE			
Keywords	**Pace**	**Additional rules**	**Cost**
Cavalry (replaces Infantry), Unit counts as having Cavalry CC Weapons	7	The captain must select the Virgo Zodiac Sign	1UP

PLAYING WITH OPEN LISTS

A War Transformed is a friendly game, designed to be played amongst friends and with the objective of having fun and seeing great stories emerge on the tabletop.

As a rule, players are encouraged to play with open lists, sharing the details of their Patrols and their intentions with regards to Orders, Hermetic Lodges, special items and the like with each other. However, some players, particularly those with a background in more competitive games, may prefer to maintain the element of surprise – this is absolutely fine – but just be sure to agree the parameters of the game with your opponent beforehand, discussing whether to have open or closed lists before beginning the process of assembling your forces!

Chapter Nine
COMMON UNIT LISTS

UNIQUE UNITS

CAPTAIN
Free, One Per Patrol
Nation – No restrictions

In many of the belligerent nations, it is the upper classes that furnish the army with commanders. These young men are raised on tales of derring-do and the promise of martial glory, but often die a horrific and ignoble death, mown down by machine gun fire or blasted apart in some muddy field. Those lucky few that survive usually have an aptitude for command and common sense.

Alongside them are men who have dragged themselves up from the other ranks through talent and determination. Such officers were formerly rare, but have become less so as the attritional nature of bitter, mechanised warfare means that ever more recruitment is necessary. No matter their social station, the senior officers of the Doggerland Front are renowned for their bravery, leading from the front in attacks that often seem suicidal.

CAPTAIN

P	MS	Z	W	ST
5	High	9	3	4

Keywords	Activation Keyword
Infantry	Unique (Leader)

Regulation Equipment

Revolver, Standard issue CC weapon

Aura

Over the top – Units within 10" may use the Captain's Zeal when making Pinning Tests

Orders

Rally – Select a Broken infantry or cavalry unit that is within 10" to make a Zeal Test. If the Test is passed then the unit is no longer Broken
(1 Command Token)

1 CSM	2 CSMs	3 CSMs
Staggering: P reduced to 3	**Trembling:** MS reduced to Low	**Madness:** Cannot issue Orders

CAPTAIN UPGRADE TABLE

Free

The unit may select up to three Orders or Ruses from the Orders Chapter

The unit may exchange its Regulation Equipment for:
Self-Loading Pistol

1 Upgrade Point

The unit may exchange its Regulation Equipment for:
Pistol Carbine

Options

The unit may choose a Zodiac Sign

The unit may choose an item from the Special Items List

The unit may choose a Mount

INFANTRY LIEUTENANT

1 Selection Point

Nation – No Restrictions

Leading from the front is an important part of what it means to be an officer in this transformed war. Surrounded by horrors both mechanical and supernatural, the men under a Lieutenant's command must be led with iron will.

It is the infantry in any Patrol that perform the most vital tasks, defending and seizing objectives, as well as securing the breaches punched in the enemy lines by both assault troops and artillery. Infantry form the core of any Patrol and can be relied upon for almost any task given to them.

INFANTRY LIEUTENANT

P	MS	Z	W	ST
5	High	8	3	3

Keywords	Activation Keyword
Infantry	Unique (Leader)

Regulation Equipment

Revolver, Standard issue CC weapon

Aura

Desperate Glory – Devastating Tests made against units of infantry within 10" are made on a d10 (the target number remains 1)

Orders

Take Aim! – A selected infantry unit within 10" may reroll any rolls of 6 generated whilst Shooting this Phase (1 Command Token)

Rally – Select a Broken **infantry** unit that is within 10" to make a Zeal Test. If the test is passed, the unit is no longer Broken (1 Command Token)

1 CSM	2 CSMs	3 CSMs
Staggering: P reduced to 3	**Trembling:** MS reduced to Low	**Madness:** Cannot issue Orders

INFANTRY LIEUTENANT UPGRADE TABLE

Free

The unit may exchange its Regulation Equipment for:
Self-Loading Pistol

1 Upgrade Point

The unit may exchange its Regulation Equipment for:
Pistol Carbine, Repeating Carbine (AVLs only)

The unit may add:
Body armour (Freikorps and German Empire Only)

Options

The unit may choose an item from the Special Items List

CAVALRY LIEUTENANT

1 Selection Point

Nation – No Restrictions

   Since the first days of the war, it has been apparent that victory will come at the point of bayonet – that a great, sweeping assault is the only sure path to breaking the stalemate.

   After the events of The Shattering, the great powers have found that the kind of concentration of troops that they once enjoyed is no longer possible. The big push, once the surest route to victory, is an unreachable dream in a post-Summersisle world – the logistical and manpower challenges are simply too great.

   Now, the doctrine of the assault has changed. No more the headlong rush of thousands in a human wave, instead, small groups of carefully selected and trained veterans, immured to the dangers of the incoming fire, move to seize critical objectives at breakneck speed. Amongst these, the critical importance of cavalry is once again being recognised.

CAVALRY LIEUTENANT

P	MS	Z	W	ST
7	High	8	3	3

Keywords	Activation Keyword
Cavalry	Unique (Leader)

Regulation Equipment

Revolver, Standard issue CC weapon

Aura

Brave Boys – Devastating Tests made against units of cavalry within 10" are made on a d10 (the target number remains 1)

Orders

Chaaaarge! – A selected cavalry unit within 10" may move an additional d3" when Charging this Phase (1 Command Token)

Rally – Select a Broken **cavalry** unit that is within 10" to make a Zeal Test. If the Test is passed, the unit is no longer Broken (1 Command Token)

1 CSM	2 CSMs	3 CSMs
Lamed: P reduced to 5	**Trembling:** MS reduced to Low	**Madness:** Cannot issue Orders

CAVALRY LIEUTENANT UPGRADE TABLE

Free

The unit may exchange its Regulation Equipment for:
Self loading pistol is one upgrade (available to all)
Brutal CC weapon and body armour is another (avaible to French and Freikorps only)

Options

The unit may choose an item from the Special Items List

WITCH

Free, one per patrol

Nation – No Restrictions

There are some who can reach through the veil and harness the forces of the spiritual world. These individuals, called Witches, wield enormous power, their intercession changing the course of many of the battles fought across the Doggerland Front. The rituals they employ to win the attention and favour of the gods are as varied as their beliefs and origins, but all must supply the gods with the thing which they most crave – blood.

Many Witches enjoy the caché of power and the comforts of society. Held in high regard, they live in the dugouts afforded to officers, surrounded by the instruments of their arcane trade. Dressed in fine cultic robes, or even well-tailored uniforms, they cut quite the figure amongst the muck and blood of the front. Others, touched as they are by forces so far beyond human understanding, give themselves completely to the spirit world. Living outside the confines of the trenches in groves or hovels hastily scratched from the earth, they clad themselves in little more than foetid skins and charms, gibbering to themselves in strange tongues.

Both men and women may be born with the innate connection to the world of spirits required to become a successful practitioner of witchcraft. For some, their powers come to them as naturally as breathing, but others must work hard to achieve mastery of the arcane arts.

WITCH

P	MS	Z	W	ST
5	Medium	7	3	3

Keywords	Activation Keyword
Infantry, Witch	Unique (Leader)

Regulation equipment

No CC weapon

Abilities

Control – Select a Rampaging creature within 15" and make a Zeal Test. If the test is passed, the creature stops Rampaging and comes under your control (1 Command Token)

Commune – The unit generates an additional Manifestation Dice – (1 Command Token)

Curse – Select an enemy unit within 15" to make a Zeal Test. If it fails, the unit receives a Combat Stress Marker (1 Command Token)

Banish – Select an enemy creature within 15". It immediately takes d6 MS Low Hits (1 Command Token)

1 CSM	2 CSMs	3 CSMs
Staggering: P reduced to 2	**Trembling:** MS reduced to low	**Shaken:** Cannot use abilities

WITCH UPGRADE TABLE

Options

The unit may choose an item from the Special Items List

LINE UNITS

INFANTRY SECTION

2 Selection Points

Nation – No Restrictions

Between the rise of industry and the return of magic, the face of war has fundamentally changed.

However, one constant remains: the men who fight. Standing in the midst of a swirling maelstrom of death and madness are fathers, sons, and brothers. All have differing motivations – some fight for a vision or ideology, others for a taste of adventure, still more out of naught but desperation. Where once there were ploughmen, bank clerks, poets, and porters, now there are Tommies, Poilu, and Lakenpatsher. Men who may have never had a realistic chance of leaving their hometown are now blasted apart in the far flung reaches of the globe, torn to shreds by artillery, machine guns, and stranger forces besides.

Alongside these men are those whose journey to the Doggerland Front has been even longer. Colonial troops, drawn from every corner of the map to these northern shores, fight as bravely as any European soldier. Some bring with them martial traditions no less ancient than those of their masters, others come from newly minted nations and fight with all the vigour expected of warriors of young countries.

Despite all the technological advancements of the preceding century, it is still the infantry that perform the heavy lifting on all fronts of the war. The sheer numbers of men brought to the front in the earliest days means that a stiffened core of veterans can be found on all sides of the engagement. With every day, fresh recruits are brought to the front by train and wagon, swelling the ranks as quickly as they can be diminished.

As the logistical challenges of the post-Shattering world deepen, it is increasingly common to see soldiers fighting in makeshift uniforms – battledress from the early war is rummaged from storerooms and patched, darned, and repaired to make up the shortfall. Some are unfortunate enough to fight in a patchwork of military and civilian clothes. Alongside these are men who serve in regiments where the cultic influence is particularly strong, leading to even stranger modes of dress!

INFANTRY SECTION				
P	**MS**	**Z**	**Mod**	**ST**
5	Medium	6	8	2
Keywords		**Activation Keyword**		
Infantry		Line (Regulars)		
Regulation Equipment				
Rifles, Standard issue CC weapons				

INFANTRY SECTION UNIT UPGRADES

Infantry Sections are incredibly versatile and can be upgraded to carry equipment that can radically alter their battlefield role. Many of these weapons require a pair of soldiers, one to carry ammunition or vital equipment and another to operate the weapon itself. When Infantry Sections are upgraded, a defined number of men are replaced by the operators of these special weapons, though some are also wielded by a single individual. Others, like grenades and their equivalents are small enough that both upgrade men carry them, but they must forgo the weapons they would otherwise carry.

Light Machine Gun Crew

3 Upgrade Points. Two models in the unit are upgraded.

Nation – German Empire and Freikorps only

At the section level, a Light Machine Gun Crew can give Infantry Sections some additional punch. Used defensively, Light Machine Guns can bloody the nose of assaulting troops as they close in, whereas, on the attack, they can be used to strafe trenches or force defenders to keep their heads down and cover an advance.

There are numerous designs, though all are comparatively crude and prone to breakdowns, jams, and overheating. Combining cumbersome mechanisms with heavy ammunition, these weapons need a crew of two to utilise effectively, denying the man forced to carry the load the opportunity to carry a weapon themselves, but the additional firepower afforded by a Light Machine Gun is well worth the exchange.

LIGHT MACHINE GUN CREW				
P	MS	Z	Mod	ST
5	Medium	6	2	2
Keywords		**Activation Keyword**		
Infantry		N/A		
Regulation Equipment				
Light Machine Gun (1), Standard issue CC weapon				

Bombers

2 Upgrade Points. Two models in the unit are upgraded.

Nation – No restrictions

Hand Grenades are one of the most effective tools for assaulting enemy positions, enabling Infantry Sections to clear trenches whilst themselves remaining in a modicum of safety behind cover.

Grenades are extraordinarily widespread amongst the armed forces fighting on the Doggerland Front and produced in mind blowing quantities by all of the belligerents. However, more often than not. they are carried by specialists called Bombers. Laden with grenades, they act in support of more conventionally armed troops, loosing their deadly cargo where directed and dispatching enemies in a hail of shrapnel fragments.

BOMBERS				
P	MS	Z	Mod	ST
5	Medium	6	2	2
Keywords		**Activation Keyword**		
Infantry		N/A		
Regulation Equipment				
Hand Grenades (2), Standard issue CC weapon				

Fire-Bottle Team

3 Upgrade Points. Two models in the unit are upgraded.

Nation – American Volunteer Legions

When the American Volunteer Legions first arrived in Europe, few had access to proper military equipment, often having to make use of stores of obsolete weaponry or producing their own improvised responses to the terrors of combat in the mechanised age.

One such innovation was a direct response to the lack of explosives available to the newly arrived American troops; when enemy trenches were captured or abandoned towns scrounged, stores of fuel, alcoholic spirits, and other flammable chemicals were often utilised to make simple incendiary bombs. Terrifyingly effective, these weapons have been widely adopted.

FIRE-BOTTLE TEAM

P	MS	Z	Mod	ST
5	Medium	6	2	2

Keywords	Activation Keyword
Infantry	N/A

Regulation Equipment	
Fire Bottles (2), Standard issue CC weapon	

Rifle Grenadier

4 Upgrade Points. One model in the unit is upgraded.

Nation – American Volunteer Legions, British Empire, and French Republic

Despite their extraordinary utility, grenades are limited by the strength of the thrower's arm. Within months of the war starting, crude methods of launching grenades far further than they could be thrown were developed spontaneously in the trenches, but the most effective of these were simply charges fitted with a rod and pushed down the barrel of a rifle. When loaded with a blank cartridge, these grenades could be fired by soldiers on the move, either braced against an object or angled against the ground.

These improvised grenade launchers proved an effective force multiplier, leading to the development of more refined versions and the widespread use of these versatile weapons, which fill the gap between Bomber teams and Trench Mortars.

RIFLE GRENADIER

P	MS	Z	Mod	ST
5	Medium	6	1	2

Keywords	Activation Keyword
Infantry	N/A

Regulation Equipment	
Rifle Grenades (1), Rifle, Standard issue CC weapon	

Anti-Tank Rifle Grenadier

4 Upgrade Points. One model in the unit is upgraded.

Nation – British Empire

Until the events of The Shattering, the British had relied on heavier field guns and light mortars to knock out enemy machine gun posts and strong points. Consequently, the British Empire has no real answer to the 37 mm guns utilised by the other belligerents fighting on the Doggerland Front. Whilst these powers have rapidly embraced the evolving role of trench cannonry in an anti-tank role, the British empire has no weapon system to adapt.

The answer to this has been the development of rifle grenades designed to penetrate armour. These weapons have a short range and cannot be fired accurately in a parabolic arc, so the men tasked with bringing them to bear must exhibit extraordinary bravery, standing toe-to-toe with these snarling iron behemoths whilst taking careful aim.

ANTI-TANK RIFLE GRENADIER				
P	MS	Z	Mod	ST
5	Medium	6	1	2
Keywords		**Activation Keyword**		
Infantry		N/A		
Regulation Equipment				
AT Rifle Grenades (1), Rifle, Standard issue CC weapon				

Pioniere

3 Upgrade Points. Two models in the unit are upgraded.

Nation – German Empire

If one grenade can cause massive damage, then what can six do when strapped together?

This is the crude logic behind the use of grenade bundles, a battlefield modification allowed by the unique design of the German *stielhandgranate*. By removing their handles, the charges from a number of grenades can be wired together to create a huge lump of explosive material, a charge capable of causing devastating damage to living flesh and disabling machinery.

PIONIERE				
P	MS	Z	Mod	ST
5	Medium	6	2	2
Keywords		**Activation Keyword**		
Infantry		N/A		
Regulation Equipment				
Explosive Charge (1), Standard issue CC weapon				

Automatic Rifleman

3 Upgrade Points. Two models in the unit are upgraded.

Nation – British Empire, French Republic, and Russian Empire

These weapons make a compromise between rate of fire and manoeuvrability, useful in both defence but also, crucially, in attacking enemy positions. Comparatively light, they can be brought to bear on the move, taking a terrible toll on huddled defenders crouched in trenches.

As with their bulkier cousins, their designs are often crude. Some are simple conversions of an existing weapon that enables it to fire at a faster rate, while others are imperfect approaches to the problem of rapid fire that are prone to frequent jams and misfires. Though light enough to be portable, their bulky magazines mean they still require a dedicated loader.

AUTOMATIC RIFLEMAN

P	MS	Z	Mod	ST
5	Medium	6	2	2

Keywords	Activation Keyword
Infantry	N/A

Regulation Equipment	
Automatic Rifle (1), Standard issue CC weapon	

NCO

1 Upgrade Point. One model in the unit is upgraded.

Nation – No Restrictions

Few men in the trench are more feared, or more respected, than Non-Commissioned Officers. These men are usually of humbler birth than the officers above them, but often have a considerably greater well of practical combat experience to draw on than their superiors. As the war grinds on and the upper classes are bled white by the attrition of modern combat, a greater number of NCOs are enjoying unprecedented autonomy, with the fresh-faced but toffee-nosed recruits sent to lead them having to lean on their greater combat experience to lead their men to victory.

NCO

P	MS	Z	Mod	ST
5	Medium	6	1	2

Keywords	Activation Keyword
Infantry	N/A

Special Rules	
Follow Me Lads – Units containing an NCO receive Advantage-1 to Zeal when making Pinning Tests	

Regulation Equipment	
Rifle, Standard issue CC weapon	

COLONIAL ASSAULT TROOPS

2 Selection Points

Nation – British Empire and French Republic

Colonial troops are drawn from the vast empires of the belligerent nations, but none are more storied than the *Tirailleurs Sénégalais* of France and the Gurkhas fighting in the service of the British Empire.

These courageous fighters are particularly adept in close quarters where they can scythe their way through enemies with alarming ease. Their heavy, machete-like coupe coupes and kukhris prove a formidable tool for clearing trenches of foes.

In some instances, though not all, their uniforms differ substantially from those of troops from the home territories. Units where there is a corps of veterans from the earliest days of the war are notable in this regard, but many units will simply have a distinctive detail to their uniform, or a unique piece of headgear to distinguish them from their fellows.

COLONIAL ASSAULT TROOPS

P	MS	Z	Mod	ST
5	Medium	6	8	2

Keywords	Activation Keyword
Infantry	Line (Assault)

Regulation Equipment	
Rifles, Brutal CC weapons	

CONVENERS

1 Selection Points

Nation – No Restirctions

Alongside the trained soldiery march fanatics, devotees of a particular god or followers of a charismatic Witch. These men and women are unflinching in their dedication, prepared to charge headlong against any defences in the hopes of securing glory and sacrifice for their deity.

Many have little choice. The homes they once knew are devastated by the calamity of The Shattering, with whole towns and villages reduced to ashen wastes where nothing can grow. The only hope of reclaiming the lost fertility of their homelands is the intercession of the gods, whose favour can only be bought with offerings of blood and bone.

CONVENERS

P	MS	Z	Mod	ST
5	Low	5	8	2

Keywords	Activation Keyword
Infantry, Foolhardy, Impetuous, Undisciplined	Line (Rabble)

Regulation Equipment	
Standard issue CC weapon	

ELITE UNITS

LANCERS

2 Selection Points

Nation – British Empire, French Republic, German Empire, Freikorps, and Russian Empire Only

As autumn gave way to winter in the fateful year of 1914, the mobile phase of the hostilities on the Western Front, with the belligerents racing to sea, was over. In place of grand manoeuvre, there were now only trenches, barbed wire, and death. Though cavalry had played a prominent part in the initial stage of the conflict, its battlefield role diminished rapidly.

With The Shattering rapidly introducing a whole new front in the war and overextended commanders forced to leave great stretches of the trenches unguarded, the role of cavalry has been reassessed. On the freshly drained seabed or newly barren farmlands of Holland, charging cavalry can patrol much greater distances than men on foot, or disrupt and harry enemy forces as they march.

LANCERS				
P	**MS**	**Z**	**Mod**	**ST**
7	Medium	7	4	3
Keywords		**Activation Keyword**		
Cavalry, Charger		Elite (Assault)		
Regulation Equipment				
Cavalry CC weapons				

FLAMMENWERFER TEAM

3 Selection Points

Nation – German Empire, Freikorps

Perhaps no other weapon, save for the choking chemical gas that drifts across the battlefield, inspires so much terror as the flamethrower. Little more than a stout pipe connected to a tank of flammable material by a tube and a pump, it spews forth burning gouts of fire and noxious fumes, clearing trenches and consuming men with ease.

The men who crew these terrifying weapons must be hard as iron – the pitiful screams of roasting soldiers and sight of charred flesh can irrevocably scar even the hardiest mind.

FLAMMENWERFER TEAM				
P	**MS**	**Z**	**W**	**ST**
5	Medium	6	2	2
Keywords		**Activation Keyword**		
Infantry, Weapon Team		Elite (Support)		
Regulation Equipment				
Flamethrower (1), No CC weapons				

SNIPER TEAM

1 Selection Point

Nation – No restrictions

Snipers are a constant menace in the trenches, where men live in constant fear of a distant shot breaking the eerie silence that hangs over their lives. Prayers of protection are often heard when it is feared that a Sniper Team is operating close by.

Working in teams of two, Snipers watch and wait for opportunities to sow maximum disruption by wounding or killing men in leadership roles. As the war has become increasingly mobile, some have taken to active stalking.

SNIPER TEAM				
P	**MS**	**Z**	**W**	**ST**
5	Medium	6	2	2
Keywords		**Activation Keyword**		
Infantry, Sniper, Camouflaged, Vanguard, Weapon Team		Elite (Support)		
Regulation Equipment				
Marksman's Rifle (1), Revolver (1), Standard issue CC weapon				
1 CSM	**2 CSMs**		**3 CSMs**	
Lamed: P reduced to 2	**Destroyed Cover:** Loses the Keyword camouflaged		**Injured Spotter:** The unit loses the Keyword sniper	

TRENCH RAIDERS

2 Selection Points

Nation – No Restrictions

From the earliest days of the war, trench raiding was an important facet of life on the Western Front, giving young officers a chance to test their mettle and prove their worth to commanders by taking captives or seizing intelligence.

As the trench lines have extended northwards as the North Sea retreats from Doggerland, nations' abilities to garrison their trench lines have been sorely tested. Many are only loosely defended, with additional forces brought up only to participate in planned offences. These newly porous frontiers have precipitated ever bolder raiding, with many commanders now setting their sights far beyond the frontlines of the enemy, striking even into the largely demilitarised areas beyond.

With the shortages resulting from the myriad challenges of post-Shattering logistics, raiding has become a practical necessity to bolster meagre supplies in leaner times. However, it has also developed a highly ritualised component in the aftermath of The Shattering – captives, trophies, and seized cultic objects are all highly valued prizes on both sides of the wire, with many seeing participation in a successful raid and the taking of a captive for sacrifice as a rite of initiation.

TRENCH RAIDERS

P	MS	Z	Mod	ST
5	Medium	6	8	2

Keywords	Activation Keyword	
Infantry	Elite (Assault)	
Regulation Equipment		
Revolvers, Brutal CC weapon		

Trench Raider Unit Upgrade

3 Upgrade Point. Two models in the unit are upgraded.

Nation – No Restrictions

RAIDER BOMBERS

P	MS	Z	Mod	ST
5	Medium	6	2	2

Keywords	Activation Keyword	
Infantry	N/A	
Regulation Equipment		
Hand Grenades (2), Revolver (2), Brutal CC weapon		

ARMOURED CAR

3 Selection Points

Nation – No restrictions

The first Armoured Cars were little more than civilian vehicles, hastily adapted to the purpose of war. Jury-rigged armour, fitted heavily and imperfectly to the frame, the form of the vehicle was adapted so that a gunner could fire from a position of relative safety on the move.

With experience, Armoured Car builders refined their designs, improving the positioning of armour so as to deflect and redirect fire away from the crew and vulnerable mechanical components. Many of this new generation of Armoured Cars, built on the chassis of powerful vehicles and boasting efficient, modern armaments seem to herald the new direction of 20th century warfare – clean lines and cold resolve, sleek and barbarous weapons for an age of machines.

In the opening stages of the war, Armoured Cars had taken the role of light cavalry, ranging ahead to reconnoitre and engage the enemy only where necessary. As the war of manoeuvre gave way to the impasse of the trench, the importance of these machines waned. In the aftermath of The Shattering, Armoured Cars have found new purpose, responding quickly to the threat of enemy patrols and breaking through the thinly held lines of this new frontier to harass and delay the enemy until the main force arrives.

ARMOURED CAR				
P	**MS**	**Z**	**W**	**ST**
9	Medium	6	3	3
Keywords		**Activation Keyword**		
Wheeled Vehicle, Car, Armoured, Turret		Elite (Vehicle)		
Regulation Equipment				
Heavy Machine Gun (1), No CC weapons				
1 CSM		**2 CSMs**		**3 CSMs**
Damaged Transmission: Can only Move at half its Pace value (rounded down)		**Injured Gunner:** The Heavy Machine Gun produces four Attack Dice instead of eight		**Lost Wheel:** Can no longer Move

PROCESSIONAL GROUP

2 Selection Points

Nations – No restrictions

Cutting through the din of fighting, the blare of instruments and shouted cries signal the presence of an idol of the gods. Celebrants dance and shout, spinning like dervishes in the smoke of burnt offerings. Borne on litters, or carried aloft on shoulders, terrifying images are glimpsed between vigorous limbs and swirls of fragrant incense.

Processional Groups carry cultic idols into battle, festooned in flower garlands and laden with sacrificial offerings. These objects may be an image of the god, a relic of some past event, or even some grisly token of a previous sacrifice, but no matter the form they take, their presence on the battlefield has the same effect, inspiring the faithful and fuelling the fire of hatred for the enemy.

Many are accompanied by dancers, musicians, or cult figures, often costumed or masked in elaborate raiments and steeped in the symbolism of that cult's worship. To observe a Processional Group is often an eerie sight, the celebrants, festooned in charms and ribbons, whirling to and fro in an ecstatic trance, shouting imprecations to their god in long forgotten tongues.

PROCESSIONAL GROUP

P	MS	Z	W	ST
5	low	8	3	4

Keywords	Activation Keyword
Weapon Team, Infantry	Elite (Rabble)

Regulation Equipment

No CC weapons

Special rules

Celebrants – Despite not having the Activation Keyword unique, this unit may act as a Supporter in Close Combat.

Sacred Idol – If this unit is acting as a Supporter, all friendly units in the Close Combat gain the Keyword **unyielding**

1 CSM	2 CSMs	3 CSMs
Broken Trance: Saving Throw reduced to 2	**Damaged Idol:** Disadvantage-1 to Zeal Tests for all friendly units within 12"	**Broken Idol:** Advantage-1 to Zeal Tests for all enemy units within 12"

CANNONADE UNITS

HEAVY MORTAR TEAM

3 Selection Points

Nation – French *Republic, German Empire, and Russian Empire only*

Though developments in siege guns in the preceding century had stalled international enthusiasm for mortars, they had seen some development in Germany. Tasked with knocking out defensive positions in trench lines, they proved considerably more effective than the heavy artillery employed at the rear. Their utility proven, Germany's enemies rushed to produce their own equivalents, or to seize German mortars for themselves.

HEAVY MORTAR TEAM				
P	**MS**	**Z**	**W**	**ST**
0	Medium	6	3	2

Keywords	Activation Keyword
Infantry, Weapon Team	Cannonade (Support)

Regulation Equipment
Heavy Mortar (1), Standard issue CC weapons

1 CSM	2 CSMs	3 CSMs
Injured Spotter: All Direct Hits rolled on Scatter Dice must be rerolled (once per Shooting Attack)	**Damaged Range-Finder:** Trench Mortar rounds now Scatter 6" rather than 4"	**Injured Loader:** The Trench Mortar can no longer make Shooting Attacks

FIELD GUN

5 Selection Points

Nation – No restrictions

By far the deadliest weapon of the whole war, artillery can claim a higher death toll than any other weapon. Though the biggest guns are far behind the lines, some Patrols make use of their smaller cousins, giving access to the kind of firepower that can make short work of enemy defences.

FIELD GUN

P	MS	Z	W	ST
0	Medium	6	4	2

Keywords	Activation Keyword
Infantry, Weapon Team	Cannonade (Artillery)

Regulation Equipment

Field Gun (1), Standard issue CC weapons

Special Rules

Crippling Shot – If a Template generated by a Field Gun covers more than 50% of the base of a unit with the Keyword tracked vehicle or wheeled vehicle, that unit must take a Disabling Test (see page 106)

1 CSM	2 CSMs	3 CSMs
Injured Spotter: All Direct Hits rolled on Scatter Dice must be rerolled	**Mishandled Rounds:** All Critical Hits must be rerolled	**Injured Loader:** The Field Gun can no longer make Shooting Attacks

3.7 CM GUN TEAM

2 Selection Points

Nation – French Republic, German Empire, and Russian Empire only

The Hague Convention of 1899, re-ratified in 1905, forbade the use of exploding or expanding bullets. In prohibiting exploding munitions that were small enough to reasonably be considered to be bullets, it effectively defined the minimum calibre of exploding munitions as 3.7 cm.

In the wake of these restrictions, the nations of the world rushed to develop man portable weapons that could be used to dislodge a machine gun nest or destroy field fortifications. Some of these weapons were mounted on carriages, others on a bipod for use by a prone gunner, but all were in the near ubiquitous 3.7 cm calibre, or a very near equivalent.

As the war progressed, the utility of these weapons in an anti-tank role was realised. Special munitions designed to punch through armour were rapidly developed to counter the increasing presence of tanks on the battlefields of Europe, as well as the return made by armoured cars as the war became more mobile. The German Empire was the first to recognise the need for dedicated anti-tank support at the infantry level, introducing the 3.7 *Tankabwehrkanone* (TAK), but this recent development has been closely followed by the French and Russians, who developed a similar round for their 37 mm mle.1916 and 1915 pattern 37 mm trench guns, in addition to using captured German munitions.

3.7CM GUN TEAM				
P	**MS**	**Z**	**W**	**ST**
0	Medium	6	3	2

Keywords		**Activation Keyword**	
Infantry, Weapon Team		Cannonade (Artillery)	

Regulation Equipment			
AT Cannon (1), Standard issue CC weapons			

1 CSM	**2 CSMs**	**3 CSMs**
Broken Sights: Range reduced to 38"	**Injured Spotter:** All Direct Hits rolled on Scatter Dice must be rerolled	**Injured Loader:** The AT Cannon can no longer make Shooting Attacks

TRENCH MORTAR TEAM

2 Selection Points

Nation – British Empire and German Empire

Unlike the other great powers, the British focused their mortar development on increasingly portable versions that sacrificed firepower for mobility, speed of deployment, and rapidity of use. The Stokes Mortar was the result of the rapid development of a portable answer to the German *Minenwerfer*, which used a considerably smaller, fin-stabilised shell and could be quickly broken down and reassembled by gunnery crews on the move.

The German military quickly recognised the utility of these smaller weapons and began to produce an equivalent weapon, the *Granatenwerfer* 16, under licence from their Austro-Hungarian allies. These fast-firing spigot mortars mirrored the role of the British light mortars and are used to offer support to their fast-moving stormtroopers, whose battle doctrine means they cannot afford to wait for larger and more ponderous ordnance to be dragged across no man's land.

TRENCH MORTAR TEAM

P	MS	Z	W	ST
4	Medium	6	3	2

Keywords	Activation Keyword
Infantry, Weapon Team	Cannonade (Support)

Regulation Equipment	
Trench Mortar (1), Standard issue CC weapons	

1 CSM	2 CSMs	3 CSMs
Injured Spotter: All Direct Hits rolled on Scatter Dice must be rerolled	**Damaged Range-Finder:** Trench Mortar rounds now Scatter 6" rather than 3"	**Injured Loader:** The Trench Mortar can no longer make Shooting Attacks

MACHINE GUN TEAM

2 Selection Points

Nation – No restrictions

Perhaps no other weapon has had such a great impact on war as the machine gun. Laying down a hail of flying death, a small team of men can accomplish the work of an entire company. Machine guns are devastating defensive weapons, well suited to use in gun emplacements where they can work in concert to wither an assault to nothing with intersecting fields of fire. However, their lack of mobility makes them tempting targets for light artillery!

MACHINE GUN TEAM				
P	**MS**	**Z**	**W**	**ST**
3	Medium	6	3	2

Keywords		**Activation Keyword**
Infantry, Weapon Team		Cannonade (Support)

Regulation Equipment

Heavy Machine Gun (1), Standard issue CC weapons

1 CSM	**2 CSMs**	**3 CSMs**
Hot Barrel: Rolls of 4 are now treated as a Miss	**Feed Jammed:** The Heavy Machine Gun produces four Attack Dice rather than 8	**Overheated:** The Heavy Machine Gun can no longer make Shooting Attacks

MINDLESS UNITS

HARROWED

1 Selection Point

Nation – No restrictions

With the rise of magic, such terrors exist on the front that even seasoned veterans turn their backs and flee. These men do not lack for courage, but they suffer from one fatal human flaw – the instinct for self-preservation. However, the strange forces unleashed after The Shattering meant that a variety of methods now exist for creating soldiers devoid of the troublesome desire to continue living.

Harrowed are created in a variety of ways. The war means that an abundant supply of corpses, in varying states of completeness and decay, are available for practitioners of dark magic. In some instances, the discorporated spirits of the newly dead are imperfectly re-tethered to their own former mortal shell. In others, a greater spirit is called forth and shattered, like the pieces of a mirror, before being forced into a number of host bodies. The more materially minded might use psychoactive drugs to chemically lobotomise the troublesome or deviant or, following the pioneering work of Humbert North, create mindless automata from the tissue of both the living and dead.

Some Harrowed are little more than dolls, crude representations of human beings made in wood, clay, or some other spiritually conductive material. Much like a corpse, these marionettes can be animated with the spirits of the recently deceased and sent against the foe with an eerie creak and clatter.

Regardless of their origins, Harrowed are used by commanders to screen their more valuable troops. Soaking up machine gun fire like sponges, they will continue to advance until they are literally torn to shreds.

HARROWED				
P	**MS**	**Z**	**Mod**	**ST**
3	Low	4	8	1
Keywords		**Activation Keyword**		
Infantry, Unnaturally Tough		Mindless (Rabble)		
Regulation Equipment				
No CC weapons				

Chapter Ten
FRENCH REPUBLIC UNITS

Nowhere else has suffered the ravages of war like France. Along her northern border, little remains but muddy wasteland and churned sludge left in the wake of some of the fiercest fighting of the war, choked with grasping thickets and dank vegetation. Her towns are rubble, her forests splintered shards, and her once fertile fields now pitted moonscapes, strewn with wreckage, untilled, and barren. And yet, amidst this ruination, the French people are resolute, determined to see the fight to the end and exact their bloody revenge.

Though her countryside is devastated, and she suffers from the shortages of food common in this strange new world, France suffers less from political instability than her contemporaries. Perhaps the French people have put aside their grievances to speed the war to its successful conclusion. France is blessed with a syncretism not seen elsewhere on the continent; her native people are more accepting of the disparate rituals introduced by colonial troops than is the case elsewhere. Whilst the other nations of Europe tend to look down on these imports, the French soldiery has embraced them wholeheartedly.

France is host to many thousands of refugees from Belgium, displaced by the fighting in the earliest years of the war. More recently, the displaced inhabitants of the Netherlands have made the long and arduous journey into France, swelling the makeshift camps and shanty towns hastily erected to receive them. With the Netherlands' neutrality simultaneously trampled by British and German troops as the seas receded, their homes became the new frontline in the recommenced war on the Western Front. The camps they now inhabit have proved fertile recruiting grounds for the French army to swell its ranks, with many foreign battalions organised and equipped by France. Nowadays, even some regular army units from Belgium and the Netherlands, with their own equipment and uniforms, can occasionally be spotted amongst French forces. Though these are often led by French commanders, many more are autonomous and only notionally under the jurisdiction of French High Command.

UNIQUE UNITS

RENAULT FT TSF
Free, Replaces Captain

The FT17 is arguably the most successful tank of the war, spawning a number of variants designed to fulfil different battlefield roles.

One of the most unusual of these is the FT *Télégraph-Sans-Fils* or TSF. These tanks completely eschew any armaments, instead carrying large and cumbersome wireless equipment so that communication can be maintained with command even as a force punches through the frontlines and into enemy territory. In the wide expanse of Doggerland, small patrols supported by these curious tanks can maintain near constant communication with command, enabling French forces to coordinate much more effectively.

RENAULT FT TSF

P	MS	Z	W	ST
7	High	9	3	3

Keywords	Activation Keyword
Tracked Vehicle, Car, Armoured, Fortress	Unique (Leader)

Regulation Equipment

No CC weapon

Special Orders

Fast Assault – A Renault FT17 within 12" may be activated in the Cannonade Phase (3 Command Tokens)

Orders

Rally – Select a Broken unit of infantry or cavalry that is within 10" to make a Zeal Test. If the Test is passed, the unit is no longer Broken (1 Command Token)

Special Rules

Tank Commander – Unlike other unique units, this Captain may only be activated once per Round and cannot act as a Supporter

1 CSM	2 CSMs	3 CSMs
Damaged Transmission: Can only Move at half its Pace value (rounded down)	**Blown Track:** Can no longer Pivot	**Madness:** Cannot issue Orders

RENAULT FT TSF UPGRADE TABLE

Free

The unit may select up to one Order or Ruse from the Orders Chapter

The unit may choose a Zodiac Sign

Options

The unit may choose an item from the Special Items List

THEOSOPHIST

Free, Replaces Captain

In the smartest salons in Parisian society, the indolent rich of *la Belle Epoque* have embraced of the mysteries of the East. Many are devotees of the infamous Madame Devinsky, herself an enigma, but one possessed of indisputable power.

Madame Devinsky has, for a number of years, been in near constant telepathic communication with a brotherhood of impossibly ancient beings, wise sages brimming with the millenia old wisdom of far-flung civilisations. Her followers devote themselves to the theosophy that she espouses, gaining great spiritual power in exchange. In the aftermath of The Shattering, this compact seems to have strengthened and her followers are capable of wondrous feats of magic, though the demands that Madane Devinsky hands down from her masters have become increasingly dark and bizarre with each passing season.

THEOSOPHIST

P	MS	Z	W	ST
5	High	9	3	4

Keywords

Keywords	Activation Keyword
Infantry	Unique (Leader)

Regulation Equipment

No CC weapon

Aura

Tranquillity – Friendly unique units within 10" may ignore the consequences of a chosen Combat Stress Marker effect on a roll of 1 on a d6 (the roll must be made at the start of each Activation)

Orders

Rally – Select a Broken infantry or cavalry unit that is within 10" to make a Zeal Test. If the test is passed, the unit is no longer Broken
(1 Command Token)

Special Rules

Astral Projection – At the start of the game, after all units have been placed, position an additional model in contact with this unit. The new model is now Activated in place of the unit and gains the Keyword wisp, however the original model remains on the table and may be the target of Shooting Attacks, or engaged in Close Combat. Should the original model be destroyed, both models are immediately removed from the board.

1 CSM	2 CSMs	3 CSMs
Staggering: P reduced to 3	**Trembling:** MS reduced to Low	**Madness:** Cannot issue Orders

THEOSOPHIST UPGRADE TABLE

Free

The unit may select up to two Orders or Ruses from the Orders Chapter

The unit may choose a Zodiac Sign

Options

The unit may choose an item from the Special Items List

LINE UNITS

RENAULT FT17
4 Selection Points

    With its well-protected engine, insulated from the crew compartment and situated at the rear of the tank; its turret capable of turning to face any target; and its relatively high speed, the FT17 is one of the most advanced tank designs on the battlefields of the Western Front.

    With the great shifts in battlefield tactics in the wake of The Shattering, the breakthrough capabilities of the FT17 and the battlefield support that it can offer to infantry far from their own line have made it one of the most valuable tools available to French commanders. Many a squad of *Poilu*, pinned down by some unseen enemy, have been heartened by the roar and clatter of an FT17's engine.

    By comparison to the lumbering and deeply flawed heavy tanks produced in France, the nimble little FT17, though lightly armed and armoured, is efficient, reliable, and brimming with charisma.

RENAULT FT17

P	MS	Z	W	ST
7	Medium	6	3	3

Keywords	Activation Keyword			
Tracked Vehicle, Car, Armoured, Turret, Fortress	Line (Vehicle)			

Regulation Equipment				
Heavy Machine Gun (1), No CC weapons				

1 CSM	2 CSMs	3 CSMs
Damaged Transmission: Can only Move at half its Pace value (rounded down)	**Blown Track:** Can no longer Pivot	**Engine Destroyed:** Can longer no Move

RENAULT FT17 UPGRADE TABLE

1 Upgrade Point

The Heavy Machine Gun may be swapped for AT Cannon

SCHNEIDER CA1

5 Selection Points

The French have had mixed luck in the development of tanks. The small FT17 has proven immensely successful, whilst its hulking cousin, the *Saint Chamond*, has developed a reputation for being unreliable, dangerous, and, frankly, inefficient. Now, so few of these great, ponderous beasts are left that they are a rare sight indeed, seldom glimpsed on the Doggerland Front.

Between these two extremes sits the Schneider CA1. Considerably smaller than the heaviest vehicles on the battlefield, it is nonetheless large enough to carry a more formidable array of weapons than its smaller FT17 counterparts. With its beaked nose for cutting through wire, it is well-suited for the task of breaking the enemy lines and cutting down entrenched enemies with its side-mounted guns. Though smaller than the super-heavy tanks of Britain and Germany, its main gun is still of a considerable calibre, and with this armament it is more than capable of going toe-to-toe with the larger tanks of the enemy, providing it has room to manoeuvre.

SCHNEIDER CA1

P	MS	Z	W	ST
5	Medium	6	4	4

Keywords	Activation Keyword
Tracked Vehicle, Tank, Fortress, Armoured	Line (Vehicle)

Regulation Equipment

Front – AT Cannon (1)

Left – Heavy Machine Gun (1)

Right – Heavy Machine Gun (1)

No CC weapons

1 CSM	2 CSMs	3 CSMs
Damaged Transmission: Can only Move at half its Pace value (rounded down)	**Blown Track:** Can no longer Pivot	**Engine Destroyed:** Can longer no Move

ELITE UNITS

VITIATED SPIRIT

2 Selection Points

When the moon was shattered, many of the spirits of the earth's wild places were awakened. Once called nymphs, these liminal creatures dwelt on the margins of both worlds, occupying both our material reality and the spiritual world, intrinsically linked to the place they inhabit. They often appeared to men as beautiful maidens, their bodies reflecting the changing seasons.

Many once claimed a tiny patch of nature as their own, slumbering there in the long ages since man began to turn his back on the old ways. Now, roused from their dreamless sleep by the calamity of the Summerisle Incident, the spirits of France find their forests reduced to splinters, their brooks poisoned, and their lakes befouled.

Mirroring the terrible corruption of their homes, their bodies have become corrupted by the artefacts of war. Coils of wire snake through their bodies and muck and filth oozes from suppurating wounds on their flesh. Stricken with grief and driven half mad by the terrible pain of their transformation, those humans that are touched by the spirit world can readily corrupt them for their own ends, twisting the spirits' rage to madness and directing their hatred of man against their own enemies.

When turned in this way, these entities become a terrifying force. Endowed with powers beyond human understanding, the corrupting taint of war proceeds them like a black pall.

VITIATED SPIRIT				
P	**MS**	**Z**	**W**	**ST**
5	Medium	6	4	4

Keywords	Activation Keyword
Man-Sized Creature, Bramblekin, Disturbing, Sylvan, Elemental Resistance	Elite (Creature)

Regulation Equipment

Brutal CC Weapons

Abilities

Growth – The unit causes a patch of wire or thicket to sprout from the ground anywhere within 6". This terrain feature remains in place for the remainder of the game unless it is destroyed by a tracked vehicle (1 Command Token)

Ensnare – Select an enemy infantry unit within 10" to make a Zeal Test. If the test is failed, the unit becomes Pinned (1 Command Token)

1 CSM	2 CSMs	3 CSMs
Madness: Gains the Keyword impetuous	**Blinded:** MS reduced to Low	**Broken Bough:** Loses Brutal CC weapons

CUIRASSIERS

2 Selection Points

In the earliest days of the war, the heaviest French cavalry fought in a way barely changed from the days of Napoleon. The romance of shining breastplates and plumed helmets soon met the stark reality of modern warfare. As casualties mounted, a number of radical changes were made to both the uniforms and equipment of the *Cuirassiers*.

However, in wake of The Shattering, the changed nature of combat and the vast, fluid frontier means that many of these units have returned to their old tactics and, in some cases at least, their old uniforms as well. Though a breastplate may be little defence against a machine bullet, it can ward against the disembowelling claw of a creature from the dark forests, or the thrust of a cultist's blade.

A charge of *Cuirassiers* makes for a terrifying sight, with the sound of thundering hooves known to turn the bowels of even the stoutest soldier to water in an instant. The psychological impact of the *Cuirassiers'* presence on the battlefield can sometimes be enough to turn the tide of an engagement, and for this reason they are still prized by French commanders.

CURASSIERS				
P	**MS**	**Z**	**Mod**	**ST**
7	High	7	4	3
Keywords		**Activation Keyword**		
Cavalry, Intimidating		Elite (Assault)		
Regulation Equipment				
Brutal CC weapons, Body Armour				

Chapter Eleven
GERMAN EMPIRE UNITS

Before the calamity of the Summerisle Incident, attrition gripped Germany by the throat. Its allies seemed on the verge of annihilation and it was embroiled in a bitter struggle on two fronts. Though The Shattering was calamitous for all the nations fighting on the Western Front, perhaps Germany alone can be said to have benefited in some small way.

As the cataclysm wracked the land, in many places the war was put on a mutual, though unofficial, hiatus. This brief reprieve gave Germany some respite from the bitter struggle and an opportunity to right itself. Though the guns of the Western Front fell silent for a time, the same was not true everywhere. With so many hardened and veteran troops freed from the trenches, Germany lent aid to their embattled allies the Austro-Hungarian Empire, enabling them to tame the Italians to their south, finally breaking their indomitable will in the Dolomites in the spring of 1917.

The Shattering left many European states reeling, but German unity was preserved by compromises and accommodations. The doors of power were opened a crack and voices from alternative political ideologies and ethnic minorities were offered a seat at the top table. Their power harnessed, the worst excesses of revolutionary thought were staved off, though the tension between the traditional military aristocracy and these new radical politicians bubbles just beneath the surface.

By declawing those on the fringes, the German Empire has bought itself the time to prosecute the war to a successful conclusion.

Many, particularly on the right, seethe with quiet fury at the betrayal of the German nation. Though some still serve the Kaiser, many more have broken away, with whole portions of the army throwing in their lot with the *Freikorps* – bands of warriors who have completely abandoned the German state and instead fight for a twisted ideology.

A young nation, the German Empire lacks the homogeneity and deep-rooted traditions of Britain and France, though it has a strong and active martial tradition, with an officer corps amongst the best in the world. Its social elite have embraced the old gods more out of pragmaticism than any genuine spirituality, but among the common soldiery, the old practices have been enthusiastically revived.

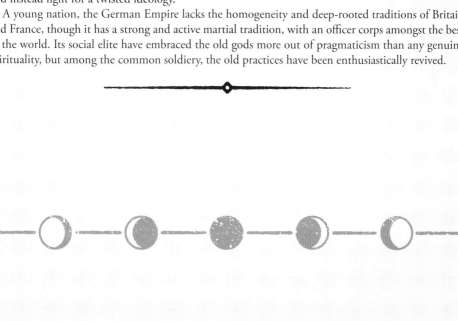

TAKTIKER

Free, Replaces Captain

Though the reality of magic cannot be denied, there are many that hold little truck with sorcery, preferring to put their faith in steel. In the military academies of Germany, aspiring officers are first-and-foremost taught to win wars by conventional means, with little recourse to spirits and sorcery.

Though battles call for bravery, wars are a game of logistics and supply – the commander best placed to leverage his materiel the sure victor.

Preparedness is the mark of a great leader, but a war on such scale must have supply to match. A hundred thousand shells? A hundred million bullets? The cost is no object – your opponent must be pummelled until they collapse from exhaustion, or the sheer weight of their dead.

TAKTIKER

P	MS	Z	W	ST
5	High	9	3	4

Keywords	Activation Keyword
Infantry	Unique (Leader)

Regulation Equipment

Revolver, Standard issue CC weapon

Aura

Material Supremacy – Units with the Keyword artillery that are within 10" may reroll Scatter Dice (once per Shooting Attack)

Orders

Rally – Select a Broken infantry or cavalry unit that is within 10" to make a Zeal Test. If the Test is passed then the unit is no longer Broken
(1 Command Token)

Special Rules

For as long as this unit remains in play, roll an additional d3 for any attempt to win Priority Activation in the Cannonade Phase.

1 CSM	2 CSMs	3 CSMs
Staggering: P reduced to 3	**Trembling:** MS reduced to Low	**Madness:** Cannot issue Orders

TAKTIKER UPGRADE TABLE

Free

The unit may select up to two Orders or Ruses from the Orders Chapter

The unit may exchange its Regulation Equipment for:
Self-Loading Pistol

The unit may choose a Zodiac Sign

1 Upgrade Point

The unit may exchange its Regulation Equipment for:
Pistol Carbine

Options

The unit may choose an item from the Special Items List

ARMANIST

Free, Replaces Captain

Many secret societies exist in Germany, with a good number of them popular among the educated elite. In university towns and fashionable drawing rooms, occult beliefs, often with a racial dimension, were in vogue long before the outbreak of war. Some were little more than glamorous gentleman's clubs, the lure of forbidden magic adding a frisson of danger to the prospect of membership, but others were dedicated, dangerous, and engaged in clandestine politics.

Chief among these is the Ultima Nord Society, a cultic body dedicated to unlocking the secrets of the ancient Germanic people. Within this secret organisation are those that believe in *Vril*, a mystic energy controllable by those with sufficient discipline and resolve. These adherents believe that *Vril* has its source and greatest concentration in subterranean spaces deep beneath the earth, within the last refuges of a mighty race driven underground long ago. On the Doggerland Front, they hope to find some clue to entering these sanctuaries amongst the scattered traces of the elder race that once inhabited it.

Armanist

P	MS	Z	W	ST
5	High	9	3	4

Keywords	Activation Keyword
Infantry	Unique (Leader)

Regulation Equipment

Revolver, Standard issue CC weapon

Aura

Invigorating Energy – Any unit within 10" with the Activation Keyword mindless count as having Fearsome CC weapons

Special Orders

Magnetism – A selected unit with the Activation Keyword mindless may move an additional d6" in the direction of the player's choice during the compulsory moves subphase (1 Command Token)

Abilities

Blood Manipulation – Select an enemy unit and roll a d6, adding an extra d3 if the unit is within 12" or an extra d6 if the unit is within 6". Compare the result of the roll with the target's Zeal. For every point above the target's Zeal, the unit takes one MS Medium Hit (1

1 CSM	2 CSMs	3 CSMs
Staggering: P reduced to 3	**Trembling:** MS reduced to Low	**Madness:** Cannot issue Orders

Armanist Upgrade Table

Free

The unit may select up to two Orders or Ruses from the Orders Chapter

The unit may exchange its Regulation Equipment for:
Self-Loading Pistol

The unit may choose a Zodiac Sign

1 Upgrade Point

The unit may exchange its regulation equipment for:
Pistol Carbine

Options

The unit may choose an item from the Special Items List

LINE UNITS

A7V

6 Selection Points

A clumsy, lumbering behemoth, the A7V is an imperfect response to the more refined super-heavy tanks used by the British. However, it is still more than capable of being used as an armoured fist to punch through enemy lines whilst protecting and supporting advancing infantry.

Whilst German High Command realises the limitations of the A7V, planned replacements are still in production. Consequently, this ungainly monster must plug the gap whilst its cousins are being built, a duty it performs well enough to have earned some affection from the men who serve in its shadow.

Though notionally the fastest super-heavy tank serving on the Western Front, in practice the A7V is the slowest. It must be driven with care over rough ground, its high centre of gravity and low ground clearance requiring a ponderous advance, lest the crew risk toppling it over or getting caught on an obstacle.

A7V

P	MS	Z	W	ST
4	Medium	6	5	4

Keywords	Activation Keyword
Tracked Vehicle, Behemoth, Fortress, Armoured, Select fire	Line (Vehicle)

Regulation Equipment

Front – AT Cannon

Left – Heavy Machine Gun (2)

Right – Heavy Machine Gun (2)

Rear – Heavy Machine Gun (2)

Standard issue CC weapon

Special Rules

Top-Heavy – an A7V cannot cross trenches or foxholes

1 CSM	2 CSMs	3 CSMs
Damaged Transmission: Can only Move at half its Pace value (rounded down)	**Blown Track:** Can no longer Pivot	**Engine Destroyed:** Can longer no Move

HAXENJÄGER

2 Selection Points

Germany's response to many of the terrors of the transformed world is pragmatic, often preferring the reliability of machines and mechanisms to the whims of magic – where the gods are fickle, cold iron gives certainty. The question of how best to deal with the presence of magic on the battlefield is answered by German troops with a kind of brutal practicality -to remove the threat of magic, simply hunt down and kill the witch.

Highly specialised troops who don the heaviest armour, the Haxenjäger appear like knights of old as they trudge across the battlefield. The solid plates of iron with which they protect themselves is ward against both bullets and the curses of witches. Their implacable march fills the heart of any magic user with dread, for their purpose on the battlefield is solely to kill witches, seeking them with a purpose as hard as the iron that covers them.

Only the bravest souls will volunteer to act as Haxenjäger – clad in heavy and cumbersome armour, daubed with sigils of warding and protection, they make slow progress across the battlefield oblivious to the death flying all around them, resolute in their purpose…

HAXENJÄGER				
P	**MS**	**Z**	**Mod**	**ST**
4	Medium	6	4	4

Keywords	Activation Keyword
Infantry, Impenetrable	Line (Assault)

Regulation Equipment	
Brutal CC Weapons, Body Armour	

Special Rules

Witch hunters – This unit is immune to the effects of a witches "curse special ability" and may reroll any failed to hit rolls made against a target with the key word witch.

Bulky – this unit must pass the same test as a tracked vehicle in order to travel over mire, taking a test on a D10 for each model in the unit and losing a model for each result of 10.

ELITE UNITS

STOßTRUPPEN

3 Selection Points

A hardened cadre of toughened veterans, *Stoßtruppen* (stormtroopers) are the iron core around which Germany remodelled her army when hostilities resumed in the aftermath of The Shattering.

In a break with conventional tactics, where troops would break through only to wait to be reinforced, the *Stoßtruppen* are well trained, equipped, and provisioned units whose task it is to break through the enemy lines and claim objective after objective until victory has been assured. Often they are old hands, long established on the front and numbed to its horrors. Those with the mental fortitude and combat skill are carefully selected and retrained for this specialist role.

As dedicated close combat units, *Stoßtruppen* carry the newly developed machine pistol This radical new weapon is portable enough to be brought to bear by men on the move, but is extremely effective at fighting in close quarters, especially when combined with the savage training and brutal melee implements of the *Stoßtruppen*.

STOßTRUPPEN				
P	**MS**	**Z**	**Mod**	**ST**
5	Medium	7	4	3
Keywords		**Activation Keyword**		
Infantry		Elite (Assault)		
Regulation Equipment				
Machine Pistols, Brutal CC weapons, Body Armour				

T-GEWEHR TEAM

1 Selection Points

In the race to come up with viable solutions for defeating armour, one of the most innovative solutions is the Mauser *Tankgewehr* 1918 – a high-calibre rifle designed to penetrate armour and disable either vital components or crew.

Though it functions almost identically to any other rifle on the battlefield, every component of the T-Gewehr has been strengthened and massively increased in size in order to accommodate such a large projectile, resulting in a huge, ungainly, but otherwise mechanically conventional, firearm. As a result, transporting both the ammunition and weapon itself is an arduous task, hampering the mobility of the gun crew.

T-GEWEHR TEAM

P	MS	Z	W	ST
4	Medium	6	2	2

Keywords	Activation Keyword
Infantry, Sniper, Weapon Team	Elite (Artillery)

Regulation Equipment		
Anti-Tank Rifle (1), Standard issue CC weapons		

1 CSM	2 CSMs	3 CSMs
Injured Spotter: Range reduced to 20"	**Crooked Sights:** Rolls of 3 are now treated as a Miss	**Warped Barrel:** Can no longer make Shooting Attacks

Chapter Twelve
BRITISH EMPIRE UNITS

The British Isles and their people are steeped in magic, but nowhere is its character so often determined by class. In the rarefied setting of an officer's dugout, libations of claret are offered to antique statues imported at exorbitant cost, whilst a few yards away the lower ranks dedicate paltry sacrifices to crudely carved idols of gods so ancient that their names and likenesses are long-forgotten. These divisions run so deep that they threaten to tear the country apart. The crumbling edifice of British unity is held together by co-opted legend, folklore, and myths of national origin, all given new immediacy by the return of magic. Britain imagines herself a valiant crusader, armour-clad and beset by monsters, but the truest threat is the canker within.

Whilst many of the most prominent of the Hermetic Lodges trace their roots back to Oxford and Cambridge, beside this decadent glamour is a great lineage of witches and cunning folk stretching back into the depths of the past. Among the lower rungs of society, in rural places isolated by geography and neglected by the march of industrialisation, the old ways and gods have been kept safe from civilisation for countless generations. In ceremonies little changed for millennia, the ancient spirits of the earth are placated with sacrifice with song handed down through the ages.

When the war began, Britain brought forth untold numbers of men to her defence from her sprawling Empire, some willing, some coerced. Now effectively stranded by the calamitous effects of The Shattering, these men struggle to rebuild their lives. With sea routes vanished and many ports now inaccessible, trade between nations has become increasingly difficult. For Britain, whose population exceeds her resources, the situation is grave. In towns and factories inflamed by shortages, violence has become commonplace, threatening to spill out into the country at large; the war must be brought to a swift conclusion, lest the whole facade come crumbling down.

UNIQUE UNITS

CUNNING PERSON

Free, Replaces Captain

Cunning Folk have long operated at the edge of societies as healers, apothecaries, and maledictors for hire. Some gained great renown and prestige, their power and knowledge greatly prized, whereas others were reviled, protected from the ire of the communities they lived alongside only by the fear they inspired. Their lives were simple, living off the land a little way from the tiny and isolated villages they served.

As the countryside emptied and towns and cities swelled ever further, the poor and marginal communities in which the Cunning Folk lived were squeezed out or dried up. Many of the old ways were lost as the farms and stockyards emptied. The numbers of those with knowledge of the craft dwindled too, pushed aside in favour of modernity. As man's connection to the earth was severed, so the power of the Cunning Folk diminished.

However, the horrors awakened by The Shattering have upended the march of progress, and so the spirits of the land rise up to claim their birthright and the old oaths are uttered once again.

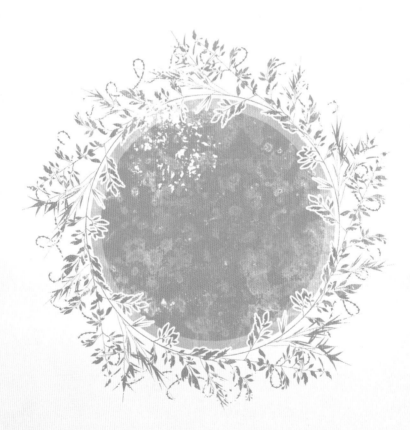

CUNNING PERSON

P	MS	Z	W	ST
5	Medium	9	3	4

Keywords	Activation Keyword
Infantry, Divinely Favoured	Unique (Leader)

Regulation Equipment

Revolver, Standard issue CC weapon

Aura

Fey Soul - Infantry units within 10" gain the Keyword bramblekin

Special Orders

Blood And Bone – Select two friendly multi-model units within 6" of one another. Choose one, remove a Combat Stress Marker and then have this unit make a Zeal Test. For every point the Test is failed by, the other selected unit takes a Wound with no Saving Throw allowed (1 Command Token)

Frost And Fire – Select an enemy unit within 10" to take Disadvantage-1 to any Saving Throws made against Shooting Attacks for the remainder of the Round (1 Command Token)

1 CSM	2 CSMs	3 CSMs
Staggering: P reduced to 3	**Trembling:** MS reduced to Low	**Madness:** Cannot issue Orders

CUNNING PERSON UPGRADE TABLE

Free

The unit may select up to two Orders or Ruses from the Orders Chapter

The unit may exchange its Regulation Equipment for:
Self-Loading Pistol

The unit may choose a Zodiac Sign

Options

The unit may choose an item from the Special Items List

163

MESMERIST

Free, Replaces Captain

Magic has deep roots in Europe, but this is perhaps nowhere more immediately obvious than in Britain. In her dark and mysterious forests and among her brooding circles of stone, the whispered names of long forgotten gods can almost be heard on the wind.

In the preceding century, just as the last sparks of autochthonous magic were being extinguished by the clearances of rural communities in the name of industrial progress, well-heeled Britons were discovering the occult for the first time. At the same time, the magically inclined could step into any museum and see a panoply of strange idols and exotic gods, looted from far-flung lands and carried to the heart of the Empire. A world of potential waiting to be grasped and directed by those with the will.

In time, temples to a host of ancient gods sprang up near fashionable spas and university towns. To some, these were a curious and salacious diversion, a season's dalliance. To others, they were a path to terrible power.

MESMERIST

P	MS	Z	W	ST
5	High	9	3	4

Keywords	Activation Keyword
Infantry	Unique (Leader)

Regulation Equipment

Revolver, Standard issue CC weapon

Aura

Conduit - Units of Spiritualists within 10" may reroll failed Saving Throws (once per Hit)

Orders

Rally – Select a Broken infantry or cavalry unit that is within 10" to make a Zeal Test. If the Test is passed then the unit is no longer Broken (1 Command Token)

Abilities

Psychic Blast – Generate a Medium Template within 15" of the unit. Every model caught beneath it takes an MS Medium Hit (1 Command Token)

1 CSM	2 CSMs	3 CSMs
Staggering: P reduced to 3	**Trembling:** MS reduced to Low	**Madness:** Cannot issue Orders

MEMERIST UPGRADE TABLE

Free

The unit may select up to two Orders or Ruses from the Orders Chapter

The unit may exchange its Regulation Equipment for:
Self-Loading Pistol

Options

The unit may choose a Zodiac Sign

The unit may choose an item from the Special Items List

MARK IV

6 Selection Points

The British were largely responsible for the development of the first real tanks, unleashing them against German defenders with limited strategic success but extraordinary acclaim. Since the earliest tanks coughed and sputtered their way across the Somme, continuous development has led to the more refined, but no less heavily armed, monster that is the Mark IV.

As with all larger tanks on the Doggerland Front, the Mark IV is designed to break through the enemy lines before unleashing a broadside of fire against the enemy from a position perpendicular to their lines. Though far from perfect, these British tanks are the only ones that are truly capable of accomplishing this task.

MARK IV

P	MS	Z	W	ST
4	Medium	6	5	4

Keywords	Activation Keyword
Tracked Vehicle, Behemoth, Fortress, Armoured	Line (Vehicle)

Regulation Equipment

Front – Heavy Machine Gun (1)

Left – AT Cannon (1), Heavy Machine Gun (1)

Right – AT Cannon (1), Heavy Machine Gun (1)

Standard issue CC weapon

1 CSM	2 CSMs	3 CSMs
Damaged Transmission: Can only Move at half its Pace value (rounded down)	**Blown Track:** Can no longer Pivot	**Engine Destroyed:** Can longer no Move

MARK IV UPGRADE TABLE

Free

The unit may exchange both of its AT Cannons for:
Heavy Machine Gun

1 Upgrade Point

The unit may be upgraded with the following special rules:
Tadpole Tail – May reroll failed tests when crossing mire (see page 102)

MEDIUM MARK A WHIPPET

5 Selection Points

The natural extension of the development of heavy tanks capable of breaking the lines in larger engagements is the creation of lighter vehicles capable of ranging ahead of the main force and harassing the enemy. This niche is already occupied by armoured cars and, though these surprisingly nimble vehicles have the edge in speed, they have several limitations – they are unable to tackle difficult terrain as easily as a tank and their armaments and armour must be comparatively light due to their smaller engine size.

A larger weapons platform that is capable of moving at a reasonable speed over rough ground, a halfway-house between an armoured car and a tank, addresses this requirement perfectly. The appropriately named Whippet is a deceptive machine. Though it appears to be a cumbersome beast like its larger cousins, it is nonetheless capable of fairly rapid movement and, crucially, conducts itself well over fairly tough terrain. The fast and tough Whippet has become the bane of many Patrols that have strayed out into the wide expanse of the Doggerland Front, cutting down isolated groups of men before retreating at speed in the face of an advancing column.

Though the Whippet boasts an impressive complement of guns in its turret, it is manned by too small a crew to bring every gun to bear at any given time; the gunners must move between positions and cannot be everywhere at once!

MEDIUM MARK A WHIPPET

P	MS	Z	W	ST
5	Medium	6	4	3

Keywords	Activation Keyword
Tracked Vehicle, Tank, Armoured, Fortress	Line (Vehicle)

Regulation Equipment

Front – Heavy Machine Gun

Left – Heavy Machine Gun

Right – Heavy Machine Gun

Rear – Heavy Machine Gun

Standard issue CC weapon

Special Rules

Limited Crew – The Whippet's armaments may only be fired from two Faces per Activation. When Activating the Whippet, the commanding player must choose which two Faces its weapons will be fired from, clearly declaring their intentions before rolling any dice.

1 CSM	2 CSMs	3 CSMs
Damaged Transmission: Can only Move at half its Pace value (rounded down)	**Blown Track:** Can no longer Pivot	**Engine Destroyed:** Can longer no Move

MAY QUEENS

2 Selection Points

As winter loosens her icy grip and the first flushes of spring creep across the land, the Queens of May are crowned. Chosen from amongst the most beautiful girls in any village, to be crowned a Queen of May is an incomparable honour – a vessel of the Triune Goddess herself.

Festooned with flower garlands and bedecked in the gifts of the new season, May Queens personify the vibrancy of the season of growth. These handmaidens of the Triune Goddess serve as her heralds, ushering in the new season, but also as executioners of her divine will, scything their way through victims – both willing and otherwise. As the world falls increasingly deep into environmental collapse and the need to secure fertility becomes more acute, the May Queens have found their way onto the battlefields of the transformed war.

Possessed by a vital spirit, in battle May Queens lead fighters in their ecstatic dance. Whirling and twisting as they advance, they present a difficult target for defenders who must watch aghast as they approach with alarming speed, the air alive with the hum of swinging sickles. When they close with the enemy, they become a blur of violence, dispatching enemies with a preternatural and deadly grace.

MAY QUEENS				
P	MS	Z	Mod	ST
5	High	8	4	3

Keywords	Activation Keyword
Infantry, Divinely Favoured, Fast target	Elite (Assault)

Regulation Equipment
Brutal CC weapons

Abilities
Rites Of Spring – The unit Moves an additional distance, chosen by their commanding player, up to a maximum of 6". For every inch moved in excess of the unit's Pace value, roll a d6. For each result of 6, this unit takes an MS Low Hit (1 Command Token)

SPIRITUALISTS

2 Selection Points

Across the Doggerland Front, hideous creatures are drawn to the fighting by the call of witches and the scent of blood. For centuries, individuals have stumbled through in places where the veil is naturally thin, giving rise to the tales of monsters that mankind has used to scare its children for untold generations. The Shattering has changed all that, weakening the veil between the spirit world and our material plane sufficiently that many of these horrors, the strongest denizens of the spirit world, can simply force their way through. Such is the violence of these events that the tears they leave behind can never fully heal.

Through these doorways pour forth a host of lesser spirits. Too weak to will their way into the material realm for themselves, they can nonetheless take advantage of the paths made by others, like infantry following a tank through crushed wire. Some are formerly human spirits, fragmented and incomplete, still haunting the battlefields on which they died, but more are of an even greater age. In the cold places beyond death, the warmth and light of our world is like a beacon to which these spirits are instinctively drawn. Dazed and disoriented, they rush through the tears to re-join the world they once knew. Some soldiers at the front, even before The Shattering, spoke of apparitions and angels, or even the warriors of the distant past, coming to aid them in their most desperate hour.

Spiritualists can harness the energies of these returning souls, bending them to their will. Though an individual spirit has little more presence in our world than a whisper, a host of spirits bound to one another is a potent force indeed.

SPIRITUALISTS

P	MS	Z	Mod	ST
5	Medium	6	4	3

Keywords	Activation Keyword
Infantry	Elite (Rabble)

Regulation Equipment	
No CC weapons	

Abilities

Guardian Spirits – Select a spot within 10" to Manifest Guardian Spirits, placing a Marker there. Any Friendly unit within 6" of the Marker gains Advantage-1 to any Saving Throws. If a vehicle, friend or foe, passes over it, the presence of iron drives the Guardian Spirits away and the Marker is immediately lost. You may have multiple Guardian Spirit Markers on the table simultaneously (1 Command Token)

Unquiet Spirits – Select a spot within 10" to manifest Unquiet Spirits, placing a Marker there. Any enemy unit with the Keyword infantry or cavalry that moves within 6" must make a Zeal Test, generating a Combat Stress Marker if failed. If a vehicle, friend or foe, passes over it, the presence of iron drives the Unquiet Spirits away and the marker is immediately lost. You may have multiple Unquiet Spirit Markers on the table simultaneously (1 Command Token)

Chapter Thirteen
FREIKORPS UNITS

Emboldened by years of fighting, held sway by new political visions and the imagined glories of an ancient past, many German soldiers who return from the front find their way into the ranks of the *Freikorps*. These men, embittered by the compromises made to shore up the German state in the wake of The Shattering, fight for a new vision of their country, free of the "pervasive" influence of dissidents, non-Germans, and other so-called "enemies within". Though they may make common cause with the armies of the Kaiser to drive foreign armies out of German lands, violence between the two groups is not uncommon and it is generally understood that a great reckoning is on its way.

With the resurgence of the old gods, the ranks of the *Freikorps* have swelled, bolstered by romantic nationalists and zealous new converts seeking to embrace their ancient traditions. Beneath lighting-blasted oaks in sacred groves, these men forsake their old oaths and pledge themselves to a life of fighting in service of both old gods and a new utopia. The White Lady is their leader, a witch of extraordinary power; from the heart of the dark forests in which she makes her home, she directs the *Freikorps* to make war on both old enemies and erstwhile friends…

No other faction has so embraced the new reality of a world transformed by magic. Where others quail at bloody sacrifice, considering it a necessary evil to win the favour of pernicious gods, the *Freikorps* revel in it. Ancient rites and barbarous customs are revived with gusto unseen elsewhere, and many an ancient grove rings to the crack of splintering ribs or the thud of the falling axe.

With little access to mechanised production, the *Freikorps* rely more on personal valour and divine protection to fight their enemies. Though their stores of munitions and weaponry are bolstered by defections and plunder, they can claim ownership of little in the way of fighting vehicles or ordnance. To supplement their shortcomings in this respect, they lean increasingly on guerrilla tactics, ambush, and surprise. When the situation requires greater force of arms, the *Freikorps* can call on horrifying creatures, twisted abominations of flesh made possible by crude experimentation and dark rituals.

UNIQUE UNITS

ORDENREITER

Free, Replaces Captain

Before the war, a great many organisations existed in Germany dedicated to promoting the racial purity of the nation, defending against the insidious march of political dissenters, deviants, and minorities. Though many stopped short of escalating to anything more than hate-filled rhetoric, some enthusiastically encouraged and engaged in violence. As the moon shattered and the world fell to pieces, they threw in their lot with the disgruntled veterans who were in open revolt against the German state, with many prominent individuals becoming key leaders in the movement.

A number of these clubs patterned themselves after knightly orders. The bold Teutonic warriors of yore, fighting heroically against hordes of Asiatic barbarians, provided a fairy-tale prototype for their own brawling and vitriol. When Germany enjoyed a series of key strategic victories over Russia in the early stages of the war, the folk memories of *Grunewald* were awakened – soldiers at the front became avengers of an ancient stain; the newly formed "knightly orders" the inheritors of the lineage of Jungingen, heirs to a glorious past and an iron will.

ORDENREITER

P	MS	Z	W	ST
7	High	9	3	4

Keywords	Activation Keyword
Cavalry	Unique (Leader)

Regulation Equipment

Brutal CC weapon, Body Armour

Aura

Armour Of Faith – All friendly units with the Keyword cavalry within 10" gain the Keyword impenetrable

Special Orders

Crush the Weak – All units within 10" can move an additional 2" when Charging if their target is of Lower MS (1 Command Token)

Orders

Rally – Select a Broken infantry or cavalry unit that is within 10" to make a Zeal Test. If the Test is passed then the unit is no longer Broken
(1 Command Token)

1 CSM	2 CSMs	3 CSMs
Staggering: P reduced to 5	**Trembling:** MS reduced to Low	**Madness:** Cannot issue Orders

ORDENREITER UPGRADE TABLE

Free

The unit may select up to two Orders or Ruses from the Orders Chapter

The unit may exchange its Regulation Equipment for:
Cavalry CC weapon and Body Armour

The unit may choose a Zodiac Sign

Options

The unit must take a Mount, either a free Horse or an upgraded one at the stated cost

The unit may choose an item from the Special Items List

SKIN CHANGER

Free, Replaces Captain

Through a process long thought forgotten, a man can inhabit the skin of a beast. Those changed in this way are called Skin Changers, touched by the spirit of the Horned God himself.

It begins with a hunt, seeking the hide of a creature possessed of a rare ferocity. Bears, wolves, and even boars are tracked and ritually slaughtered, their skins cut away and prepared for the ceremony by which a man becomes a beast. Attended by witches of immense power, the would-be Skin Changer is flayed, the thread of their life held fast by prayer alone. Once their muscle and sinew is exposed to the sky, they are sown into the skin of the hunted beast. In time, hunched in terrible pain, alone in some clearing, their form begins to mould into that of the creature whose skin they now inhabit.

Though powerful intoxicants stay some of the agony, the process can easily break even the strongest will and many succumb to death long before the transformation takes hold.

Those that survive become towering hulks of muscle, possessed of raw animal strength and human intelligence. Alike in form to neither beast nor man, they stand apart – true avatars of the wild.

SKIN CHANGER

P	MS	Z	W	ST
6	High	9	4	4

Keywords	Activation Keyword
Medium Creature, Infantry, Disturbing	Unique (Leader)

Regulation Equipment

Brutal CC weapon

Aura

Aspect Of The Beast – Friendly units within 10" gain an additional Attack Dice when fighting in a Close Combat

Special Orders

Wilde Jagd – All units within 12" are immune to pinning in the coming round (3 Command Tokens)

Special Rules

The presence of these avatars of the wild grants an additional d3 to any attempt to Manifest a Prowler

1 CSM	2 CSMs	3 CSMs
Lamed: P reduced to 3	**Injured Claws:** MS reduced to Low	**Madness:** Gains the Keyword impetuous

SKIN CHANGER UPGRADE TABLE

Free

The unit may select up to one Order or Ruse from the Orders Chapter

The unit may choose a Zodiac Sign

Options

The unit may choose an item from the Special Items List

ELITE UNITS

HARII

2 Selection Points

Among the ranks of the *Freikorps* are men of such devotion that they appear to have abandoned all reason. Freed of many of the trappings of modern warfare, they fight much as their ancestors did in the mythic past.

Though they differ from *Korps* to *Korps*, many will enter a trance-like state before battle. Sometimes this is brought about through intense fasting and other devotional acts, but more often than not it is simply the result of ingesting one (or many) of the various psychoactive plants and fungi common to the magic-charged woods of the post-Shattering world.

Harii are covered in incised tattoos and grisly tokens of their past deeds; indeed, many in the *Freikorps* cultivate a deliberately terrifying appearance to intimidate their enemy. Some of the most famed of these fearsome warriors paint every inch of their skin jet black, fighting otherwise completely naked and trusting to the gods for all the protection they need. The appearance of these merciless fighters on the battlefield can be shattering to morale and many a trench and salient has been abandoned at the mere suggestion of dark figures looming in the darkness.

With bodies daubed in symbols of protection and warding, calling to the gods to strengthen their arms or witness their valour, they charge heedlessly into the enemy, leaving a bloody tide in their wake.

HARII				
P	**MS**	**Z**	**Mod**	**ST**
5	High	8	4	3

Keywords	Activation Keyword
Infantry, Vanguard, Divinely Favoured, Unyielding	Elite (Assault)

Regulation Equipment
Fearsome CC weapons

Special Rules
Berserkergang – Before battle is joined, this unit ingests a quantity of psychoactive substances, driving them into a state of frenzy! When the Harii are first Activated to Charge, they immediately gain the Keyword insensible and can reroll all misses in Close Combat (once per Attack Die). However, at the start of each subsequent Elite Phase, if the unit is not in Close Combat, they generate a Combat Stress marker. The effects last until the end of the game.

WECHSELBÄLGER

2 Selection Points

The *Freikorps* have little care for the moral strictures of the old world. In the wake of The Shattering, they seek to create a new world order, one that values strength above all things. Through dark magic, the form of man can be manipulated. The flesh can be moulded like clay, the spirit bent and hammered into new shapes.

By subjecting a soldier to the most hideous of agonies, a new breed of warrior can be created. Through a crude process of vivisection and ancient ritual, warriors that are neither man nor beast are born deep in the dark forests where the *Freikorps* dwell. Some appear as hybrid creatures, with recognisable aspects of the unfortunate beasts from whom their constituent parts were "donated", whilst others are simply monsters, hideous parodies of misshapen flesh.

Whatever form they take, *Wechselbälger* combine brute strength and low cunning. Working in a pack, they are capable of tearing through enemies with ease and shrugging off blows that would kill a lesser creature without much consequence.

WECHSELBÄLGER

P	MS	Z	Mod	ST
6	High	7	4	4

Keywords	Activation Keyword
Infantry, Terrifying, Unyielding	Elite (Assault)

Regulation Equipment

Brutal CC weapons

Special Rules

Hideous – The presence of Wechselbälger is terrifying even to their allies. The unit must be placed first during deployment, with any friendly unit except a Skin Changer, or one with the Activation Keyword mindless, having to start the game at least 12" away from them

Savage – For purposes of Attack Dice generation, any Zeal modifiers affecting this unit are ignored.

Leader Of The Pack – If a Skin Changer is destroyed within 12" of this unit, this unit gains the Keyword impetuous for the remainder of the game.

WECHSELBÄLGER UPGRADE TABLE

2 Upgrade Points

The unit may be upgraded to have one of the following Keywords:
Aquatic
Ophite
Bramble Kin
Sylvan

BAUMKRIEGER

3 Selection Points

There is little that science can offer when a man loses a limb. Against shells and bombs, bodies are blasted apart with shocking regularity, with medicine at a loss to heal either body or soul. However, where science has failed, it is said that magic offers a solution; in the dark and haunted forests along the Rhine, an ancient rite is practised to restore what has been lost.

In the gaping wound where a limb once was, a seed is sown beneath the flesh. Amidst chants and incantations, it sprouts beneath the skin, its roots boring between ribs and snaking through the viscera, seeking for nourishing blood. In weeks, a seed becomes a sapling, which must be trained, pruned, and trimmed to the shape of the missing limb. With time, where once a ravaged stump protruded, a strong new limb sprouts forth. Bough becomes bone – stout as an oak and lithe as an ash.

It is said that the rite takes weeks, the agony driving men to the brink of madness and often beyond.

Some give themselves up completely as the pain overtakes their senses, but those who do soon find themselves much changed. As the roots spread through their bodies, they succumb to the force of the spirit growing within them. Many choose death, but some few surrender to their fate. In time, they become more tree than man, colossal hulks of living wood, the scraps of what was once a human entwined in their bark and branches, nothing more than a vestigial reminder of the shape they once inhabited.

The huge and otherworldly creatures that result are known as *Baumkrieger*. A terrifying sight, they are directed against the enemy in the hopes that whatever human part remains gives vent to its unthinking, hopeless rage.

BAUMKRIEGER				
P	MS	Z	W	ST
3	High	6	5	5

Keywords	Activation Keyword
Large Creature, Terrifying, Impenetrable, Sylvan	Elite (Creature)

Regulation Equipment
Fearsome CC weapons

Abilities

Lurch – The unit rushes forward, too fast for its ungainly form. The unit moves 8" in a chosen direction, but the commanding player must roll a d6, generating a Combat Stress Marker on a roll of 6

1 CSM	2 CSMs	3 CSMs
Madness: Gains the Keyword impetuous	**Blinded:** MS reduced to Low	**Broken Bough:** Loses the number of attacks generated in close combat is reduced to 2

178

MINDLESS UNITS

PANZERKAMPFBIEST

1 selection point

With little access to the materiel necessary to produce machines of war, the *Freikorps* rely on ingenuity and blood magic to level the playing field when fighting opponents with modern weapons.

In the mechanised armies of their enemies, tanks are used to breach holes in enemy lines so that infantry can pour in behind. The tank gives some cover to the men who follow in its wake, but moves slowly and, though heavily armoured, is vulnerable to larger weapons or counterattacks by enemy infantry, who can dispatch the crew within in short order.

The witches of the *Freikorps* find that their dark forests offer them solutions to many of the problems of modern warfare. The *Freikorps* often hunt, the very act honouring the spirits of the forest and the savage gods they worship. When particularly ferocious beasts are identified, the greatest prize is to take them alive. These living hulks of muscle and rage serve the *Freikorps* as *Panzerkampfbestien*, their already formidable forms transformed by scalpel and sorcery.

Rendered temporarily dormant by potent draughts of herbs and fungi from the deep forests, they are covered in crudely wrought plates of metal, covered in sigils and fetishistic tokens. When they awake, disoriented and enraged, these armoured beasts are goaded towards the enemy to charge their lines, shrugging off incoming fire as they come.

PANZERKAMPFBIEST				
P	**MS**	**Z**	**W**	**ST**
5	Medium	5	2	4
Keywords		**Activation Keyword**		
Intimidating, Medium Creature		Mindless (Rabble)		
Regulation Equipment				
Brutal CC weapon, Body Armour				

Chapter Fourteen
AMERICAN VOLUNTEER LEGION UNITS

All across the United States, the call to action rings out in meeting halls and labour camps. Wherever strong-armed men and women are found, recruiters ply their trade. In books, pamphlets, and speeches, recruiters from across Europe, whether German, British, or French, tell of a glorious and righteous struggle, where brave Americans can lend their service to free the world from the forces of tyranny.

When American volunteers first land in Europe, they are often shocked by the reality of the war that greets them. Far from glorious, the grim reality of combat, transformed by both magic and mechanisation, soon becomes apparent. The reality of fighting on the Western Front bears little relation to the tale that they had been told.

The American Volunteer Legions serve alongside the fighting men of all of the European powers, their ranks often swollen by recruits from the peripheral powers of the European continent, of Ireland, Spain, Scandinavia, and elsewhere. A melting pot of different peoples, the AVLs often have a character all of their own, as varied as their reasons for fighting. Some are little more than a rag-tag band of mercenaries, militants, or millenarians, but many more are professional militia, well equipped and motivated to fight boldly for their cause.

Some are equipped by the patrons for whom they fight, outfitted in either the national uniforms of their employers or custom-made clothing specific to the organisation they serve. Many more come to the front with little but the clothes on their back and crude civilian weaponry. What they might lack in professional equipment, the fighting men of the AVLs more than make up for with ingenuity, quickly adapting to the new realities of the Doggerland Front and embracing its technological innovations. They can often be seen at the frontlines where the fighting is thickest, but also alongside partisans in occupied areas or leading guerrilla actions against isolated platoons.

UNIQUE UNITS

MERCENARY CAPTAIN

Free, Replaces Captain

War has always drawn men looking for adventure, excitement, or simply a means of escape – for some, the opportunity to escape from a life with few options, even into a situation of great danger, seems preferable to a future without the prospect of improvement. Men join the American Volunteer Legions for a host of reasons, but perhaps a lack of prospects at home is the most common.

The AVLs are a mixed bunch, but the vast majority are professional outfits led by officers with some previous military experience. The nations of Europe, their militaries decimated and their industry and trade on the verge of collapse, call out for able-bodied men from across the world to serve.

For many old soldiers, struggling to make a living themselves, the opportunity presented by service on the Doggerland Front is too good to pass up. Some lead little more than a rag-tag band, but most are polished and well-drilled military units, either equipped by their host nations or by the organisers themselves. For this reason, uniforms can be extremely varied, particularly in Legions where there is a strong ideological component to recruitment. Some legions even wear uniforms and carry equipment indistinguishable from that of the United State's own armed forces, with soldiers either supplying their own from the souvenirs of their previous service, or quartermasters making illicit deals with stores of materiel back home.

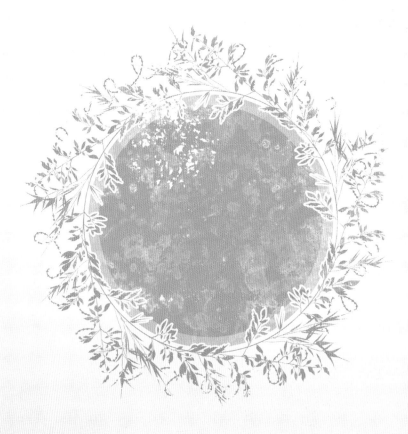

MERCENARY CAPTAIN

P	MS	Z	W	ST
5	High	9	3	4

Keywords	Activation Keyword
Infantry	Unique (Leader)

Regulation Equipment

Revolver, Standard issue CC weapon

Aura

Money Talks – Units of Gunslingers within 10" can roll a d10 whenever they gain a Combat Stress Marker. On a roll of 1, the Combat Stress is ignored.

Orders

Rally – Select a Broken infantry or cavalry unit that is within 10" to make a Zeal Test. If the Test is passed then the unit is no longer Broken
(1 Command Token)

1 CSM	2 CSMs	3 CSMs
Staggering: P reduced to 3	**Trembling:** MS reduced to Low	**Madness:** Cannot issue Orders

MERCENARY CAPTAIN UPGRADE TABLE

Free

The unit may select up to three Orders or Ruses from the Orders Chapter

The unit may exchange its Regulation Equipment for:
Self-Loading Pistol

The unit may choose a Zodiac Sign

Options

The unit may choose an item from the Special Items List

MILLENARIAN PREACHER

Free, Replaces Captain

Europe is not the only place steeped in magic; there are many places in the United States where the veil is thin and the energy of the spirit world may seep through.

Living alongside such a tear in the veil, many see the terrors of the spirit world on an almost daily basis. To live in such a place feels like bearing witness to the end of days, leading to apocalyptic cults regularly springing up. Though all are convinced of mankind's impending annihilation, there are differing interpretations of exactly when and, crucially, in what form the conflagration will occur. These varied beliefs are often heavily influenced by regional traditions, or the demographics of the place from which the adherents hail.

Though many of these congregations stay in the United States, some few are driven to Europe and the war by prophetic vision, coming to the aid of one side or another depending on their inclination. European militaries are often all too happy to indulge their desire to fight, their wild fanaticism making up for their shortcomings in training and equipment.

MILLENARIAN PREACHER

P	MS	Z	W	ST
5	High	9	3	4

Keywords	Activation Keyword
Infantry, Divinely Favoured	Unique (Leader)

Regulation Equipment

Revolver, Standard issue CC weapon

Aura

Fire and Fury – Units of Coveners may reroll any Pinning Test (once per Test)

Abilities

Lay On Hands – Select a friendly unit of Coveners within 6" which has taken casualties in this Round. If successfully cast, roll a d10 for each casualty suffered, returning any model on roll of 1 (1 Command Token)

Rite of serpents – Select a unit of Coveners within 10". Any unit, friend or foe and including the selected Coveners, that is within 3" takes 4 MS Low Hits (per unit) and the selected Coveners gain the Keyword ophite for the remainder of the game (1 Command Token)

1 CSM	2 CSMs	3 CSMs
Staggering: P reduced to 3	**Trembling:** MS reduced to Low	**Madness:** Cannot issue Orders

MILLENARIAN PREACHER UPGRADE TABLE

Free

The unit may select up to two Orders or Ruses from the Order Chapter

The unit may exchange its Regulation Equipment for:
Fearsome CC Weapon

The unit may choose a Zodiac Sign

Option

The unit may chose an item from the Special Items List

ELITE UNITS

TRENCH FIGHTERS
3 Selection Points

Unfit for the brutal reality of combat on the Western Front, the first waves of American Volunteer Legionnaires suffered enormously on all sides. Armed with weapons laughably unsuited to the fighting of modern warfare and completely unprepared for the presence of magic on such a scale, they were cut down in droves. In response, the organisers of these groups looked for some way to even the odds and give American fighters a cost-effective means of defeating their more experienced foes.

Repeating shotguns had been widely available in the United States for a number of years by this time and had proven effective support weapons in close quarters against foes in many of America's colonial adventures. Cheaply acquired, they are supplied to troops in large quantities to supplement the equipment contributed by the Legion's host nations. Their operation is simple and often familiar to the men who wield them, many of whom have experience with similar weapons. In close proximity, these simple weapons are brutally effective, capable of scything down the defenders of a trench with extraordinary ease.

TRENCH FIGHTERS				
P	**MS**	**Z**	**Mod**	**ST**
5	Medium	6	8	2
Keywords		**Activation Keyword**		
Infantry		Elite (Assault)		
Regulation Equipment				
Self-Loading Shotguns, Standard issue CC weapons				
Special Rules				
Sportsmen - If any member of this unit is within the Template of a Hand Grenade (after Scattering) roll a d10. On a result of 1, the grenade is shot out of the air and treated as though it were a dud.				

GUNSLINGERS

2 Selection Points

When the Old West died, so too did a way of life. But even as the last traces of the frontier were brought to heel, new frontiers emerged where gunmen of exceptional skill could ply their bloody trade.

Some turned their attention to America's southern neighbour, caught in the throes of a bloody civil conflict, others to climes further afield, but all sought out places where their talent and taste for violence could earn them their keep. In the wake of The Shattering, new opportunities present themselves and none is more lucrative, or holds a greater promise of brutality, than the Doggerland Front.

Even the most ideologically fanatical of the AVLs will countenance unscrupulous fighters if they are of sufficient renown. Many have a reputation that precedes them, and their presence in a Legion can be a powerful draw for wide-eyed young men and women seeking adventure.

GUNSLINGERS

P	MS	Z	Mod	ST
5	High	7	4	3

Keywords	Activation Keyword
Infantry	Elite (Assault)

Regulation Equipment	
Revolver, Brutal CC weapons	

GUNSLINGER UPGRADE TABLE

1 Upgrade Point

The unit may exchange its Regulation Equipment for:
Repeater Carbines

2 Upgrade Points

The unit may be upgraded to have any one of the following Keywords:
Trick Shot
Far Sighted
Vanguard

ROUGH RIDERS

2 Selection Points

When the call for men went out throughout the United States, many who heeded it did so out of a sense of adventure. The desire to serve, to test one's mettle, and to show true quality was one that would have been familiar to those who heard a similar, earlier call to arms. Many recruiters invoked the spirit of the volunteer cavalry when signing men up to fight in Europe, recalling the spectre of San Juan Hill and regaling their listeners with tales of Colonel Roosevelt and the daring exploits of his men.

The spirit of that time is alive and well in the men who join the volunteer cavalry. Some are young, with little prospect of advancement and few responsibilities, but many are older – veterans of campaigns both foreign and domestic, unwilling or unable to settle into the rhythms of civilian life. Whilst some serve out of a genuine conviction for a cause, for every young ideological firebrand or old convert tying up loose ends at the close of their life, there are two more that are simply in it for the money.

ROUGH RIDERS

P	MS	Z	Mod	ST
7	Medium	7	4	3

Keywords	Activation Keyword
Cavalry, Vanguard, Hit and Run	Elite (Assault)

Weapons and equipment	
Revolvers, Standard issue CC weapons	

ROUGH RIDERS UPGRADE TABLE

1 Upgrade Points

The unit may exchange their Revolvers for:
Carbine

CANNONADE UNITS

IMPROVISED FIGHTING VEHICLE

3 Selection Points

Though armoured cars are not an uncommon sight among the American Volunteer Legions, they are expensive beasts to run and maintain. Many legions make use of largely unmodified civilian vehicles instead, their extra speed and manoeuvrability much prized by commanders for lighting fast operations where the element of surprise affords some protection against oncoming fire.

Like any vehicle used on the Doggerland Front, their mobility is compromised when operating on rougher ground. For that reason, this class of fighting vehicle tends to be seen in the urbanised battlegrounds on either side of the newly drained channel, or somewhere just back from the hundreds of miles worth of trenches snaking through France. However, where road infrastructure still supports them, these lightly armed, fast-moving vehicles can make a real impact.

IMPROVISED FIGHTING VEHICLE				
P	MS	Z	W	ST
10	Medium	6	3	4

Keywords	Activation Keyword
Wheeled Vehicle, Car, Open Top	Cannonade (Vehicle)

Regulation Equipment

Light Machine Gun (1), Rifle (2), Standard issue CC weapon

Special Rules

The Light Machine Gun of an Improvised Fighting Vehicle uses the In Cover weapon profile

1 CSM	2 CSMs	3 CSMs
Damaged Transmission: Can only Move at half its Pace value (rounded down)	**Injured Gunner:** The Light Machine Gun produces 3 Shooting Attack Dice rather than 6	**Lost Wheel:** Can no longer Move

Chapter Fifteen
RUSSIAN EMPIRE UNITS

Their schemes thrown into disarray by the terrifying events of The Shattering, Prince Felix Yusopov and his fellow conspirators met at his palace to redraw their plans for the assassination of Grigory Rasputin. None of these prominent noblemen were ever seen alive again, but the details of their grisly, ritualistic murder both thrill and disgust the Russian court, already rocked by the reports coming in from across the nation of receding seas, horrific creatures, and strange magic.

Rasputin himself is now beyond reproach, always at the side of the Tzarina; few would dare to point the finger of blame at him, though bizarre rumours continue to swirl around the court. The Tzar himself is increasingly withdrawn, confined to his rooms by an inexplicable illness. With each day that passes, he retreats further from public view, the Tzarina often acting as an intermediary between her bedridden husband and his staff. Many question the sanity of the Tzar's decisions, but few have the courage to openly voice their dissent in the febrile atmosphere of the terrified court.

The Russian Empire is dangerously close to total environmental collapse. The frozen far north of the country has not thawed in two summers and the icy climate seems to expand further south with every passing week. Fleeing the country's wild northern fringes, refugees pour south in search of food and shelter. The men are pressed into military service, often with the promise of new homes for their families on their return, but the influx of people is putting additional pressure on the already beleaguered towns and villages in the Russian heartland. Russian forces, pushing west into what was once the Baltic Sea in an attempt to strangle Germany into submission, regularly come into contact with British and French forces, often raiding their supposed allies in search of supplies. These incidents are quietly brushed under the carpet by both sides for fear of a diplomatic incident but, in some locations, the situation has deteriorated into one of open hostility.

Russian forces suffered enormously in the early stages of the war, suffering several major reverses against German forces. They have struggled militarily since those initial defeats but, in the aftermath of The Shattering, the changed paradigm of the conflict has come to increasingly favour Russian tactics, organisation, and equipment. This reversal of fortunes, coupled with vicious crackdowns, seem to have declawed the most pernicious of revolutionaries, but the spectre of change ever lurks at the margins of Russian society.

UNIQUE UNITS

SHAMAN
Free, Replaces Captain

The low thud of a drum and a piercing ancient chant signals the approach of troops from Russia's frozen frontiers, a wide expanse of taiga stretching from the doorstep of Europe to the heart of Asia.

Peopled by herders, nomads, and hunters, this is a land that never forsook the old ways. Though notionally brought to heel by the servants of God and Tzar long before, their isolation offered them some protection against the otherwise inexorable march of progress. The gods of this wild place dwell in the dark groves of pine, beneath the pitchy, sluggish waters of its rivers, and in the unfathomable minds of the beasts that range the tundra.

It is the Shamans of these nomad tribes, men of extraordinary power, through whom those gods speak. For them, the veil that separates this world and the other can be traversed as easily as a swimmer can dive beneath the surface of a lake. With aptitude and training, man can reach through and make contact with the beings that dwell just beyond the veil of the spirit world. When a Shaman enters the trance by which they commune with the spirits, their power manifests in our reality, invigorating hearts and strengthening limbs.

SHAMAN

P	MS	Z	W	ST
5	High	9	3	4

Keywords	Activation Keyword
Infantry	Unique (Leader)

Regulation Equipment

Brutal CC weapon

Auras

Wolf – Siberian Hunters within 10" of this unit may reroll any 6's rolled in Close Combat (once per Attack Die)

Bear – Siberian Hunters within 10" of this unit gain the Keyword mighty blow, but lose their Saving Throw

Eagle – Siberian Hunters within 10" of this unit reroll any 6's rolled in Shooting Attacks (once per Attack Die)

Special Rule

Great Spirit – In the Command Phase, the commanding player must choose which Aura the unit will produce this round

Orders

Rally – Select a Broken infantry or cavalry unit that is within 10" to make a Zeal Test. If the Test is passed then the unit is no longer Broken (1 Command Token)

1 CSM	2 CSMs	3 CSMs
Staggering: P reduced to 3	**Trembling:** MS reduced to Low	**Cowering:** Aura has no Effect

SHAMAN UPGRADE TABLE

Free

The unit may select up to two Orders or Ruses from the Order Chapter

The unit may exchange its Regulation Equipment for:
Fearsome CC weapon

The unit may choose a Zodiac Sign

Options

The unit may choose an item from the Special Items List

HETMAN
Free, Replaces Captain

Few of The Russian Empire's many ethnic minorities are as intrinsically bound to the armies of the Tzar as the Cossacks, hosts of fiercely proud horsemen with a reputation for their skill at arms.

These bands are led by officers from the same host, often democratically selected by their peers from the most respected families. These commanders hold the rank of *Hetman*, an ancient title used from the earliest days of Cossack culture. Generally, those selected as *Hetman* have significant military experience and are fine riders and fighters in their own right.

Since the events of The Shattering, the huge changes to the lines of battle, along with the shortages of both food and manufactured goods, caused by the changes that Summerisle wrought have meant that the density of soldiers at any point along the front is much reduced. This, in turn, has caused a rapid change in the mobility of the war, and the Cossacks, always much prized by the Russian military, are now held in even greater esteem for the success of their wild charges.

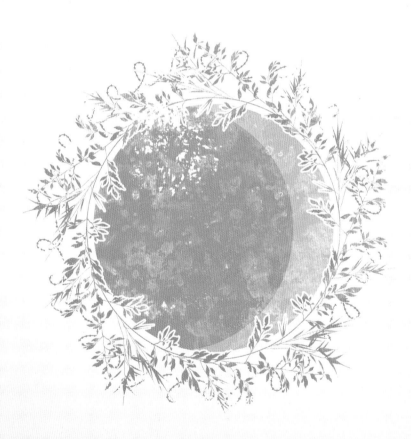

HETMAN

P	MS	Z	W	ST
7	High	9	3	4

Keywords	Activation Keyword
Cavalry	Unique (Leader)

Regulation Equipment

Brutal CC weapon, Revolver

Aura

Gu-Rai! – Units of Cossacks receive Advantage-1 to any Saving Throws made in Close Combat

Special Rules

Host – A Patrol led by a Hetman can allocate the SP cost of Lancers to line when building a Patrol

Orders

Rally – Select a Broken infantry or cavalry unit that is within 10" to make a Zeal Test. If the Test is passed then the unit is no longer Broken
(1 Command Token)

1 CSM	2 CSMs	3 CSMs
Lamed: P reduced to 5	**Trembling:** MS reduced to Low	**Madness:** Cannot issue Orders

195

HETMAN UPGRADE TABLE

Free

The unit must take a Mount, either a free Horse or an upgraded type at the stated cost

The unit may select up to two Orders or Ruses from the Orders Chapter

The unit may exchange its Regulation Equipment for:
Self-Loading Pistol (1)

The unit may choose a Zodiac Sign

Options

The unit may choose an item from the Special Items List

LINE UNITS

CONSCRIPTS

2 Selection Points

As the war began, Russia's army was far larger than that of any other belligerent, though decades of systemic neglect had left it poorly equipped. Few Russian fighting men had access to sufficient ammunition, supplies, or even uniforms when compared to their foes, but the Russian Empire was determined that sheer numbers and the indomitable spirit of the Russian people could carry the day.

Though the Tzar has a great number of hardened, experienced, and professional soldiers at his command, the average Russian soldier is of a different kind. Poorly equipped, these Conscripts are held in little esteem by their commanders, and few are expected to survive long enough for their deficiencies in supply to count for much!

Many are sent to the front in a rag-tag assemblage of civilian and military clothing. Weapons are in particularly short supply, with standing orders for any man not issued a rifle to claim one from their compatriots when they inevitably fall in battle.

What they lack in access to material, they more than make up for in fighting spirit, attacking bravely and defending with implacable tenacity, even in the face of almost certain death.

CONSCRIPTS				
P	**MS**	**Z**	**Mod**	**ST**
5	Medium	6	12	2

Keywords	**Activation Keyword**
Infantry, Undisciplined	Line (Regulars)

Regulation Equipment
Rifle, Standard issue CC weapons

Special Rules
Shortages – Although the unit is comprised of 12 models, only 8 Rifles are available to it. This means that the unit can roll a maximum of eight Attack Dice during Shooting Attacks and suffer up to four Wounds before its ability to Shoot is diminished.

ELITE UNITS

COSSACKS
2 Selection Points

Few classes of soldier have as storied a reputation as the Cossacks, their ranks drawn from a small number of ethnic minorities. The majority of Cossack units are levied from groups living a semi-settled life of hunting and nomadic grazing in the western territories near the Russian Empire's vast European border, hugging to either side of the Carpathians where the falling rains make for rich pasture. Many of these groups have been in service to the Tzar for centuries, earning them a special place in the annals of Russia's military history.

In addition to these western Cossacks, there are many hosts of nomadic horsemen from considerably further east. Organising themselves into hosts and performing a similar battlefield duty, they too are moulded by a lifetime in the saddle.

COSSACKS				
P	**MS**	**Z**	**Mod**	**ST**
7	High	7	4	3
Keywords		**Activation Keyword**		
Cavalry		Elite (Assault)		
Regulation Equipment				
Brutal CC weapons, Carbines				

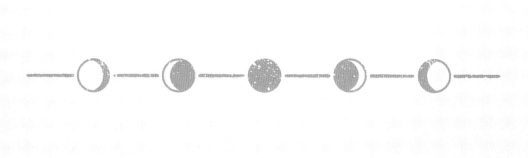

SIBERIAN HUNTERS

3 Selection Points

The ecological crisis caused by the Summerisle Incident has hit the Russian Empire hard, particularly on its northern fringes. In the high plains and forests of Siberia, the Spring of 1917 never arrived. The isolated people of these places, desperate to pasture their herds, began the great journey south in droves.

A lifetime of living off the land has given these men a particular set of skills much prized by Russian commanders. Well-versed in the art of hunting, they are exceptional shots to a man, capable of great feats of marksmanship. Moreover, a lifetime of stalking prey has given each an almost preternatural ability to make themselves hidden, easily concealing themselves even in a largely flat and featureless landscape. Operating in small teams, they range ahead of the main force, scouting out enemy positions and reporting back to their commanders, or infiltrating beyond the line to accomplish specific objectives.

SIBERIAN HUNTERS

P	MS	Z	Mod	ST
5	High	7	4	2

Keywords	Activation Keyword
Infantry, Camouflage, Hit and Run	Elite (Support)

Regulation Equipment
Marksman's Rifles, Standard issue CC weapons

Special Rules

Trackers – This unit is adept at hunting, well used to stalking its quarry across the tundra. Though their weapons do not have the Keyword quickfire, Siberian Hunters may Move and Shoot in a Normal Activation without penalty

CANNONADE UNITS

TACHANKA

3 Selection Point

The war on the Eastern Front was always considerably more mobile than in the west – fought over an area many thousands of square kilometres wide, the enormity of the porous, ever shifting frontline made the static lines of the Western Front impossible. Garrisoning such a vast frontline, spanning from the Baltic to the Black Sea, was impossible even for such a huge military force as that of the Russian Empire.

Over this vast and sparsely populated area, highly mobile forces reigned supreme. The *Tachanka*, a civilian cart pulled by a team of three or more horses and mounted with a heavy machine gun, is the Russian answer to the requirement of firepower on the move. Capable of crossing difficult terrain more easily than armoured cars, Tachankas can be used in support of cavalry operations, lending enhanced firepower to mobile fighting forces who must, per force, be more lightly armed.

After the hiatus in the fighting caused by The Shattering, a resurgent Russia found that the catastrophe has caused the Western Front to more closely mirror the conditions that first inspired the use of these converted carriages. With considerably lower concentrations of men to garrison a vastly lengthened front, the immutable and impenetrable trench lines of 1916 are gone – the *Tachanka* is in its element.

Tachanka				
P	**MS**	**Z**	**W**	**ST**
7	Medium	6	3	3

Keywords	Activation Keyword
Cavalry, Car, Weapons Team, Undisciplined	Cannonade (Support)

Regulation Equipment
Heavy Machine Gun (1), Standard issue CC weapon

Special Rules
The unit is treated as a vehicle for the purposes of Close Combat Attack Dice generation and, like a vehicle, it can never Charge or Move through woods In all other regards it acts as a single-model cavalry unit, following the special rules for cavalry in every other respect, including terrain. Just like other cavalry units, the unit has no facing and can be the target of Orders which do not explicitly mention vehicles

1 CSM	2 CSMs	3 CSMs
Hot Barrel: Rolls of 4 are now treated as a Miss	**Feed Jammed:** The Heavy Machine Gun produces 5 Shooting Attack Dice rather than 10	**Overheated:** The Heavy Machine Gun can no longer make Shooting Attacks

Chapter Sixteen
SPECIAL ITEMS

Any Captain, Lieutenant, or Witch is entitled to carry Special Items, though some are only available to specific units. No Patrol may include more than one of the same item, nor can any unit carry more than one. Each Faction also has its own Special Item that is not available to any other Faction.

COMMON SPECIAL ITEMS

Branch Of Ash
1 Upgrade Point

A short staff of ash, keen and straight. This ashen limb strikes out at any that harbour pox or pestilence.

The efficacy of ash against venomous creatures is well attested to. This weapon lends the power of this most vital tree to the arm of its wielder, allowing any failed Close Combat Attacks with this weapon made against a unit with the Keyword **ophite** to be rerolled (once per Attack Die).

Branch Of Elm
1 Upgrade Point

A stout club of elm, bound with studs and hardened in fire. This survivor of countless battles seems to almost revel in slaughter.

The elm's ancestral hatred of mankind lends extra power to the blows that the bearer of this weapon rains down on their foes. Any Close Combat Attack Dice rolls of 6 made with this weapon can be rerolled (once per Attack Die).

Witchbone Whistle
1 Upgrade Points

Who is this who is coming?

A grisly token of a black day, its call cuts through the din, shrill and keen. All Orders issued by the bearer can be made at a 12" range rather than 10".

A Dancer's Skin
2 Upgrade Points

Lily white her skin, lithe her limbs and lissom her dancing – who could ask for a more fitting sacrifice?

This item grants its wearer a dancer's grace, allowing them to Move, including to Charge, through any terrain, except **impassable**, as though it were **open ground**.

Crown Of Horns
1 Upgrade Points

A knotted circlet of antler, horn, and bone, the Lord of the Hunt often wore this magnificent crown as a token of his wild fief.

Any who wears this crown becomes an avatar of the Lord of the Hunt, an ancient aspect of the Horned God and the King of Beasts. Units with the Keyword **cavalry** must make a Zeal Test in order to Charge a unit within 10" of the bearer, including the bearer themselves.

Natterjack Boots (On-Foot only)

1 Upgrade Point

Ignoble it may be, one can often find safety by crawling on one's belly.

Fashioned from the skin of toads, these boots mould their wearer to the shape of this unclean beast. The unit gains the Keywords **aquatic** and **ophite**, but has -1 Pace.

The Witchfinder's Spicule

2 Upgrade Points

Little more than a wooden handle and a cold iron spike, it betokens the colder heart that once wielded it so deftly.

Once a treasured heirloom of a hidden order, this ancient tool has somehow found its way into different hands. Though it now serves new masters, it still yearns for flesh to pierce. The wielder has the Keyword **sniper** when targeting a Witch with a Shooting Attack.

Toadstone Ring

1 Upgrade Point

Glittering and flawless, deep and dark – a perfect jewel lurking amidst gore and gristle

Within the head of a toad is a precious gem – one that can protect the body from any contagion or poison. The bearer is immune to Critical Hits generated by units with the Keyword **ophite**.

Hagstone Pendant

1 Upgrade Point

A drop at a time the venom falls, scouring and boring so that the skin may fall away.

When a serpent wishes to shed its skin, it will gnaw at a stone until it pierces a hole through which it may pass. When worn as an amulet, these stones grant protection from creatures of the spirit world. For each Combat Stress Marker generated by a Haunter against the bearer roll a d10; on a result of 1, the Marker is ignored.

WITCH ONLY

Secespita

1 Upgrade Point

Ancient beyond measure, this broad blade has tasted the blood of aeons.

A relic of a long dead empire, this sacrificial knife still yearns for the taste of blood. Any models removed from the board in a Close Combat in which the bearer takes part, even as a Supporter, generate a Manifestation Die. This special item counts as a Brutal CC weapon in Close Combat.

Bolino

1 Upgrade Points

Cruel and cold, a beckoning finger of bitter steel calls you forth to the altar.

A ritual knife in the form of a hook, the bearer can change the result of a single Manifestation Die rolled by them up or down by 1. This special item counts as a Brutal CC weapon in Close Combat.

Artavo

1 Upgrade Point

A clenched fist, bone white knuckles grasping jet black.

A ritual blade with an ebony handle, the bearer can choose to roll an additional d3 in any Manifestation attempt, but takes a Wound if they do. This special item counts as a Brutal CC weapon in Close Combat.

Elephant Gun
2 Upgrade Points

This weapon is designed to fell even the largest animals.

WEAPON		
Name	**Keywords**	**Weapon type | (number of shots) | Effective Range/ Maximum Range**
Elephant Gun	Small Arms, Big Hitter	Precision | (1) | 30"

Very Pistol
2 Upgrade Points

Firing a flare on a parachute, this pistol provides officers with a way of illuminating the path of an assault.

Grants the bearer the following Order:

- ⊗ **Very Pistol** – Place a Large Template anywhere within 30" of the bearer and scatter it d6". For the remainder of the Round, any unit partially within this Template loses the Keyword **camouflage**. (1 Command Token)

Carrier Pigeon
1 Upgrade Points

With 50,000 men getting killed a week, who's going to miss a pigeon?

This specially trained bird can carry Orders to distant units with considerable speed.

Once per game, a single unit at any distance from the bearer may be the target of an Order, regardless of its stated range.

CAPTAIN ONLY

Wristwatch
4 Upgrade Points

A comparatively recent affectation, these precision-made instruments help officers coordinate attacks down to the second. The bearer may reroll any failed attempt to use a Ruse in the first Command Phase once.

Stopwatch
2 Upgrade Point

What gentleman would be complete without one?

The bearer may roll an additional d3 when attempting to use a Ruse in the first Command Phase.

Swagger Stick
1 Upgrade Point

"Follow me lads!"

When using the first Order or Ruse of the game, roll a d3; on a result of 1, refund one Command Token.

FACTION SPECIFIC SPECIAL ITEMS

GERMAN EMPIRE
White Serpent Band
1 Upgrade Point

In ancient times, it was said that the flesh of a white serpent granted knowledge of the speech of beasts.

Made in the image of a tiny snake, this ivory ring can give a man some semblance of that creature's power. One unit with the Keyword **cavalry** within 10" of the bearer can reroll any Zeal Test once, including Battle Shock.

FRENCH REPUBLIC ONLY
Token of Jean Chastel
1 Upgrade Point

In the face of true savagery, only the blessed may prevail.

Taken from the grave of the famous hunter, beasts cower before this ancestral stain. Saving Throws made by **creatures** against Shooting Attacks made by the bearer are always taken at Disadvantage-1.

BRITISH EMPIRE ONLY
The Barb Of Long Lankin
1 Upgrade Point

A crude spike of beaten metal, hideous and cruel. Stolen away from beneath a gibbet and blackened in ashes, it burns with the heat of centuries of malice.

This ancient blade is a relic of a terrible deed. Its bearer can pass unseen through any ward or protection, needling through the smallest of cracks. The bearer may Move through a terrain feature as though it were **open ground**, even as part of a Charge. The bearer must take a Zeal Test before any such Move, gaining a Combat Stress Marker if they fail.

FREIKORPS ONLY
Oaken Limb
1 Upgrade Point

A limb, strong and hale, sprouts forth where once there was none – what matters the price?

This bearer generates an additional Attack Dice when in Close Combat, but gains the Keyword **sylvan**.

AMERICAN VOLUNTEER LEGION ONLY
Keseberg's Prize
1 Upgrade Point

As they rode over the mountains, they fell into darkness.

Pillaged from a grave and heavy with a bitter curse, this raiment blackens the heart of any who wears it. Once per game, the bearer may recover any Wounds by nominating a friendly unit within 6" and inflicting an equal number of Wounds. As soon as the item is used, the unit gains the Keyword Bloodthirsty.

RUSSIAN EMPIRE ONLY
Skull Lantern
1 Upgrade Point

Good mother, could you spare a brand?

A grisly lamp to light the way in any darkness, it may reveal that which is unseen. Any unit within 20" of the bearer loses the Keyword **camouflage**.

Chapter Seventeen
SCENARIOS

In *A War Transformed,* players can fight a variety of battles, all of which have different Objectives and reward different styles of play. This chapter provides details for how to set up, play, and win the scenarios of *A War Transformed.*

CHOOSING A SCENARIO

The first step in any game of *A War Transformed* is choosing a Scenario to play. Choosing between them can be as simple as picking one that you like the sound of, randomising the decision (a d6 can be a great solution), or even playing through a series over the course of a few games. There are six scenarios to play through, ranging from a straightforward engagement to a pitched, high stakes assault on an enemy position.

OPTIONAL RULES

Once you've decided on both the number of Selection Points and the scenario that you are going to play, decide whether you want to play with any of the following optional rules. These aren't mandatory, nor will omitting them impact your enjoyment of the game, but they can add a little spice to the experience!

EXTRA MANIFESTATION DICE

Sometimes it can be fun to get some **creatures** on the table early, and the best way to do that is to start the game with a pool of additional Manifestation Dice! A good way to decide on a figure is to base it on the number of Selection Points in play.

EXTRA MANIFESTATION DICE TABLE	
Number of SP	**Additional Manifestation Dice**
Fewer than 10 SP	d3 additional manifestation dice
Between 10 and 15 SP	3 additional manifestation dice
Between 16 and 20 SP	2d3 additional manifestation dice
21 or more SP	d3+3 additional manifestation dice

DIVINE PROTECTION TOKENS

Combat in *A War Transformed* can be brutal, to say the least, so consider having a pool of three Divine Protection Tokens that can be discarded throughout the course of the game to let you reroll a failed Saving Throw on a **unique** unit.

ENGAGEMENT

Recommended with up to 25 SP per side

In **Engagement**, two sides meet and fight each other in a straight contest to determine who is the victor.

SETTING UP THE TABLE

Players take it in turns to place terrain features across the table. **Engagement** games are best played on a table that has lots of room for manoeuvre, so try to create lots of open areas for your units to move freely, whilst also making sure that there is still lots of Cover for them to duck behind as they advance.

Recommended Terrain:

- ⊛ A maximum of three pieces of **impassable** terrain features
- ⊛ A maximum of eight special terrain features
- ⊛ No limit to **obstacles**

DEPLOYING

Units are positioned along the opposing long edges of a 6' x 4' table, with players taking it in turns to place a unit at a time.

To determine which player will deploy a unit first, each player rolls a d10 – the player with the lowest score places their unit first. In **Engagement** both players can choose to deploy their units anywhere within their Deployment Zone, in any orientation that they wish.

VICTORY CONDITIONS

Engagement lasts up to six full Rounds, with the victor being the last man standing or the player with the most remaining Selection Points worth of units at the end of the sixth Round.

To determine how many Selection Points you have left, count your remaining units, comparing these with their original recruitment cost in Selection Points. A captain counts for 3 points and a Witch for 2. Any Broken units only count for half their Selection Point value.

PLAYER A'S *12"* DEPLOYMENT ZONE

PLAYER B'S *12"* DEPLOYMENT ZONE

TRENCH RAID

Recommended with up to 10 SP per side

In **Trench Raid**, one side attempts to make off with Objectives, such as captives, intelligence, supplies, or trophies, from the other side's fortifications. You can decide who plays the Attacker and Defender with a dice roll, or play two games, one as either side, to decide the ultimate victor!

SETTING UP THE TABLE

Trench Raid is played on a slightly smaller table, at just 4' x 4'. The first step is to determine who will play on which side. The Defender sets up first, placing their fortifications as they wish in the whole of their half of the table. The Attacker then places as many **obstacles** as they wish to cover their advance.

Trench Raid is best when there are lots of **trenches** and fortifications to advance against, so try to use as many of these features as possible. After the terrain is set out, both players place three Objectives each, taking it in turns with the Attacker going first.

Recommended Terrain:

- ☻ No **impassable** terrain
- ☻ At least six **trenches** or **buildings**
- ☻ No limit to **obstacles**

DEPLOYING

The Attacker's units are positioned along their table edge, whilst the Defender's units are positioned within their 24" x 36" Deployment Zone.

The Defender places all of their units first, representing the Attacker's careful reconnaissance of the enemy positions.

SELECTION RESTRICTIONS

In **Trench Raid**, neither side can choose any units with the Keywords **cavalry**, **tracked vehicle**, or **wheeled vehicle**, with the exception of **unique** units.

VICTORY

Trench Raid lasts up to six full Rounds, with the victor being the last man standing or the player who has accumulated the most Objective Points at the end of the sixth Round.

The Attacker gains 2 Objective Points for each Objective their units are in contact with, while the Defender gains 1 Objective Point for each Destroyed enemy unit. Tally up how many points each player has gained and add the Selection Points total any for remaining units, remembering that any Broken units only count for half, a Captain counts for 3, and a Witch for 2.

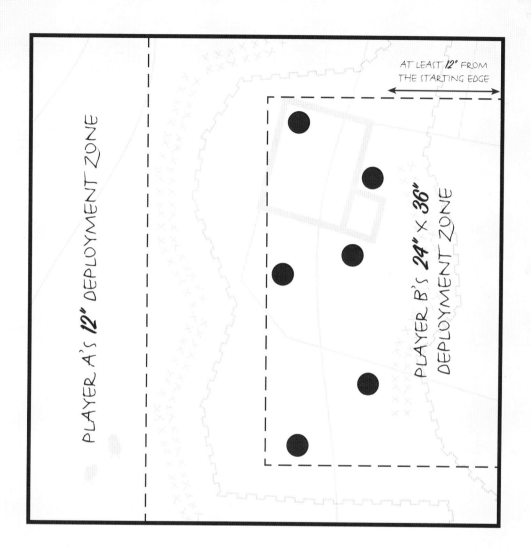

PLAYER A's 12" DEPLOYMENT ZONE

AT LEAST 12" FROM THE STARTING EDGE

PLAYER B's 24" × 36" DEPLOYMENT ZONE

Objective

6 OBJECTIVES ARE PLACED, 3 AT LEAST 12" FROM THE STARTING EDGE AND THREE BETWEEN 18" AND 24" OF THE TABLE EDGE, WITHIN THE 24" × 36" DEPLOYMENT ZONE

NO MAN'S LAND RECOVERY

Recommended with up to 20 SP per side

In **No Man's Land Recovery**, an operation sees two Patrols meeting to fight each other over scattered objectives.

SETTING UP THE TABLE

Players take it in turns to place terrain features over the whole table., before deciding which player will start on which side. **No Man's Land Recovery** is best played on a table that has lots of room for manoeuvre, so try to create lots of open areas for your units to move freely, whilst making sure that there is still lots of Cover for them to duck behind as they advance. After the terrain is set out, players place three Objectives each anywhere in the space between the two Deployment Zones, rolling to determine who places first and taking it in turns.

Once this is done, roll to determine who starts on which table edge.

Recommended Terrain:

- ⊛ A maximum of three pieces of **impassable** terrain
- ⊛ A maximum of eight special terrain features
- ⊛ No limit to **obstacles**

DEPLOYING

Units are positioned along the opposing long edges of a 6' x 4' table, with each player taking it in turns to place a unit at a time.

In **No Man's Land Recovery**, both players can choose to deploy their units anywhere within their deployment zone, in any orientation that they wish.

VICTORY

No Man's Land Recovery lasts up to six full Rounds, with the victor being the last man standing or the player who has accumulated the most Objective Points at the end of the sixth Round.

Both players gain 1 Objective Point for each Objective that they have an **infantry** unit in contact with and 2 Objective Points for each Objective that they have an **infantry** unit in contact with when there are no enemy units within 6". Tally up how many points each player has gained and add the Selection Points total any for remaining units, remembering that any Broken units only count for half, a Captain counts for 3, and a Witch for 2.

PLAYER A'S *12"* DEPLOYMENT ZONE

PLAYER B'S *12"* DEPLOYMENT ZONE

DEFENCE

Recommended with up to 20 SP per side

In **Defence**, the Defender attempts to hold an isolated objective, whilst the Attacker attempts to seize it from them. The Attacker and Defender may be decided with a dice roll or play two games, one as either side, to determine who is the ultimate victor!

SETTING UP THE TABLE

Before determining who plays on which side, players take it in turns to place terrain over the whole table.

Recommended Terrain:

- A maximum of eight special terrain features
- No limit to **obstacles**

With the battlefield laid out, divide the table into three 2' x 4' strips and flip a coin to determine which of the strips on either end of the table the Attacker will start from, this is Segment 1. The Objective must be placed somewhere on a line straight down the centre of Segment 2.

Roll again to determine which player will place the Objective along the line!

THE OBJECTIVE

Once the player who is placing the Objective is determined, use a d3 to decide its nature.

DEFENCE OBJECTIVE TABLE	
d3 Roll	**Objective**
1	A place of great spiritual power. Place a locus of some kind as the Objective. The Defender may deploy anywhere in their half of the table.
2	An abandoned tank. Place a model of a tank or similar in a mire as the Objective. The tank counts as impassable terrain. The Defender may deploy up to half of their Patrol by Selection Points (rounded down) anywhere in Section 2, but the remainder must be in Section 3
3	A downed reconnaissance aircraft or wounded messenger pigeon with vital intelligence. The Defender deploys within 12" of the table edge in Segment 3

DEPLOYING

The Attacker's units are positioned within 12" of their table edge, whilst the Defender's position is determined by the Objective Table. Players should roll to see who deploys first, with the player with the lowest score deploying first.

VICTORY

Defence lasts up to six Rounds, until the Objective has been seized by the Attacker, or one side is Destroyed completely.

The Attacker may seize the objective if the Defender has no units (not counting Broken units) within 6" of it after the end of the fourth Turn.

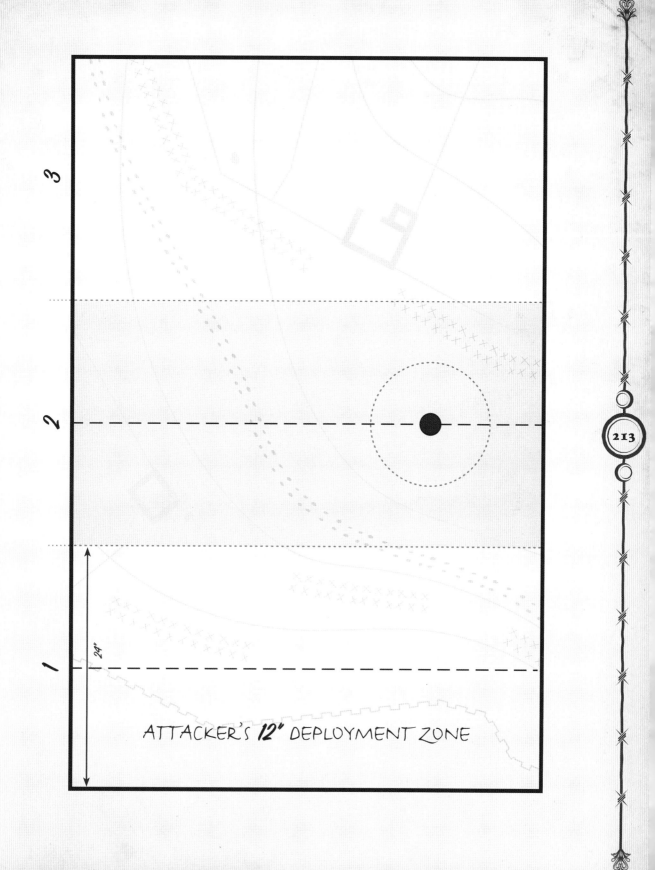

ATTACKER'S *12"* DEPLOYMENT ZONE

24"

1

2

3

THE BIG PUSH

Recommended with up to 30 SP for the Attacker and up to 20 SP for the Defender

In **The Big Push**, two unequal sides fight in a massive contest to either seize or defend a vital sector of the Doggerland Front. Forces should be skewed to favour the Attacker to the tune of 50% more Selection Points.

The Defender may ignore the usual restrictions to unit selection, selecting whatever proportion of **cannonade** and **elite** they choose. Neither side may have more than two **vehicle** units in their Patrol.

SETTING UP THE TABLE

Players should take it in turns to place terrain features over the whole table. **The Big Push** is designed to replicate a huge assault against a salient or heavily defended section of **trench**, and is best played on tables with lots of Cover for the Defender and the ability to concentrate a huge force to assault them

Recommended Terrain:

- ☜ No **impassable** terrain
- ☜ As many **foxholes**, **trenches**, and sections of **wire** as your collection will allow
- ☜ No limit to **obstacles**

Flip a coin to decide who will place the first Objective, then take it in turns to place three Objectives within 12" of the Defender's table edge, with each Objective being at least 12" apart.

DEPLOYING

The Defender places all of their units first, with the Attacker following on after that. In **The Big Push**, both players can choose to deploy their units anywhere within their deployment zone.

SPECIAL RULES

For each Selection Point the Attacker has more than the Defender, the Attacker must deploy at least one Selection Points worth of units in Reserve. For example, if the Defender has 18 Selection Points worth of units and the Attacker 27, at least 9 Selection Points worth of units in the Attacker's Patrol must be deployed in Reserve.

Units deployed in Reserve are left off the table initially, but are placed anywhere within 12" of the Attacker's table edge at the end of the Compulsory Movement Subphase on the third Turn. Reserve units do not generate Command Tokens until the next Command Phase after they are deployed.

> *The Command Tokens generated by the Attacker can never exceed those generated by the Defender by more than three* – any additional Command Tokens are discarded.

VICTORY

The Big Push lasts for up to six Rounds, until one side is Destroyed completely, or the Attacker has secured two or more of the Objectives. The Attacker can secure an Objective by having a unit that is neither in a Close Combat or Broken begin a Turn in contact with it. If, at the end of six Turns, the Attacker has not secured two Objectives, the assault is repulsed, and the Defender is victorious.

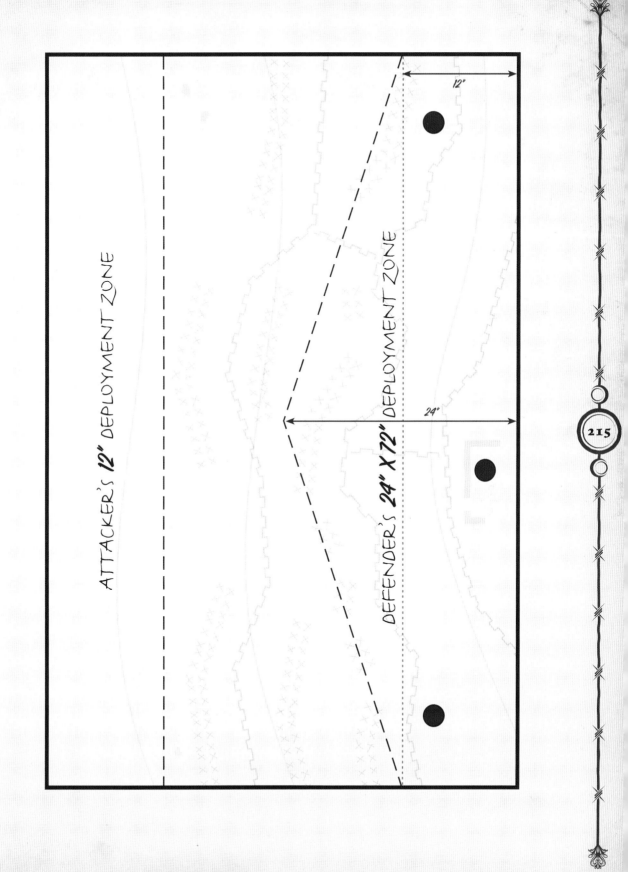

ATTACKER'S *12"* DEPLOYMENT ZONE

DEFENDER'S *24" X 72"* DEPLOYMENT ZONE

12"

24"

GAS! GAS! GAS!

Recommended with up to 25 SP per side

In **Gas! Gas! Gas!**, two sides duke it out whilst a roiling cloud of Witch Gas rolls across the battlefield.

Wherever the veil between realities has been rent, the energies of the spirit world bleed into our reality. In some situations, these aetheric particles can become suspended in water vapour and pulled into the atmosphere, accumulating in vast storms. Thick and murky, these clouds of gas roll over battlefields, disrupting the carefully laid plans of many commanders. Witch Gas attacks and corrodes modern technology, seeping into engines, magazines, and fuel tanks and rendering whatever is within inert.

SETTING UP THE TABLE

Players take it in turns to place terrain features over the whole table. **Gas! Gas! Gas!** is best played on a table with lots of open areas for your units to manoeuvre freely, whilst making sure that there is still lots of Cover for them to duck behind as they advance.

Recommended Terrain:

- A maximum of three pieces of **impassable** terrain
- A maximum of eight special terrain features
- No limit to **obstacles**

DEPLOYING

Units are positioned along the opposing long edges of a 6' x 4' table, with each player taking it in turns to place one unit at a time.

To determine which player will deploy a unit first, each player rolls a d10 – the player with the lowest score places their first unit first. In **Gas! Gas! Gas!**, both players can choose to deploy their units anywhere within their deployment zone, in any orientation that they wish.

WITCH GAS

Once both players have finished deploying their units, flip a coin to determine which of the short table edges the Witch Gas starts on. During the game, the Witch Gas moves across the table from one side to the other by one 12" segment per Turn.

Any unit partly within the segment that the Witch Gas occupies is counted as within it. Units that are within Witch Gas cannot make Shooting Attacks, and **vehicle** units cannot Move either. Additionally, any unit that is within Witch Gas gains the Keyword **camouflage**.

VICTORY

Gas! Gas! Gas! lasts up to six full Rounds, with the victor being the last man standing or the player with the most remaining Selection Points worth of units at the end of the sixth Round.

To determine how many Selection Points you have left, count your remaining units, comparing these with their original recruitment cost in Selection Points. A captain counts for 3 points and a Witch for 2. Any Broken units only count for half their Selection Point value.

12" X 48" SEGMENT

PLAYER A'S *12"* DEPLOYMENT ZONE

PLAYER B'S *12"* DEPLOYMENT ZONE

WEAPON REFERENCE

―――――――――◆―――――――――

RANGED WEAPONS TABLE

Name	Keywords	Weapon type | (number of shots) | Effective Range/Maximum Range
Anti-Tank Rifle	Ordnance	Anti-Tank Rifle | (1) | 45"
Anti-tank Rifle Grenade	Ordnance, Direct Fire	Anti-Tank | (1) | 25"
AT Cannon	Ordnance, Direct Fire	Anti-Tank | (1) | 72"
Automatic Rifle (Bipod) Not in Cover	Small Arms	Machine Gun | (4) | 15"
Automatic Rifle (Bipod) In Cover	Small Arms	Machine Gun | (4) | 25"
Carbine	Small Arms, Quickfire	Standard Issue | (1) | 20"/25"
Explosive Charge	Arcing Shot, Small Arms, Devastating, Disabling	High Explosive | (Large Template) | 8"
Field Gun	Small Arms, Arcing Shot, Devastating, Big Hitter	High Explosive | (Large Template) | 72"
Fire Bottle	Small Arms, Arcing Shot, Horrifying, Quickfire	Flame Weapon | (Small Template) | 6"
Flamethrower	Horrifying, Small Arms, Quickfire	Flame Weapon | (Projected Fire Template) | 10"
Hand Grenade	Small Arms, Arcing Shot, Devastating, Quickfire	High Explosive | (Small Template) | 8"
Heavy Machine Gun	Small Arms, Devastating	Machine Gun | (8) | 36"
Heavy Mortar	Small Arms, Arcing Shot, Devastating	High Explosive | (Medium Template) | 72"

Light Machine Gun (Bipod) Not In Cover	Small Arms	Rapid Fire | (6) | 15"
Light Machine Gun (Bipod) In Cover	Small Arms, Devastating	Machine Gun | (6) | 25"
Machine Pistol	Small Arms, Quickfire	Rapid Fire | (3) | 15"
Marksman's Rifle	Small Arms, Armour-Piercing	Precision | (1) | 48"
Pistol Carbine	Small Arms, Small Calibre, Quickfire, Swift	Standard Issue | (2) | 18"/22"
Repeater Carbine	Small Arms, Quickfire	Standard Issue | (2) | 20"/25"
Revolver	Small Arms, Quickfire, Swift	Standard Issue | (1) | 10"/14"
Shotgun	Small Arms, Quickfire	Close Quarters | (1) | 10"
Self-Loading Pistol	Small Arms, Small Calibre, Quickfire, Swift	Standard Issue | (2) | 10"/14"
Self-Loading Shotgun	Small Arms, Quickfire	Close Quarters | (2) | 10"
Rifle	Small Arms, Quickfire	Standard Issue | (1) | 25"/30"
Rifle Grenade	Small Arms, Arcing Shot, Devastating, Unstable Projectile	High explosive | (Small Template) | 25"
Trench Mortar	Small Arms, Arcing Shot, Devastating	High Explosive | (Small Template) | 48"

Close Combat Weapons Table

Name	Effect
No CC weapons	Saving Throws made against Close Combat Attacks with this weapon are made at Advantage-1
Standard issue CC weapons	This unit has no special armament, making its Close Combat Attacks without any bonuses or penalties
Fearsome CC weapons	This unit can make Critical Hits in Close Combat.
Cavalry CC weapons	In the first Close Combat Phase after a unit armed with this weapon Charges, their opponent must reroll all successful Saving Throw rolls once.
Brutal CC Weapons	For every roll of 1 made in Close Combat, this unit generates an additional Attack Die. Resolve this straight away as though it were part of your initial Attack. Any further rolls or 1s do not generate additional Attack Dice.

Template Blast Reference

Template Type	Size
Small Template	3" diameter
Medium Template	4" diameter
Large Template	6" diameter
Projected Fire Template	2" wide and 10" long

CREDITS

---◆---

ACKNOWLEDGEMENTS

With huge thanks to everyone who helped bring the Doggerland Front to life, but particularly to Edward Parry and Joost Noppen for their tireless energy, enthusiasm, and patience right from the start.

To my wife, thank you for your support, belief, and encouragement —without you this would have been just another idea.

AUTHOR

Having achieved his MA in the History of Art with a research project on medieval imagery in commemoration of the Great War, **Freddy Silburn-Slater** now earns a living as a copywriter, specialising in tabletop gaming and historical subjects. He lives with his wife in rural Suffolk.

ILLUSTRATOR

Dimitris Martinos is an illustrator/comic artist born and based in Athens, Greece. He initially started drawing as a child around the 1980s, inking hundreds of black and white pages inspired by World War II comics. He has worked for Modiphius on Achtung! Cthulhu, and for the French comic publisher Delcourt.

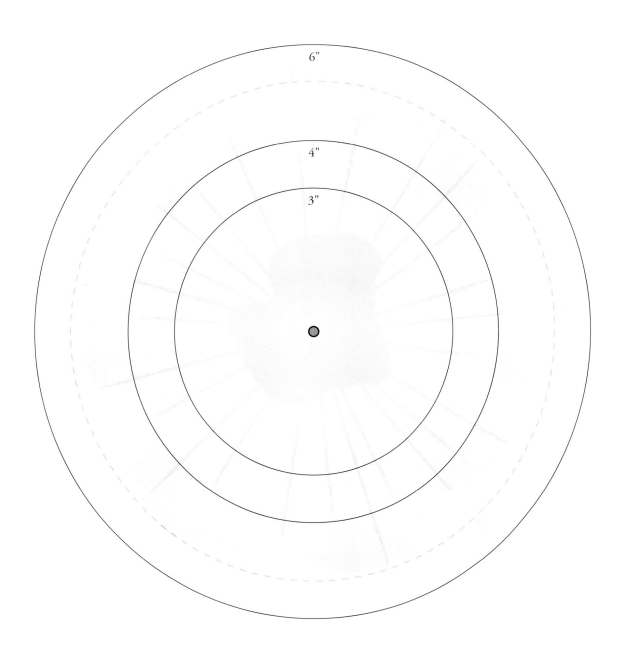